Bonds of Affection

Bonds of Affection

Rohn Federbush

authorHOUSE®

AuthorHouse™
1663 Liberty Drive
Bloomington, IN 47403
www.authorhouse.com
Phone: 1 (800) 839-8640

Published by AuthorHouse 09/03/2015

ISBN: 978-1-5049-4786-2 (sc)
ISBN: 978-1-5049-4785-5 (e)

Print information available on the last page.

Tied together as hostages in a bank robbery, an ex-race-car driver, Gina Branson, shares the shock of the bank guard, Thomas Woods, as he witnesses the murder of his twin brother. Once freed, the roller coaster of Tom's grief and rage alienates them on issues of retribution and clemency. Bound to each other from their first flicker of interest, the couple weathers both the bank-robbery trial and the death of Gina's ailing mother to a final testing of their faith, trust and affection.

Rohn Federbush

ACKNOWLEDGEMENTS

Alcoholics Anonymous

CHAPTER ONE

NASCAR Race, Brooklyn, Michigan
Friday, July 13th

Splintered flashes alerted Gina Branson to the scream of tearing metal and the reek of flaming gasoline. The racecar to her right melted into the retaining wall. The rear-view mirror promised another skyrocketing chassis might land on the tail of her car. Gina pressed the gas pedal into the floorboard, praying for deliverance.

Disintegrating parts and flying debris thoroughly wrecked her racer. As Gina climbed out, she brushed the door handle good-bye before fleeing to the infield. Searing smoke from burning tires and fuel intensified her tears for the two drivers who had vanished in the battle of speed, space and steel.

"Why are we doing this?" Gina asked the ambulance nurse mopping warm blood from her injured right shoulder.

"Good question," the female attendant said. "Maybe you should ask yourself."

* * *

When Gina returned to her hotel in Ann Arbor, the desk clerk waved a letter at her. "From Illinois."

"Mother," Gina whispered, taking the letter.

In her room, yellow roses Gina ordered before the race adorned the entry-way table. She buried her face in the fragrant bouquet, thanking the Lord for His intervention, yet again.

The bed felt too soft for her tense body. She kicked off her boots, but her toes refused to relax. She tore the letter open with her teeth because her shoulder hurt too much to use her right hand. The penmanship wasn't her mother's. Gina re-examined the envelope where the address label identified home. Holding in another rose-scented breath of air, Gina read the note from Florence Kerner, her mother's nurse, spelling out the diagnosis, "pancreatic cancer."

* * *

Geneva's City Bank, Illinois
Friday, September 28th

Gina rubbed the bridge of her nose acknowledging defeat might be at hand. The black-and-white marble tiles on the bank's floor summoned the checkered flag she had ceased to pursue. As a racecar driver Gina taught herself to take violent hits. Perhaps the Lord wouldn't answer her fervent prayers for a deluge of ready cash. She ducked her head and released the arms of the chair as she'd learned to let go of the steering wheel for unavoidable collisions.

Gina's financial history would soon blink to life on the loan officer's computer screen. Would their high-school flirtations fifteen years earlier sufficiently influence Jonas Woods? Gina had trailed behind a bevy of football fans following every move of any coach's dream, the Woods twins – Thomas and Jonas. She predicted Jonas's dark eyebrows would raise when he reviewed her negative credit reports.

Her checkbook was as empty as her credit cards were overflowing because of her mother's continuing medical costs. To help with household expenses, Gina found a job as a school bus driver. Now, she hoped the bank would give her a loan on her mother's equity in the house to fix its leaky roof and the ancient plumbing, as well as cover the mounting medical debts. Would Jonas want her to have the money?

Gina smiled at him for all she was worth.

Jonas's head moved closer to his computer screen as he scrutinized her unbelievable amount of debt. Gina had no friends or extended family to tide her over the financial rough patch. As a race-car driver, she never felt a part of the gang. Despite her loyal team, she'd raced alone competing against men. Now she was experiencing the same need for individual courage.

Across the aisle, a bank guard lifted his head toward the balcony at the noise of the vault door swinging open. Gina recognized the guard as Jonas's twin, Thomas. His mouth was drawn in a thin line of concentration. Tom's dark blue uniform barely fit his gigantic frame. Then she met his eyes. The combined black of iris and pupil immersed her in their languid pool…until dollar bills starting falling from overhead.

A single hundred dollar bill landed on the knee of Gina's white wool trouser. Ignoring the delighted hubbub from the other bank patrons, Gina didn't move lest it sail away. The Lord might revoke the miracle of pennies from heaven. How many pennies in a hundred dollars? How many pennies did she need to fix the roof? Maybe she could just glue the coppers to the shingles to keep the rain out.

Jonas jumped up, shoving clumps of the showering bills into *his* pockets. Maybe he needed money as much as she did. Obviously, neither of them had been taught the proper etiquette for an actual, finite miracle. Jonas danced into the aisle with his arms lifted over his head catching the falling money.

Then noise and spraying bullets cut across his middle, folding him onto the floor.

Loud barks of orders rained down from the balcony. "Every one, stay where you are. Drop your gun!"

Unable to move, Gina watched Tom throw his useless gun at the bank's glassed-in entrance as he rushed to his fallen twin.

"Don't move!" The same hoarse voice descended on them. "Get down there," he shouted to his accomplice. "Tie them up!"

The money stopped its descent.

Jonas wasn't moving. Blood pooled around him.

Tom's left knee would soon touch his twin's blood. Tom lifted Jonas's dark curls, searching for a pulse in his neck, but his shoulders slumped in resignation.

Jonas was dead.

A slim youth ran at them from the stairwell, a huge coil of rope burdened one shoulder. He slammed a knife into Jonas's glass desktop, splintering the glass under the blow.

Stupid or scared, Gina thought.

The boy motioned for Tom to place two chairs back-to-back. The mute boy licked his lips as if even swallowing had become a problem. He did the best he could to tie Gina and Tom to the chairs. Then he directed the other bank clients and tellers to sit on the floor against the wrought-iron dividing fence. He looped the rope around the six frightened women.

The older robber calmly descended the stairs, pulling his black shirt over a protruding stomach. He locked the front door, rammed Tom's gun into his belt and swung his automatic weapon over his shoulder.

Gina knew how to avoid danger when her hands were gripping the steering wheel, but this situation was out of her control. *Lord'* she prayed silently, *don't let the Hospice volunteer abandon Mother if I can't return.* Who would meet their Maker first, her mother or her?

The senior thief marched behind the tellers' counters, punching buttons on the money drawers and dumping his loot into a bulging duffel bag. The younger kid had his back to the killer, who kept walking right out the back door.

When the teenager finished securing his hostages, they all heard the first police sirens. He wiped his hand over his dry mouth, realizing the older man had abandoned him.

The sirens increased in volume.

The orphaned thief found a drinking fountain near the back door. He drank for a long time, as if lost in the pleasure of quenching his thirst or unwilling to face his predicament. Finally, he straightened as police banged on the glass front door.

He locked the rear door before racing to the front entrance, screaming, "I've got nine hostages." He punched at the air toward the glass-held police.

They backed off.

"Fools." Gina heard Tom growl from the chair tied behind hers.

"He only has eight unless he's counting your brother."

"Killed," Tom snarled.

A chill went up Gina's back into her hairline as if she were bound to a wild animal. She feared Tom's anger more than their inept captor. The kid, surely younger than seventeen, came over to sit in a chair next to them where the loan desk blocked the sight of the source of all the blood.

"You don't have a gun," Gina said softly, hoping to calm both Tom and their kidnapper.

"They won't care." The kid ran his hands through his astonishing white hair.

"I'm Gina. Did any of the other people get hurt?"

"I guess I better check, huh?" He got up, then remembering some mode of goniff politeness said, "My name's Danny. Bianco."

Gina elbowed the guard.

"Tom," he snapped. "Your friend killed my brother."

"Sorry." Danny crossed the room to bend down to each of the six women tied to the divider.

"Don't talk to him," Tom whispered viciously.

"Nonsense, we have to survive."

"To make sure he dies," Tom spat.

Gina hissed back, "To gather evidence. The big guy had the gun."

Danny walked over to the water fountain, found the paper-cup rack and dispensed water to two of the ashen-faced, older women. He seemed oblivious to the scattered bills on the bank's floor.

Returning to his seat next to Gina, he asked, "What am I going to do when they need to use the bathroom?"

Gina considered his dilemma. "Move chairs behind the fence. You can tie the rope temporarily to the empty chair, and then retie it when they return."

One of the tellers reached for the cash next to her, but Danny's ropes had tethered her arms too closely to her side.

"I'm not very good at this," Danny said. "It's my first time."

"You haven't hurt anyone," Gina said, elbowing Tom to keep him quiet.

"But Uncle--."

Gina could feel Tom's back straighten with renewed interest. He said in a civil tone, "...told you someone might get hurt."

"Yeah," Danny said, elongating the word as if he were mentally feeble.

During the silent hours that followed, Danny periodically checked his captives. He did release two older women, one at a time, replacing their ends of the rope to the empty chairs. When they returned, he allowed them to sit in the more comfortable chairs before retying them. The rest of the women sitting on the floor remained calm as if inventorying their lives.

Gina did the same, praying she'd made the right decision about making Geneva her home instead of continuing to race. She was in more danger of getting shot by the police than being hurt by this un-armed teenager, but her tension was not relieved. At least in a car she had a choice of which way to turn to avoid a wreck.

God help me, she prayed.

So, she talked non-stop to Danny about her life in Geneva as a young girl, cleaning homes to buy books and clothes for high school, of never quite fitting in. She skipped over the race-car stuff, which didn't seem dire enough for the occasion. She hated knowing her rope-mate, Tom, could hear the gross failures in her life, but she persisted in the descriptions.

"My mother's house is over a hundred years old. The roof leaks. I put a bucket in one place in the attic and have to move it to another spot when the wind shifts. Mother says last winter my bedroom windows let the snow seep in. The wallpaper is peeling off the walls downstairs."

Danny only nodded.

"I'm camping out in my brother's basement until I finish my degree," Tom said in a mild tone, adding, "Have you applied to the state's Historical Perseverance Fund to help restore your house?"

"Good idea." Was it her imagination or could she feel warmth radiating from Tom's back to hers?

The phone's sudden ring made them jump.

"Better answer it, kid," Tom said without hostility.

Danny picked up the phone. "Just me," he said to some unknown question, probably about how many lawless men controlled the hostages. He frowned and looked at the headpiece.

Gina heard loud swearing.

"Would you like to speak to one of the hostages?" Danny politely held the receiver to Gina's ear.

"Hello?" More cursing on the other end answered. "Maybe you should calm down."

More invectives followed.

Tom shook his chair in frustration.

Gina told the authorities, "There are eight of us tied up, one dead man and Danny Bianco."

Danny grabbed the phone. "Did he ask for my name?"

"No, but you counted nine hostages and there are only eight."

Danny held the phone for her again.

"Can you tell me how he's armed?" a calmer policeman asked. "How many guns?"

"None," Gina said. "He tied us up before his uncle left with the money and the guns."

Danny was frowning. He hung up the phone. "They'll come in now, won't they?"

"Pretty soon, I think." She felt pity for him. "Did your uncle threaten you?" Danny seemed to nod off in his chair next to her. "Danny!" she yelled.

He woke but his eyes didn't seem to focus immediately. "Narcolepsy," he said, "too much stress and I sleep."

"Untie me, now!"

Danny stood up and then unwrapped her ropes.

Gina moved to stand in front of Tom as Danny methodically retied him to the chair. She told herself it wasn't just to check out Tom's eyes. His tone had changed from rage to something closer to a human's. He appeared less threatening than she'd imagined, even though his massive shoulders hunched forward and back under the rope constraints.

"I'm studying to be a therapist," Tom said. "You're a natural."

Gina inspected his ring finger. Single. A guilty sensation stirred in the pit of her stomach. Tom moved his bound feet, and she couldn't help noticing how massive his legs were. She shook herself, but he had caught on.

"I hope we'll have a chance to decipher that look." His face relaxed.

If she had the choice to stay glued to the moment forever, she would have, but urgent business demanded her attention.

She directed Danny, "Now, sit down with your hands on your head."

He did, so she walked unsteadily toward the front door to unlock it, holding the door open for the police as they charged in.

* * *

Tom Woods's mind cleared somewhat from the shock of witnessing his twin's death. The Geneva cops took command while maintaining a polite, solicitous manner, nothing like the reality shows on television. Tom planned not to expect too much of himself. He'd been a guard at the bank for exactly two and a half days. Jonas had given him the job to help pay for his education as a therapist, even after Tom told him he wouldn't be able to shoot the gun.

The middle-aged patrons of the bank were escorted to their cars or detained until a relative could retrieve them from their extraordinary day witnessing a murder during a bank robbery. One out of the six might experience post-traumatic symptoms, but the rest would fill out their repertoire of daily gossip for friends. Gina might get off scot-free from the turmoil because she had taken control of the situation and effectively freed them before she let in the police.

Tom repeated the day's quote from his Alcoholics' Anonymous Twelve-Steps book, "No single event can awaken within us a stranger__" The rest of the quote was lost as he took in the sight of his brother's body.

An officer pointed him to a chair facing away from his twin's inert form.

Then Tom recalled the rest of the quote, "__a stranger totally unknown to us."

Unfamiliar rage had taken hold of him and kept building in his chest, clouding his thoughts. He needed to explain to Dolly, Jonas's wife, what had happened. No words surfaced in his heated, revenge-driven brain.

The ambulance workers were preparing his brother for removal from the bank. The sound of the zipper on the body bag shook the tears out of Tom.

Gina came to his side as he fished for his handkerchief. "This is Sergeant Steve Muller." She placed her hand on Tom's bent shoulder.

A small man, Muller extended a cold hand.

"Have to tell his wife." Tom was amazed at the effort required to mouth those few words. He reached up to grasp Gina's hand where it lay on his shoulder.

Sergeant Muller stepped back as Tom stood. "I'll go with you."

Tom still held onto Gina's hand, so he asked her, "Can you come?"

"Of course," she said.

He could tell her ready agreement had surprised her.

"I need to call the Hospice worker who's with my mother, first."

Muller handed his phone to Gina, who called home, as they walked to the police car.

"Not much has to be explained, at first," Muller said. "Families recognize the seriousness of the situation when they see my uniform and the car."

No words. All Tom needed to do was show up and Dolly would know the horrible truth: Jonas was gone. Gina passed the phone back to the front seat. Everyone moved slowly as if conscious of the gravity of their mission.

"The address?" Muller asked.

"St. Charles," Tom answered. "Twenty-one forty-one Twelfth Street."

They took Route 31 north, along the river from Geneva to St. Charles. Tom imagined this was the route Mary Todd Lincoln had taken south on her way to the asylum in Batavia. Glimpses of the Fox River helped. He wanted the world to transform as much as his personal world had changed with the brutal death of his brother, but the river flowed on. The planet wasn't interested in the passing of one loan officer. Even the passing of the man who saved the Union could not dent reality for more than a moment in time.

Tom wished he knew a quiet, unsupervised place to escape. His emotions ranged from putting his fist through the police car's window to wishing he had died instead of Jonas. He could not remember which of the AA Twelve Steps would help him now, but letting go and letting God handle things had ended with his twin brother's death.

The police car pulled into the driveway of Jonas's brick ranch house.

Tom's shoes had gotten heavier.

Sergeant Muller led the way with Gina on his heels.

Tom followed, but when Dolly opened the door she only glanced at the two people in front of him before lunging at him.

"He's dead," Dolly said.

"Call your folks," Tom managed.

"I'll do it for you," Gina said as the four of them entered the house.

Dolly collapsed on the couch Muller led her to. "Punch seven. The boys are still in school."

Gina made the call then sat down next to Dolly. "They're on their way," she said and looked up at Tom.

Tom realized he was looming over Dolly. Sitting seemed a dishonorable thing to do, as if any comfort would deny the horror.

"Tom," Dolly said. "Do sit down. We don't need to get kinks in our necks, right now." That's when her tears started.

They could be sisters, Tom thought as Gina placed her hand on Dolly's cheek before embracing her. Their faces had the same cherub chin, wide blue eyes, and delicate bone structure, although Dolly's long blonde hair contrasted with Gina's short black curls. Entranced with the scene, Tom sat down opposite them. The colors affronted the propriety of the situation. Dolly's couch was as red as Jonas's spilt blood. Her bright yellow sweater and white jeans contrasted with Gina's blue blouse and white wool pants. Dolly wore white socks while Gina's high-heeled boots matched her blue blouse. Where did women find blue boots?

God help me, Tom prayed, *I'm avoiding my emotions.*

Gina broke away from her embrace of Dolly first, asking the sergeant, "Will you drive me to my mother's?"

"Wait," Tom heard himself say. "Dolly's parents are ten minutes away. They'll be here shortly, then I can drive you home."

Sergeant Muller parked himself in the chair next to the door. "Neither of you has your car. We'll wait with Mrs. Woods until the family arrives."

* * *

Gina could well understand Tom's need for company to face his brother's wife, but he couldn't seem to let go of her now. Tom paced the floor. Why had he asked to drive her home? Perhaps, keeping her at his side reminded him of a time when his brother still lived. His rapt attention engulfed her. Perhaps he found it easier to concentrate on her rather than accept his own grief.

She fetched a glass of cold water for the widow along with a soft green kitchen towel to wipe away her tears. Dolly must surely have loved her husband. Gina envied the love this husband and wife had shared. The men she met on the racecar circuit hadn't the inclination to develop a relationship with someone they competed against. So Gina had never had the opportunity to give her heart away.

When she returned with the water and towel, Tom asked, "Does your mother live in Geneva?"

"On Dean Street," she said, deciding not to bring up her mother's fatal illness.

Dolly said, "There is a Dean Street in St. Charles too, north of Main Street."

Muller interjected, "She's right you know. I got mixed up once when I was a rookie."

Dolly looked at the sergeant as if she didn't understand why a stranger was sitting by her door.

Muller smiled and then Dolly turned away as if afraid to converse with the man who had brought such bad news. "The Post Office probably gets mixed up, too.

Tom and Dolly delved into any subject with the verve necessary to escape dealing with their bereavement. So, Gina opened up too, hoping to let them breathe easier for a moment or two longer. "My mother's dying from pancreatic cancer."

She nodded at their condolence, but could tell from Muller's stillness that she'd said the wrong thing. Mentioning her mother's upcoming death was too close to Tom and Dolly's fresh loss.

Then Dolly's parents arrived. After a short phatic patch of introductions, Muller drove Tom and Gina back to their cars at the bank. Gina didn't expect Tom to remember he said he'd drive her home.

"My car is over here." Tom indicated a beat-up Escort.

Muller seemed to apologize. His face turned beet red with embarrassment. "Mrs. Woods, Dolly, certainly is a strong woman. We'll need statements from you both. Tomorrow, before ten? I'll call you at eight to remind you."

Gina's state of confusion had less to do with the traumatic morning than it did with the realization Tom Woods was a man she wouldn't mind getting to know. At least six-foot-five, his lean face and those black pools other people would call eyes were riveting. Perhaps the emotional tensions involved in his grief helped him to appear a passionate man, lightning in his veins, heat….

Tom touched her elbow. "I don't want to say good-bye yet. We need to talk about our statements for Muller."

His car was filthy with dog hairs and smelly trash. He removed a pile of bills stamped with 'overdue' in red block letters from the passenger seat and a bag of soda cans from the floor before Gina could even get. She pushed the window button to help some of the lint and stench escape as they drove toward Geneva's Dean Street.

She gave him the necessary directions, "Turn left at the bookstore on Fifth Avenue."

The drive didn't take as long as she'd hoped. Tom never mentioned their statements to Muller.

"My car is still at the bank." She pointed to her mother's two-story home, badly in need of paint.

Tom followed her up the sidewalk. "I'll pick you up for the police appointment. I can't think straight now."

"My mother's bed is in the front room," Gina explained why she didn't invite him to come in.

Then Tom grabbed her shoulders and bent down to give her the warmest, most heartfelt kiss she'd ever received. Nothing mattered except hanging onto him.

"I need you, too," she whispered when their lips parted. She could feel tears rolling down her face.

"I know." Then he smiled for a split second as if he'd forgotten his loss. "We'll hold on to each other."

CHAPTER TWO

Well, that was stupid, Tom told himself as he drove back to his brother's home. Kissing the girl to make her cry. He had nothing to offer.

A cloud of grief stormed inside him.

In order to avoid Geneva's Main Street and the sight of the bank, Tom headed west on the tree-lined side streets away from the historic district, where Gina lived.

Once he arrived at the intersection of Randall Road, he caught a glimpse of Johnson's Mound. The slight hill's bit of forest held memories of Jonas. Dark weather hung over the horizon, threatening.

Without realizing its complicity, Tom's car made the jog down Randall, south instead of north toward St. Charles, onto the two-lane paved road that ran all the way out to the forest preserve.

Even if he'd wanted to keep the bank-guard job, he'd probably disqualified himself by letting his brother be killed. He couldn't save Jonas and he wouldn't be able take care of Jonas's widow or their two boys.

He drove into the forest preserve's gravel parking lot. The years slammed back at him. His mother rounded up her twins whenever she was fighting with their dad, which was often, and drove them out to Johnson's Mound for a walk to clear her head. Tom's father had a temper fit for an emperor not a house painter. Usually his parents wouldn't speak to each other when their emotions got the better of their good sense.

A drunken driver had ended their fights and their lives.

Tom had been working at Radio Shack at the time. The electronics firm let him go after too many days lapsed after too many drunken nights. Tom's trips to AA meetings halted without finding a sponsor in the program. He'd stopped drinking, agreeing with the program's assessment: his life was out-of-control and he needed help from someone or something.

Jonas hadn't had a problem with alcohol. His addiction to avoid grieving their parents turned to cold, hard cash. Greed was almost patriotic in America, and Tom hadn't confronted his brother.

Instead, Tom started back to school. By the end of the fall term, he'd have a Masters with enough clinic hours to qualify as a therapist.

Fortunately, his parents hadn't lived to see Jonas murdered.

"Thank God," Tom said to the universe. "Thank God!"

Fall held a chill. Storm clouds overhead lowered. Tom rummaged around in the back seat of his car to find a sweater, pulling it over the bank-guard uniform.

Jonas had received a matching sweater the last Christmas their mom was alive. Tom's was red, Jonas's blue.

"Fire and ice," she had explained.

Tom walked quietly down the familiar paths where he could name nearly every type of tree. His mind still churned. How long could he survive without family? No parents, no brother, soon no home? The basement apartment he occupied in his brother's house was in jeopardy. Tom had considered the place temporary until he finished his degree and found a social worker's position.

A shift in the wind touched his brow. Tom looked up at the oaks, still holding onto their browned leaves. An early ice storm might threaten the sturdy old trees with their roots sunk deep into the hill, but for now they were hanging onto their foliage.

Tom was tired of playing it safe. Deaths appeared at random, never within his control. He wanted to tear into the world, cut out a bite of happiness before his life was swept aside.

He drove back taking Randall Road north to Route 64. He couldn't face returning to Jonas's house; instead, he turned west again toward Plato Center. As he drove through the township, he counted all the new houses replacing grain-yielding fields. Meandering around the dirt country roads, he found McDonald Road and his grandfather's farm.

The white barn stood firm against the elements. Tom had been ten when the structure was built over twenty years earlier. The house was more ancient, built before the Civil War as far as he knew. The older section had in-turned eaves with a graying stucco finish. The wooden addition boasted thick walls and inset windows. He'd helped stoke its coal furnace which used an open grate in the dining room floor and ceiling to circulate the heated air.

Sliding oak doors between the two sections of the house had hidden his grandparents' tree until Christmas morning. After Jonas and Tom dismantled all the wrappings from their presents, they were allowed outside to frolic in the snow with Grandpa's border collie, Bob.

'*Good memories,* Tom told himself. *I have good memories.*

He turned the car around in the farm lane. A wooden swing still hung from the lower limbs of the century oak. Rain started to sweep across his windshield.

* * *

Back in St. Charles on Dean Street, where his parents built a concrete block house on the last lot in town backing up to the train tracks, the new owners had rid themselves of two apple trees, one in the back and one next to the driveway. Tom could almost taste the heavily sugared pies his mother had baked. The house had been painted white, the shutters green, but the new owners changed the colors to dark browns, making the home seem even smaller.

Tom had been sober for two years, but just a taste of whiskey would hit the spot now. Apparently alcohol was an unquenchable thirst. AA members had welcomed Tom to the tables, sharing the jarring incidents in their lives. He needed their wisdom. Alcohol could use the death of his brother to call him back to a sodden, unfeeling life.

'God forbid,' he prayed, letting the tears for his lost brother flow.

Jonas's house south of Main Street, Route 64, was empty when he finally made it home. As he entered the back entrance to his basement apartment, he realized Dolly's parents, Mr. and Mrs. Stone, must have taken Dolly and the boys to their home in Wayne. His nephews, Jeffrey and Timothy loved to ride their horses.

Dolly was a stay-at-home mom and Jonas's expenses far exceeded his income. Jonas had cashed in his life insurance to pay for Tom's final year of tuition. Now, Dolly would probably have to sell the Twelfth Street house and move back in with her folks, like Gina, the girl he'd just kissed, who couldn't invite him in, because she was living with her dying mother.

Tom pulled down his suitcase and an Army-surplus duffel bag to start packing. Dolly would find the house easier to list without a tenant.

He could still feel where Gina's arms had clung to him, as he had to her. The circumstances surrounding the kiss were too serious to consider any momentary feelings for each other permanent. Tom wished he'd attended one high-school reunion to keep in touch, although Gina didn't seem the type to reminisce about teenage years.

Structure your time, Tom told himself. He could pop a TV dinner into the microwave and then comb the want ads for another brainless job and an apartment. Life and death turned on a dime and all he could do was gather his strength to deal with reality. But he was dispensable. The killer should have let Jonas dance and shot him instead. Tom was the one with the gun, yet now Dolly and his nephews had no one.

That stupid kid. Maybe he hadn't pulled the trigger, but he was involved. Tom couldn't bring Jonas back to care for his family, but the criminal at hand would pay dearly for Jonas's death. Tom would make sure Danny Bianco didn't follow his uncle's directions in any more deadly crime sprees.

Then he remembered Gina's kindness to their kidnapper while she maneuvered him to untie them. He hoped she would see the justice in putting the kid away for his entire adult life.

Jonas would have wreaked the same retribution for Tom.

The way Gina spoke to Danny during the robbery was textbook. Establish a helpful attitude; get his trust by sympathizing with his plight against the authorities, then take control of the situation.

Tom wondered if Gina had ever pursued psychological studies. He didn't know anything about the past of the woman he'd kissed with needy devotion. He would find out more at the police station in the morning, where he planned to nail Danny Bianco's hide to the wall.

* * *

Saturday, September 29th

Gina bent down to pound on Tom's bedroom window. "Nine o'clock, sleepy head," she called above the barking of the neighbor's dog.

Tom's big hand waved between the window's vertical blinds.

She went around the back of the house to the basement entrance. A battery of descending stone steps, lined with pots of bright yellow mums led to the apartment's door. She knocked hard on the door he'd left open.

"Come in," he called. "I'm in the shower."

"I've had mine," she answered quietly, but failed to stop her thoughts from rubbing suds all over his big body.

"What?" Tom asked, sticking a dripping head around the door frame.

"Coffee," she lied. "I thought you asked me to take a cup."

"Muller must have some at the station."

Before Gina could acclimate herself to the efficiency's kitchen, Tom stood fully clothed in a sport coat and jeans in the doorway to his bedroom.

"How did you get here?" Tom asked. "Your car--?"

"Mother's friend brings her yellow roses and glazed donuts every morning." Gina moved to reopen the back door. "Muller called to say he couldn't reach you. So Menasha, Mother's devoted beau, volunteered to take me to the bank for my car."

"I'll drive you to the police station." Tom ushered her out, bending his head to get through the low exit. "We need to talk."

Thick morning fog hid the brightest of the fall leaves.

"Let's take my Mustang." Gina hoped not to wreck her clean skirt in Tom's messed up car.

"You're blocking me anyway," he said.

Once Tom was ensconced in the passenger seat, Old Spice after-shave drew Gina's attention to his side of the car.

He stared back at her with those deep-set, dark eyes.

"Better keep your eyes on the road," he cautioned. "I wanted to make sure our stories about the robbery don't conflict."

"Police expect witnesses to disagree."

"I don't want Danny Bianco to see daylight again as long as he lives."

Gina remained silent for as long as she could. "Bit harsh."

"My brother won't see another minute of life. Why should a man involved in his murder go free?"

There was nothing more to say.

She hoped they'd give their statements separately. Tom wouldn't like what she planned to say in Danny's defense. Narcolepsy, for Pete's sake, and his white hair! The kid obviously had been scared to death more than once.

While they were stopped at the stop-light on Broadway, Gina tried again, "A nun at St. Patrick's told us about a friend of hers, a nun too, I guess, who visited prisoners on death row. She thought even mass murderers owned part of a pure soul. Like a handkerchief spotted with blood, the rest of the cloth, the rest of the untouched soul was still good."

The traffic light turned green.

Tom said, "That kid will turn out just like his uncle, ruthless and dangerous."

"Not necessarily."

How could this cold vengeful man kiss with such greedy heat? Had her own needs embellished her memory of their first kiss?

* * *

Kane County Courthouse, Geneva

From reading too many Sherlock Holmes mysteries, Tom expected the detective offices inside of the brick jail attached to the mid-18th century courthouse to be paneled in vintage wood, with a frosted glass door signifying Sergeant Steve Muller's quiet office. Instead, unlike the books, movies and television series, the place reminded him of his grandfather's dairy barn.

White cement blocks divided the partitions into bullet-proof windowed sections. In place of green metal shades, the rooms were illuminated with harsh fluorescent lighting. No romantic smoke fumes from pondering Sherlocks permeated the air, only a faint odor of disinfectant. He shrugged off his disappointment, content with the knowledge that criminals didn't stand a chance of escape.

Tom and Gina seated themselves across the room from a scowling desk officer. Tom took Gina's hand. They weren't the perpetrators. Why weren't they escorted into a friendlier atmosphere?

Gina smiled slightly as she stroked his cold hand.

He couldn't rehearse their story because the desk guard might hear. Tom smiled, nodding his head, willing her to remember to say only negative things about Danny Bianco.

Sergeant Muller came out of a side door and without more than a perfunctory hello, picked Gina for the first statement.

Muller and Gina were about the same height. Tom would have to step back when talking to him, not to seem intimidating with his larger size. *Stay friendly,* he told himself. But he didn't like Muller. Jealousy over Gina? Impossible! He had hardly known the girl in high-school.

Tom concluded his emotions were out of control. He shouldn't trust any of his own decisions while under the sway of grief. Afraid to ask for help, his soul ranted at the thought of a God who would allow so much evil. No humility was possible while he held onto wrath, but Tom couldn't let go of the anger in his heart. Not yet.

He knew the Bible's exhortation to Job. "Where were you when the foundations of the world were laid?"

If Tom released anger's hold, who would mourn and vindicate Jonas, the man who shared his mother's womb?

* * *

Gina smiled at Sergeant Muller when he asked if she liked hazelnut cappuccino. "I'd die for a cup."

"Against the law to bribe a witness." He handed her one of the three cups in the fast-food holder. "Do you realize you and Dolly Woods share the same facial bone structure?"

Gina shrugged and reminded herself to talk fast, so that Tom's coffee wouldn't cool off. "The boy must have gone through hell to get caught in that set up."

"St. Charles Boys' Home since he was seven. His uncle claimed the boy murdered his own prostitute mother."

The coffee didn't taste right. "That same uncle was the man who killed Jonas. I bet he's the one who killed Danny's mother and then blamed it on the poor child."

"The boy doesn't seem tough," Muller conceded.

"What about the narcolepsy? Right before he realized the police were going to storm the bank, he fell asleep. I had to yell at him to untie me."

Muller made another note. "We'll have him examined by an expert."

"What will they do to him?"

"He was involved in an armed robbery and murder."

"But I'm sure he's confessed his part." Gina reached out for Muller's hand. "Won't there be a plea bargain?"

Muller took her hand but shook his head. "He's going to plead not guilty to the murder."

"He should!" Gina drew back her hand as if burned.

"So, there will be a jury trial."

Gina brushed her tears aside. "Can I see the poor kid?"

"Call his lawyer." Muller squinted at her. "I'll have to tell the prosecutor you're a hostile witness."

"I don't care," she said, satisfied she'd done as much as she could.

* * *

Tom crossed and re-crossed his knees, finally wiping his damp hands on the sides of his jeans. He'd read the day's prayer in a steamy blur from his shower -- something about peace outstretching our understanding, or was it simply past human understanding? His own testimony might have to carry the case against Danny.

He heard Gina laugh. Couldn't have. She wouldn't laugh at this horrendous crime.

Muller and Gina returned.

Tom could smell cappuccino. His stomach growled and he was freezing from the metal chair. Before he could stop himself, he stood and kicked at a wastebasket next to the chair.

The noise shocked them all. "Sorry," he said, not meaning it.

He would have liked to play kick-the-can forever, or until his foot fell off. He sat back down but Muller motioned for him to follow.

"I'll wait." A deep frown line developed between Gina's eyebrows.

Tom followed Muller into the interrogation room.

* * *

Gina wracked her brain as she waited for Tom. Why was she determined to keep seeing him? Obviously he wanted to punish the young thief. If she'd had a brother shot before her eyes, she might refuse to acknowledge Danny had been used by his unscrupulous uncle.

Gina decided she would champion Danny, even if it meant destroying any chance of getting to know Tom. She threw her empty coffee cup in the waste basket he had upended. Perhaps she could ask him if she could attend Jonas's funeral. The longer she kept in contact the more she could influence his adverse opinion of Danny.

Tom was probably going through the anger stage of grief now. He'd get through it with the Lord's help. But would he want her to remain close as a constant reminder of the horror at the bank?

CHAPTER THREE

In no hurry to return home, Gina listened to Tom talk non-stop from the time they left Sergeant Muller's office. They'd walked to Geneva's Main Street after leaving the oak-lined square of the Kane County courthouse. The cherry trees along Main were devoid of leaves.

Even while continuing to discuss the intricacies of the trial system which might free Danny, Tom constantly made way for Gina on the sidewalk.

His deference to her space reminded her of a Hindu wedding she had attended for a racecar driver.

Wrapped in gauze veils the bridal couple had carefully circumvented a container in the floor where a votive flame flickered. The pundit priest cautioned them not to take a step into the future without considering how it might affect their partner. The groom protected the bride's skirts to assure each step was safely away from the gentle flame.

But only the groom was in the racecar when it slammed into the second turn's concrete wall. The bride stood helpless in the speedway infield as the roaring fire consumed him.

Gina realized she was more steeled against death than Tom. She'd lost every one of seven racing acquaintances. All killed in speeding cars. Maybe she had been in Geneva's City Bank for a reason other than securing a loan.

Maybe Tom needed her.

He stepped in front of her when a boy's skateboard flew at them from the low cement wall surrounding one of the cherry trees. Tom did appear bound to her in the manner of the Hindu wedding couple. Farther down the sidewalk, he stayed glued to her when a group of giggling teenage girls tried to walk between them. His actions were instinctive, unconscious, clearly those of a gentleman.

Unfortunately, his words were in conflict with everything she believed.

Sitting for an hour on the hard chairs at Wisniewski's sandwich shop where she'd paid for his coffee and Danish, didn't stop his tirade. The aromatic coffee seemed to goad him into pursuing all the ramifications of a trial by jury which he insisted this murder case needed.

Gina was not pleased with her weak defense of Danny. "I'm not a lawyer," she said. "But I do feel drawn to the boy."

"Your lack of children might predispose you to mother him," Tom was swift to point out,

His words were less than kind, but he was handsome. She liked being the center of his attention, as if she were facing down a dangerous animal. Was she protecting her young? "Danny's only fifteen."

"Didn't we call you the crusader in high school?" Tom kidded her.

"Danny's hope for justice certainly seems tipped the wrong way."

* * *

Finally she'd taken Tom back to his sister-in-law's empty house. Gina checked her face in the visor mirror. Did she look cheerful enough for her mother? She tried smiling and pulling on her short bangs, but her face fell back into a serious, even worried look. Her cheeks were still red with vexation for not sticking up more for the kid.

Well, Lord, she entreated, *help prepare Mother. She knows I've been giving my statement of the bank robbery.*

As she opened the front door of her mother's home on Dean Street in Geneva, her mother called out, "Gina?"

"Yes," she stalled in front of the hall mirror. "I'm home."

Florence Kerner, the Hospice worker, came out of the front room, which had been converted into the sick room. "Rough day at the police station?"

"Horrible. How is Mother?"

"Come on in here," her mother called. "Don't be whispering about me in the hall."

Florence patted Gina's shoulder and followed her in.

Gina leaned over and kissed her mother's forehead. "I like blue on you."

She preened in her satin bed jacket. "I put on my best. Tell me all about your visit to the halls of justice."

Florence poured Gina a cup of coffee from the carafe on the bed tray. "Let her relax a moment, Marie."

After taking a sip of the strong coffee, Gina said, "I met the man I want to marry."

She certainly knew how to get her mother's attention.

Mother clapped her hands. "About time. I wondered how long I'd have to put up with this bed-ridden existence, waiting for a hint of grandchildren."

Gina started to cry. Her tears came in great horrid bursts of sobs. She never cried in front of her mother, thinking it evil, even cruel, not to maintain a measure of cheerfulness while her mother battled the serious illness.

"Mother," she choked out. "I'm so sorry."

Mother handed a box of tissues to her. "'Bout time you showed some emotion about my leaving this dilapidated house."

Gina peeked around the tissue to find her mother smiling at her.

"You've been through a lot." Mother shook her head. "Seeing a man shot to death before your eyes."

"Florence!" Gina was shocked she'd shared the gory facts.

"Not me," Florence defended herself. "Marie insists on watching the news. They've gone over every detail of the robbery five times in the last twenty-four hours."

"So, are you in love with the guard? Or the sergeant?" Mother asked.

"I was just kidding." Even though, Gina knew her mother could see into her soul.

"No, you weren't," Mother insisted. "Which one?"

"The guard, Thomas Woods." Gina pushed her chin up to counteract any adverse opinion. "I think he would make a good friend."

"I suspect he is soft and needy after seeing his twin gunned down."

Gina wished that were true. "More vengeful than needy."

"Understandable," Mother said.

"But, Mother. The man who shot Jonas got away. Danny Bianco is just a kid and didn't even have a gun."

"Your hero thinks he should be put away forever."

"Yes," Gina felt weepy again, but checked herself. "Florence, if you can stay this evening, Tom wants to take me out for dinner."

Florence nodded.

"Would you mind meeting him, Mother?"

"Can't wait. Florence, put all these medicines out of sight. And please open the windows. I hate the smell of disinfectants."

* * *

Tom made sure he arrived on time.

Gina was biting her lower lip, but she looked great in a black short skirt and white silk blouse.

"My mother would like to meet you." Gina indicated the open archway to the front room.

The bright room was paneled with books. Facing the fireplace, Mrs. Branson sat like a queen in a high-pillowed bed next to the window.

"Thomas Woods?" the older woman's voice was strong, but her eyes were red-rimmed from illness.

"Yes, ma'am," he answered. "Pleased to meet you."

"You can call me Marie. Knew your parents when they were courting." She motioned for him to sit down on a padded stool next to the bed. "I worked with your mother at DuKane. I was secretary to the vice president back then. He was the owner's son. Younger son died in a swimming challenge. But, you don't want to know about them. Sorry, I was to hear *how* your parents perished."

Tom looked toward the hall for Gina, who was occupied with Mrs. Branson's nurse.

Marie tapped his knee to get his attention. "I'd like you to hurry this courtship along, so I can kiss a married daughter before I die."

Tom nearly flew off the stool. "Ma'am, I never--."

"Relax," she grinned impishly.

He was standing open-mouthed when Gina came back into the room.

"Mother," she scolded, "what have you been saying to Tom?"

"Nothing." Marie smiled innocently at him. "Have I said anything to upset you?"

"Of course not," Tom lied, relieved to find he was smiling at her joke. "We're just getting to know each other."

Gina was struggling with her coat.

He'd almost forgotten how to help a woman, but he managed.

Marie nodded her approval. "Hope to see you soon."

Gina eyed him suspiciously as she got into his car. "How did Mother shock you?"

"Said I better marry you before she dies." Tom laughed, until her face crumpled instead of smiling. "Sorry. Gina, I'm sorry. I know she's ill."

"Mother's such a card." Gina finally grinned. "She's entertaining herself by putting you on the spot."

"Did a very good job." He laughed again out of politeness. "Is the Cove Restaurant okay for tonight?" He tried to keep the subject light. "I wish I could kid with people like your mother does so easily."

* * *

The Cove Restaurant

The Cove Restaurant's entrance on Riverside Drive north of St. Charles was difficult to find. He remembered a guard rail proceeded the sharp left turn down a gravel path to the river. During Prohibition, gangsters had used the place to run Canadian whiskey down from Wisconsin. The Fox River Dam in St. Charles required they truck the casks into Batavia for a boat to the mighty Mississippi.

The darkness in his chest amplified the black night and the dark river behind the secluded restaurant. Tom took a moment to brace his voice for a cheerful tone. "I usually tell the punch line before I get a joke told."

"Me too. Florence told me one of Woody Allen's, 'There are a million ways to get from birth to death, and they all work.'" Gina made a face. "Sorry, that was tactless."

All he could say was, "Jokes aren't really in our future are they?"

"Serious stuff __ murder and cancer."

Tom nodded.

In the restaurant, conversation ceased until they were seated and the waiter disappeared with their order. "Beautiful Fall, isn't it?" he tried a safe topic.

Gina lifted the lemon wedge from her water before answering. "I hadn't really noticed." She sipped from the iced water and added, "I do think mothers should put winter coats on their children earlier. Of course by afternoon, the kids drag them on the ground because it's gotten too warm. I drive a school bus for Geneva's public schools."

Tom's opinion of his hostage-mate rose. She was obviously a conscientious worker.

Over vegetarian spaghetti sauce and a glass of Merlot for Gina, they both kept to safe subjects.

Tom appreciated Gina's tact when she didn't ask him to share a bottle with her.

"I worked as a Radio Shack manager before I decided to get a degree in counseling." Tom poured himself more water from the sparkling decanter on the table. "Some of the customers showed up in a state of constant suffering, those who weren't obviously on drugs. I decided to do more than plug them into electronic entertainment."

Gina's smile of understanding encouraged him to ask about her life after they took a moment to order dessert. He settled for a pineapple pudding and she chose the tiramisu.

"A racecar career might sound glamorous, but I lost too many people in horrible crashes to ignore my mother's call to come home."

Tom's fancy dessert dish was empty so he had to bring it up. "You never told me exactly what you said to Sergeant Muller."

"Didn't I?" She folded her napkin, as if she wished she could end the discussion before it started. "Muller said your sister-in-law and I have the same facial bones." Gina blushed and then changed the subject away from herself. "Danny was in juvenile detention since he was seven."

"For what?"

"Danny's uncle, the same one who shot Jonas, claimed Danny killed his own mother."

"At age seven?"

"Exactly." Gina leaned forward.

Tom couldn't help noticing the movement of her ample breasts.

"A child couldn't wield a knife with enough strength to murder anyone." Gina moved back in her chair, aligning her socially straight back.

Ruing the loss of cleavage, Tom wasn't certain he'd alerted her to his sexual focus.

Gina continued after finishing her wine, "Danny's mother was his uncle's sister. Danny might have seen his uncle kill his mother, which would explain the narcolepsy."

"Violent backgrounds produce violent felons."

"Not always," Gina said. "What about all the relatives of the presidents assassinated in this country?"

"So you defended Danny to Muller?" He tapped her wrist with his index finger.

Her blush went deep red. "I know it seems unloyal to your brother."

"Disloyal," Tom corrected. "How did Muller respond?"

"He said the prosecutor would treat me as a hostile witness."

Tom didn't want her to feel uncomfortable. "Probably why he didn't believe a word of what I said."

"What did you say?" She arched her brow and the frown line between her blue eyes reappeared.

"It doesn't matter. I told Muller Danny was dancing around making fun of us."

Gina stood, making the glassware shake. "That's an outright lie."

"Sit down." Tom handed the attentive waiter his credit card. "I'm kidding you. I told him what I saw of the second man, which wasn't much with my back turned. They are looking for him. How tall was he?"

Gina sat back down. "I couldn't really tell. I'd have to see him behind the teller's counter to know if it's him. I remember how he walked and his girth."

He studied his emptied dish, wishing he'd never mentioned the robbery. "When do we show up again for court?"

The waiter return to the table. "Sir, do you have another credit card?" The waiter handed Tom the offending one. "Your limit has been exceeded."

Tom looked at Gina, who searched her purse for the money.

Outside he apologized. "Sorry. I haven't been taking care of my finances lately. I thought there would be enough credit left. I probably won't even have a job after the robbery. Does Geneva's school district need any more bus drivers?"

"They're always asking for people. Come by tomorrow at four in the morning and we can drive to the terminal together."

"That's awfully white of you." Tonight hadn't worked out the way Tom had planned. He'd wanted to impress her since that look she gave him in the bank when she'd untied the ropes. He took her hand as he seated her in his newly cleaned car. "I hope you weren't too embarrassed."

"I'm fine," she said. "I enjoy being with you."

He stood there with the door open, not knowing what to say. No wonder her mother thought he was courting. The girl liked him.

He wondered how long he'd been standing there when Gina finally called his name. "Tom, it's okay."

"My reactions are kind of slow since the murder." After taking a deep breath, he circled the trunk and got behind the wheel. "Wouldn't it be ironic if we did become more than friends because of this?"

"Mother says life needs to continue for the living."

"I guess," Tom said, not really liking the platitude.

He glanced at this young woman who said she found him—what, likable? Her dark curls surrounded a sweet face. Long lashes flirted with her ivory cheeks, hardly the mannish mannerisms he'd expected from a racecar driver.

Gina wasn't soft. Who could discount a good heart? Still the circumstances didn't readily promote romance.

"Coming to the funeral on Friday?" Tom's stomach felt as if he'd punched himself.

"I'll be there." Then Gina reached over, curved her hand behind his head and kissed his mouth.

The kiss was sweet and long enough for him to kiss her back, embrace her and wonder what he was doing. His mind was going. Under her lilac perfume, he smelled cedar: -- rich, exotic and compelling.

"I might not have a job." Tom pushed her gently away from him.

Gina didn't back off, so he added, "And after my sister-in-law sells the house I won't have a place to stay."

"Until you finish your degree, you'll be a bus driver like I am." She straightened her short skirt over her long legs. "And you could live with us, until you find something else."

All he could do was shake his head, *No.*

"Why not? You could have a bedroom all to yourself in the attic, and the place needs a man." She laughed. "You could help move the buckets around when it rains. And Mother would love it." Gina was all smiles, oblivious to any of his problems and their differences concerning a certain juvenile delinquent.

Not possible, he wanted to say but the words wouldn't form on the lips she had just kissed.

* * *

Gina couldn't stop herself. The giant of a man had looked so helpless. She had to kiss him. Tom needed to know right then how attractive he was, how thoroughly male. He was a therapist, after all. He'd come to his senses soon and help her get Danny freed.

His response was stronger than their first kiss. His warmth infused her veins with passion and relief. The world remained fresh and untouched by the horrible events they had both witnessed, shared.

Would Tom come to live under her mother's roof, too? Maybe having him too close would ruin everything or anything which might develop between them.

* * *

St. Patrick's, St. Charles, Illinois
Wednesday, October 3rd

On Wednesday, all Tom Woods wanted to remember at his brother's funeral Mass were Father Damion's comforting words, but at the open grave site with the boys clinging to him and Dolly needing his strength, Tom couldn't recall one syllable.

Dolly's parents were grief-stricken too. Dolly was their only child and they'd loved Jonas as if he'd been their son. Maybe an Orphans' Anonymous program existed, where he could join a group of weeping adults giving their first names to strangers.

A blackbird settled on the pungent earth next to the grave, flapped its wings but didn't fly away. Another bird joined it before both birds walked off toward a slight rise and then took off flying, finally circling over the burial site.

My parents' spirits, Tom thought irrationally, *to guide Jonas home.'*

After the service ended, Gina came up to him as he stood next to Dolly.

"I don't want you to worry about Tom," she said to Dolly. "He's agreed to move in with my mother and me when you sell the house."

"Good," Dolly said.

Tom could tell Dolly was actually relieved.

He thanked Gina in his heart even if his head wouldn't yet agree to the move. Gina and he had already worked together for two days as bus drivers for the Geneva Public Schools.

Tom did look forward to the happy faces of the kids, sleepy in the morning, over-stimulated in the afternoon. He liked his new job.

Gina was a devout protector of the children. She would get out of the bus and walk around it, checking out everyone and every moving thing within range of her suspicions. The children couldn't receive better care than Gina Branson's.

And besides being capable, she was a joy to watch. Her lithe body had grace and a certain drawing power. Tom wondered if he'd change jobs immediately after he finished school. He liked just being around her.

Sergeant Muller interrupted. "Mrs. Woods, I'm sorry for your loss. I'm the investigator for the case."

"I wasn't there," Dolly said.

"No, of course not," he said, taking her glove hand and motioning toward Gina and Tom. "I needed to tell them the arraignment is tomorrow morning. Sorry again for the intrusion." Muller's face was surprisingly red as he stumbled on with his condolences. "You probably don't remember the day I brought Tom and Gina to your house."

"I remember," Dolly said and patted the somber detectives hand as it still grasped hers.

"Tomorrow? Thursday?" Tom repeated. He'd forgotten it was so soon.

"Why was it moved?" Gina asked.

"The boy's lawyer." Muller hadn't turned away from Dolly, who was studying the tops of her black shoes.

Gina didn't say any more, but Tom worried when a frown entrenched in her brow. Something was wrong, and he didn't have time to talk to her about it today.

"I'll be there," he said.

Gina nodded before grabbing for Muller's arm and speaking earnestly to him all the way to her car.

* * *

Settled into her Mustang away from the crowd of mourners, Gina called the number Muller had given her. Danny's lawyer wasn't happy about granting her permission to visit.

"I'll meet you there at four o'clock today," he finally said in a dismissive manner.

Gina looked at her cell phone. Was the lawyer's voice familiar, or just his manner of speaking down to women? Gina had planned to speak to the boy alone; to beg him to tell the police where his uncle might be hiding.

In front of another male, this lawyer, Danny might not readily give up his uncle.

CHAPTER FOUR

Home from the chilly funeral, Gina deemed her wardrobe inadequate for the task of advocating for Danny's innocence. She wanted Danny to feel comfortable enough to open up, but she needed to impress his grouchy lawyer too. She hung her coat on a peg inside the bedroom door in the attic and kicked off her modest black pumps.

Would Tom be able to live up here comfortably? He hadn't yet agreed to come, but he hadn't told her no.

Gina clutched an armload of her clothes from the attic closet and moved them to the second-floor guest room. She climbed the stairs to the attic again and embraced the oval free-standing mirror, walking it down the narrow stairs to her new bedroom.

She dusted off the high-necked black wool dress she'd worn to the funeral, trusting her black-strapped heels and sheer nylons would win the defense lawyer's attention. Her beaded necklace with the silly elephants might appeal to Danny. His lawyer needed to investigate Danny's earlier ridiculous murder charge of his mother to alleviate any prejudice in the jury trial of Jonas's killer.

* * *

Kane County Courthouse Jail, Geneva

Gina parked in a metered spot luckily vacated by a shopper laden with clothing bags. What was she doing? Mother's seventy-second birthday was on Sunday and Gina couldn't imagine an appropriate gift. She should be looking after her mother instead of trying to save Danny. Rain pelted the car. Her coat still held its funeral flowers scent. Luckily her car had its own designated umbrella.

Pushing the bar handle on the jail's entrance, Gina backed into the door and folded her umbrella so that most of the runoff would stay outside. The back of her nylons were no doubt spattered with dirty rain water. She slid her hand in turn down each calf to her ankle. The uniformed officer at the desk ignored her performance. Jails weren't meant to be welcoming, she told herself.

Luckily, she was allowed to see Danny alone, because his lawyer was still on his way.

The metal fillings in her teeth resonated with the sound of grating steel-on-steel as she was escorted through several sliding doors. The table they allowed in the visitor's room was made of heavy oak. Not one initial had been carved into the beautiful wood. Gina smoothed her damp hands over its pristine surface, before turning her wet coat inside out and folding it over the back of her chair.

She ran her hand over her hair to see if it was windblown.

The perfect present for her mother flashed in front of her. Constant visitors to Mother's beside required a semblance of order. Florence fussed with her patient's hair and makeup, but her mother might appreciate a mirror to monitor the latest traces of stress and drugs. An antique hand mirror was the answer.

Danny smiled when he first spotted Gina, then let his face fall back into its defensive mask.

She stood, but the guard motioned for her to sit back down as he stepped back to the door, arms crossed, as witness and protector.

"Are they treating you all right? Do you need anything? Is it all right that I came?"

Danny grinned at her. "Yes, yes, and yes."

"What do you need?" Gina returned his smile. She stretched out her hand to pat his folded arms before checking to see if the guard allowed that.

The guard accepted the harmless touch of comfort.

"Books," Danny said. "I'm all right if I can read." He blushed slightly. "You know take a trip and never leave the farm."

Was that a hint of a tear? Danny wiped his nose with his shirt sleeve. "I'll bring some by tonight."

At first Danny seemed delighted, then shut down defending against a possible disappointment

"I promise," she added.

Danny cracked his knuckles to break the silence. "Why did you come?"

"I'm a hostile witness for the prosecutor. You didn't hurt anyone and I want them to arrest your uncle for killing the loan officer." Gina didn't use Jonas's name, thinking the crime would seem too personalized.

Danny sat quietly as if going over her words carefully. "I don't want my uncle found out."

"Why not?" She couldn't believe it. "You could be sent away for a very long time if they can't catch him."

The boy tugged on his white hair. "He's the only family I have."

She knew that. "When did your hair turn white?"

"At the Boys' Home," he said not lifting his head. "I hit a kid with a shovel after he tried to touch me. The guards held me by my feet, head first down into a sewage cistern." Danny looked up to check out the effect of his story.

Gina wondered how long her mouth was open.

"I nearly died," he said to her shocked expression.

Then the door behind them opened and the guard stiffened.

"Alan Passantino," a wide man in a brown tweed suit said. "Danny's family lawyer."

"Gina Branson," she said without extending her hand.

"What have you been telling her?" the lawyer asked.

Danny smiled from ear to ear. His teeth gleamed in the harsh light. "Told her why I have white hair."

The lawyer explained in a monotone, "Penicillin from an infection in juvenile detention."

"I want you to look into those earlier charges," Gina said.

Passantino sat down, opened the button on his musty smelling, tight coat and shook his head. "The case is closed and Danny paid his dues to society."

"You can't believe Danny did anything like that at seven?" Gina noticed Danny had started to nod off.

"Danny, Danny," she called, "What books should I bring tonight."

Instant attention. "Robinson Crusoe and Proust," he said, then toned down his enthusiasm. "If you can find a copy."

"I'll bring you mine," she said. "It's not as if I won't be able to find you to retrieve them."

"Yeah," he said sounding retarded again. Then he perked up. Danny slid his hand to her side of the table, barely allowing his fingertips to touch her hand. "Sometimes I can't sleep."

"Could we talk before you leave?" she asked Passantino.

"Heavy case load," he said, rummaging through a briefcase on the chair away from her. "I'll call you. Now if you don't mind I should spend some time with my client."

"Of course," she said and headed for the door. "I'll leave the books at the desk tonight," she again promised Danny, who grinned heartily before lowering his head for the lawyer's interrogation.

At the desk Gina asked for Sergeant Muller. He wasn't available, but she left her number. She didn't know if the police were allowed to investigate lawyers, but she knew she didn't like Danny's.

* * *

Thursday, October 4th

At eight o'clock Thursday morning a chartered Chicago bus patiently waited in the parking lot next to the Geneva grammar school. Tom Woods's bus returned from collecting children on his run. The school scheduled an art museum tour once a month. Tom looked too big to get through the door. Lowering his head nearly to his chest, he climbed out of the bus.

"Tight fit?" Gina asked.

"Don't laugh. You're the one that got me this midget's job."

"I was laughing with you," she lied.

"Was I laughing?"

After transferring the children and their parental chaperon's to the charted bus, Gina and Tom walked to their cars, he slid his arm around her waist. "Sexy bitch."

"Me?" She knew it shouldn't, but the epithet pleased her.

"You," he said drawing her closer. "With this overtime I think I can afford a cup of coffee before we head to the court house."

* * *

Wisniewski's Coffee Shop, Geneva

Over coffee cups at Wisniewski's to keep Tom's thoughts away from the courtroom, Gina asked, "When do you plan to move in?"

He sighed. "How about Saturday, or is that too soon?"

Tom's left arm rested on their small table.

Gina explained, "Mother's seventy-second birthday is Sunday. Please come and move in the next Saturday, October the 13th? I'll tell Mother to expect a boarder." Then Gina remembered the initial state of his Escort. "You have a dog."

"Not me. I take my neighbor's dog for a walk every Sunday. His name is Mikey."

Gina's heart flip-flopped. "And your neighbor's name?"

He scratched his head, then showed his delight at remembering, "Evelyn Stiles."

"A stylish maiden?"

"Once," Tom grinned. "You can't be jealous of an eighty-six-year-old woman."

As she smiled up at the burly waitress bringing a refill, Gina noticed the walls of the place were covered with labor-intensive antiques. Whiffletrees, double oxen yokes, rusty plows, wooden hay rakes, and wire rug beaters were nailed at various angles above the wainscoting. Next to a wash board, a clothes wringer from an old washing machine hung at a precarious slant. Its shiny handle reflected the sun's bright rays.

"I wonder what the great, grandchildren of this electronic age will save for antiques?"

Tom looked around the walls. "VCR's. DVD's, IPhones?"

"Maybe the old seventy-eights in my mother's basement will be worth a penny or two." Her coffee was fresh and the exact temperature Gina liked. "The attic got cleared out when my stepdad redecorated it. The walls are lined in cedar."

"The entire attic?" Tom reached for her hand. "When we kissed, I did smell cedar. I thought I was losing my mind."

Gina appreciated the moment. She wanted to ask him if he remembered recognizing her licentious thoughts when he was tied up at the bank, but she couldn't throw away their camaraderie with words recalling the death of his brother. "What are the tools of today?"

"Keyboards and cell phones?"

They were becoming friends. Her watch read nine o'clock. Still plenty of time before the ten o'clock court date. "I need to buy my mother a birthday present. I thought a hand mirror would work."

"There's an antique shop next door."

Geneva's antique shops had invaded every nook and cranny of the original industrial town's main street. The dry-goods store was now filled with antique clocks and model sailing ships. Two grocery stores held antique toys and guns. A furniture emporium stocked stained-glass windows and claw-footed bath tubs. Even in St. Charles, the town touching Geneva's borders, the obsession with antiques provided enough market for more than a dozen historical homes to be turned into profitable shops.

Gina spied a silver hand mirror with mother of pearl roses decorating its back. "I found one," she called to Tom.

A teenage sales clerk adjusted her braless breasts for Tom's approval. Tom coughed and turned his back on the child. "I won't need a truck on Saturday."

"Don't you have very much furniture?"

"None. Just my clothes and books."

Books. He loved books too. Gina ventured, "I loaned Danny two books he asked for yesterday."

"I told you not to visit him." Tom studied the carved design in the back of an ancient rocking chair with too much intensity.

Gina's chin lifted. "I never do what I'm told." Inviting this antagonistic man to live in her mother's house might not have been such a good idea.

"Sorry," he said. "I don't know what gets into me." Then Tom turned in her direction, surveying her with those smoldering eyes. "I guess you bring out all the male testosterone symptoms."

Instant forgiveness or understanding warmed her heart. She ducked her head somewhat embarrassed at her planned revelation. "I'm constantly repeating the Lord's Prayer in my head and in the shower today."

Tom hadn't wavered in his attention.

"Anyway, I noticed the prayer doesn't have room to ask for anything specific, just daily bread." she hurried on afraid to lose her audience, "And the part about forgiving ourselves as we forgive others might mean if we can diminish the importance of our own faults in the overall scheme of things, the transgressions of others might be lessened."

Tom seemed to be digesting her words. "Dolly's priest came over to see her, but she was at her mother's. I asked him about the Lord's Prayer, because I stumbled over the same phrase, about forgiving others as we want to be forgiven. Kind of frightening if the Lord can't forgive me the way I can't forgive Danny."

Gina waited, but finally broke the silence to ask, "How did he answer you?"

As if pulled out of the bank nightmare, Tom shook himself. "Sorry. Right, the priest said something about the Lord at the crucifixion. He didn't say, 'Father, I forgive them because they know not what they do.' He was in so much pain He couldn't forgive them, like me about my brother's death. Instead, the Lord said, 'Father (you) forgive them because they know not what they do.' So I asked the Lord to forgive whoever caused my brother's death because right now, I'm too injured to conjure up forgiveness."

Gina thought she might as well confess. "I met Danny's Italian lawyer too."

Again Tom's head went down, bull fashion, but he recovered his civilized self enough to ask, "What books did the kid want?"

"Robinson Crusoe and Proust!"

"Wow. Who would have guessed?"

"Danny has trouble sleeping." She almost lost Tom's sympathetic attention again so she quickly added. "Something about the lawyer seemed too familiar."

"He got fresh with you?"

She hunched her shoulders, then tried to relax. "No. Not even friendly. Paranoia in a jail is perfectly sane, isn't it?"

Tom continued to stare at her.

She fidgeted. "A fat family lawyer, Passantino."

"Bianco," Tom said, remembering Danny's last name.

"Passantino did resemble Danny, but his eyes were cold."

"Wait just a minute."

"I'm insane," she told him. "His uncle wouldn't show up to counsel him, would he?"

* * *

Kane County Court House

At ten o'clock Tom followed Gina up the marble stairs to the round balcony where the doors to the criminal courtrooms could be found. Here were the paintings, sculpture and hallowed halls Tom had expected when he visited the police station next door. No concrete blocks were in evidence, only polished wood and brass accouterments. The tops of eight foot windows held stained glass symbols of justice, peace and harmony. All was right with the world.

The preliminary hearing room was a sea of smelly people. Lawyers and families of victims and families of criminals jostled each other. They heaved en masse toward the judge's stand when their man or woman's name was called. Waves of citizens exited the double doors as soon as bail or a decision to remand was made. Tom likened them to a field of wheat, each shaft of misery swaying with the news of one of their own, being laid low or lifted up.

When Danny was brought in wearing an orange jumpsuit, Gina was on her feet shoving people with both hands to claim a seat near the front divider. Tom followed her effective push towards the front.

Two prosecuting lawyers, a young woman and an older thin man, stood shuffling papers at a front desk to the left of the judge's view. Sergeant Muller was already seated at their table.

On the right the guards unshackled the prisoner and took their position against the exit leading to the holding cells. No lawyer stood next to the teenager.

"Case number--."

The judge held up his hand and the clerk stopped his litany. "Where is the lawyer for the defendant?"

Danny spoke in a strong clear voice. "He told me to tell you I fired him."

"Did you?"

"Well, no, sir. My uncle says there's no hope for me. It was an inside job."

Tom jumped up. The judge frowned directly at him.

Gina was on her feet too. "Judge, sir, may I speak?"

"Does it concern this young man's attorney?" Gina nodded. "In my chambers." The judge sighed deeply.

The prosecutors, Sergeant Muller, Gina and Tom all followed the clerk down the hall to Judge Joseph Wilcox's office. The judge entered from a side door. "Mr. Novak, Steffen, I'm sure your new assistant, Ms. Krisch, knows we can't have a trial set without a lawyer for the defense."

"Sergeant Muller," Gina ignored the pomp and went straight to the point. "Danny's uncle was posing as his lawyer when I visited him."

Muller went to the outer door and called one of his officers. "One moment, Judge," he waved in the judge's direction. "Issue a warrant for Alan Passantino. His address might be on the admittance sheet at the jail."

Mr. Novak called Muller over.

Tom heard them whisper, ". . . .inside job. . . . .his brother."

Tom sat down in a chair against the wall. This was going to take a while to sort out.

"Passantino is the man who killed, Jonas Woods, the loan officer at the bank." Gina spoke directly to the judge.

"How does this affect your case?" the Judge addressed the prosecutors.

"We'd like a continuance," Ms. Krisch said. "The victim did possess stolen money in his pockets."

Tom couldn't contain himself, he jumped up saying, "It was falling from the sky. None of us knew what to do. Jonas is innocent! The kid is blaming his victim!"

The judge completely ignored him. "Continuance granted. In the meantime." The judge turned to the clerk. "Appoint an attorney for the defendant."

"Judge Wilcox?" Gina moved forward.

The judge sighed again. "Yes, young lady. What is your name for the record and who are you?"

"I'm Gina Branson. I and Tom Woods, the deceased's twin brother." Gina turned and pointed at Tom, who was now standing. "We were hostages when Danny's uncle left with the money and the guns."

"Judge?" Ms. Krisch objected.

"What is it you want, Miss Branson?" Judge Wilcox asked without patience.

"I want Danny Bianco to see a court-appointed therapist. He has narcolepsy and his uncle accused him of killing his mother when he was seven. Passantino is determined to implicate the victim again!"

"Young woman," Mr. Novak began, "this is not the place--."

Judge Wilcox waved his hand for silence. "So appointed." He nodded to the clerk, then the clerk and the judge exited through a door in the back of the small room. "Interesting morning," he told the clerk.

When Tom and Gina followed the prosecutors down the hall, Tom noticed they were still shaking their heads.

Gina had a definite spring to her step.

Tom had to push himself to keep up with her. "Well, you handled that situation." Tom hooked his arm in her elbow. "Is it safe to move in with a bulldozer of justice?"

"Me?" Gina turned a radiant smile on him. "The case hasn't started."

Hard to be angry at her impish face, but he was. "Justice delayed is justice deferred," was all he could manage out of a wellspring of frustration.

Deep in Tom's soul his guilt rose, obliterating some of his anger. Gina couldn't solve what bothered him the most. He could have saved his twin, if he'd learned how to shoot. A drink would taste awfully good. The past was unchangeable. Tom searched his brain for the prayer he'd read to start his day. Ah, there it was lodged behind the word, acceptance. "Nothing gives rest but the sincere search for truth."

Gina was right. Forgiving himself would have to precede forgiveness for Jonas's murderer.

* * *

Sergeant Muller was waiting in the fresh air near Gina's car. "Let's walk over to my office for a minute."

"An inside job is ridiculous," Gina said. "Jonas reacted to the moment."

"Convince me," Muller said walking them back toward the jail to his office. "I'll run a credit check on Jonas. Did he have money problems?"

Tom tasted bile at the back of his throat. He stopped mid-stride and kicked the tire of the nearest car. *Bout broke your toe'* he told himself. "You believe that punk?"

Gina moved closer to the sergeant, her blue eyes widening.

Muller raised and lowered his forearms as if to settle the wind of hostility emanating from Tom. "Just a few questions."

Tom stormed away before he could shorten Muller by pounding him straight into the pavement. Tom stopped and yelled back over his shoulder, "You're accusing the victim!"

Muller gave up, dismissing Gina, who ran to catch up with Tom.

"Idiots," Tom spat out.

"They're wrong." Gina unlocked the car, but Tom couldn't bend his anger enough to sit down. "Lock it," he said. "Let's walk."

"Sure, sure," Gina said.

Tom headed south. How far could he walk? At this rate he'd be in Florida before nightfall. He slowed and reached for Gina's hand.

Then dropped it when she said, "Danny doesn't believe that."

He felt so tired. Adrenaline had run its course. He sat down on the low stone wall bordering St. Mary's convent school lawns.

Gina stood facing him. "Did Danny make any comment in the bank to make you believe your brother was involved?"

Tom shook his head. The sun was warm and the lawn behind his back invitingly soft. He pressed his fingertips into the grass behind him until his fingernails scraped cool soil. Jonas. Jonas was under earth and sod.

Gina watched him. Her concern and awareness of his shift of mood intrigued him. She was really beautiful. Tom wiped his hands on his jeans.

Gina stopped his inspection of the black dirt under his fingernails. "Danny didn't think that lie up by himself."

"His uncle?"

She moved a step back to reassess his reaction.

"I'm exhausted," he said.

Gina patted his shoulder. "You rest. I'll go for the car."

"No." Tom reclined on the grass, then pushed himself erect. "I can walk." They retraced their steps to the parking lot west of the courthouse square. "We walked farther than I intended." His legs were leaden sticks.

"I'm thirsty," Gina said.

"I need the facilities too," Tom said. "I think I'm going to be sick." Diarrhea threatened.

* * *

Inside the jail the desk officer recognized them. "Muller said you'd be along."

Tom headed for the john and Gina drank at the water fountain in the short hall. She remembered Danny's delay at the water fountain in Geneva's bank after his uncle abandoned the poor kid.

Muller escorted them into his office. "I agree it's nuts, Tom. But, we need to put this to rest. I don't cherish asking the widow about her husband."

Nearly crumbling into an upholstered chair along the wall, Tom held his head up with one hand.

"Danny didn't think this up by himself," Gina said.

"I agree." Sergeant Muller tapped a closed file on his desk.

They both waited for a response from Tom, who only shook his head.

"You two get out of here." Muller opened the door. "I'll call you if I need to. Try to get some rest." Muller stuck out his hand to shake with Tom.

Tom shook it moving like a zombie.

In Gina's car, Tom laid his head against the headrest. "I wonder if this is what narcolepsy feels like?"

Gina beamed at him, probably because Tom wasn't blaming Danny for his uncle's insinuation of an inside contact at the bank.

"If Jonas is suspected of being involved," Tom said, "I will be too."

CHAPTER FIVE

Dean Street, Geneva
Saturday, October 13th

Gina jumped out of bed on Saturday morning because Tom was moving in. She made her bed in the smaller room, chiding herself for being happy while Mother was in such misery.

Still in silk pajamas she peeked into the front room.

Her mother's hand hung down from the bed with her fingers clenching and unclenching. Gently grasping her hand, Gina asked quietly, "Mother?"

"Yes, dear," her mother smiled with an effort. "Time for another dose."

Gina hurried to the kitchen for a glass of iced water. 'Calm,' she insisted. 'Remain calm.'

As she handed over the open pill container and watched her shake out two pain killers, calmness was furthest from her mind. Gina wanted to hit something big. Take her car out and ram it into the nearest moving vehicle, hopefully a truck. Roll over a gravel truck at high speed, back up and smash it again.

"Gina," Mother said, tugging at the glass still in Gina's hand.

Gina released the glass.

"What were you thinking just then?" Her mother downed a double dose of pain pills. "Is that young man refusing to budge?"

"No. He's moving in." Gina tugged at her bangs. "I get angry because you're suffering. You never hurt anyone. Why should you be punished?"

"Who better?" Mother grinned then patted her hand. "I get mad, too; but then I try to pick someone to visit this on."

Silence reigned as they both thought about unforgiven enemies, strangers, evil men and mean women, who might need chastisement.

"See?" Mother reached out her arms. "Give your old mother a hug. The discomfort is manageable now. I don't see my dying as a punishment for anything I've done."

Gina noticed the whites of her mother's eyes were yellowish. "Then why does God allow pain?"

"Sometimes I think God is like a child trying to see how bad He can be to prove He's loved. I do love the Lord. I receive solace, even when the torment is the greatest, as if the universe knows of me—and cares." Mother sat up straighter on the pillows and smoothed the coverlet. "In the evenings the agony seems amplified. Isn't that strange?"

When Florence arrived, Gina pleaded, "Please call Doctor Wiggins to prescribe a self-regulated morphine drip.

"That would help." Menasha was only a few steps behind Florence. His arms were filled with three dozen yellow roses and glazed donuts for everyone.

Florence didn't seem to approve of the morphine drip. "Marie, you'd have to be careful. Maybe I should stay here in the evenings."

Mother waved at them airily. "I'd like to sleep through one night."

"Florence," Menasha said. "I believe everyone should be able to choose their time to die."

"I'm Catholic," Florence answered testily.

"Why does that matter?" Menasha asked.

Gina had been raised as an Episcopalian but knew Florence referred to suicide, which was not an option for strict adherents of the Roman Church, even in the worst, painful moments.

"Protestants get a better deal." Mother was feeling her oats.

Gina straightened the coverlet. "You're about as Protestant as Joan of Arc."

"She was the first!" Mother held up one finger.

Menasha followed Florence into the kitchen to find more vases and fresh coffee.

"Gina," Mother whispered. "I have a favor to ask." Gina embraced the slight frame of her once strong mother listening closely. "Menasha lives by himself and when I'm gone his life—well, you know. Make a match."

Gina shook her head.

Her mother swatted at Gina's arm, acting disgusted with her obtuseness. "Invite them both to dinner, here."

"Menasha has loved you for years." Gina knew his heart would be broken.

"And he'll need someone. What can it hurt?"

Gina stared at her mother. She was serious. "Okay," she finally agreed. "But they may not like each other."

"They already do," Mother continued to whisper.

Menasha and Florence were laughing when they brought the sweet-smelling roses and fragrant coffee back into the front room.

"Here's my happy pair of helpers." Mother winked at Gina.

Gina hoped her shocked expression would be interpreted as concern about other matters. "I'm off to collect our new house boy," she said as brightly as she could.

"You naughty thing." Mother laughed. "I'm looking forward to the extra hubbub."

* * *

2141 12th Street, St. Charles

No amount of pounding on Tom's basement window produced movement. Gina could hear Dolly's children so she went to the front door and knocked.

Dolly answered. "Good to see you."

"Tom won't wake up. I've been pounding."

"I'll telephone him in a minute but I need to talk to you." Dolly shut the entrance door. "The kids are busy. Come upstairs."

"Do the children help?" Gina asked.

"From missing Jonas?"

Gina could only bob her head.

"They do." Dolly hugged herself. "They take up time and make you think about everything that needs doing."

"I'd like to have about eight. I always wanted brothers and sisters."

"Tom will make a good father. Jonas was." Dolly stood at the top of the stairs as if suspended in her memories. "But Tom isn't fixated on money."

Because of Danny's charges of an inside job at the bank, Gina pursued the subject of money. "Were there money problems?"

"Not one. My parents bailed us out each month."

"Jonas accepted that?"

Dolly went perfectly still as if letting her mind search the recent past. "He would say, 'No sense running on empty.' I agreed."

Jonas's defeat as a provider must have cost him more expense of soul than his wife realized. Did Jonas help Passantino get in the bank before it opened?

"I'd like to show you something I want Tom to take with him, if you have room."

In the master bedroom, Gina admired the suite of mahogany furniture. The rose flowered bedspread matched the upholstery on a love seat and winged-back chair. The four-poster bed did not have a canopy but the mirrored wardrobe, bedside tables, two waist-high dressers and a delicate dressing table and stool all matched.

"What beautiful furniture," Gina said.

"Jonas insisted on buying all this with his parents' life insurance. I've filled the drawers with photograph albums, Christmas cards, letters, and hats. Whoever has enough clothes to fill these pieces has too much to wear. I think Tom spent his inheritance on tuition."

"You must admire the workmanship. My stepdad loved to work with wood."

"Actually, Gina, I hate it." Dolly lingered in the doorway.

"Why?"

"I sleep on the couch now." Dolly shook her head as if to clear it. "I can't wait to go home to my old bedroom at my parents'. I miss Jonas so much." Dolly ventured into the room as if it belonged to a stranger. "I never convinced Jonas I wanted *him* more than anything he could buy me. Isn't that sad? That's why I can't stand this foul furniture."

She pulled the bedspread off, folding it with jerky motions. "Jonas thought I was more passionate in this horrid bed. I was trying to convince him he was the only thing that mattered to me. He misunderstood all my renewed enthusiasm in lovemaking as proof the money accounted for my affection. Why didn't he know, really know I only loved him?"

Gina put her arms around the widow. "Some people never feel worthy of love. The attic, where Tom will be staying, has room for the set. But will he accept all of this?"

"That's the problem." Dolly pushed her hair behind her shoulders. "I'm going to cut my hair too."

"Dolly!"

"I can't help it." Dolly held her hair with both hands to the top of her head. "Jonas liked it long and now I want it short."

"Well, okay. You'll look great."

* * *

Tom refused to understand women. The two of them anyway. Dolly had ordered a truck and two movers before he'd even had his coffee. Gina had accepted Jonas's bedroom furniture for him.

"I'll pay you for it. Slowly," he promised Dolly. "Otherwise you can take it back off the truck."

The two movers stopped in their tracks. One carried pillows for the love seat and the other had a small stool. "Is he kidding?"

"Ignore him," Dolly said and the men proceeded down the steps. "Whatever. I don't want to see it again."

When she went upstairs with a vacuum, Tom zeroed in on Gina. "Why did you encourage her?"

"She's going to cut her hair, too."

"Oh," he said not understanding but giving into the illogical reasoning of women.

Gina moved closer to whisper, "Never tell Dolly that Jonas was dancing at the bank."

"You do smell like cedar." Tom settled his arms around her, nibbling at her ear.

* * *

Dean Street, Geneva

As soon as Tom had the furniture upstairs in Gina's Dean Street attic, the rain started. Gina moved the buckets to their appointed places.

"You're going to ruin all this cedar," Tom said admiring the paneled walls and ceiling of the huge attic.

"And your furniture, if I don't get the roof fixed quickly."

He bent over to light the logs in the fireplace. "Have you sent away for the historical fund application yet?"

"Been kind of busy." Gina tucked rolled-up towels around the buckets.

"I'll do that for you. Come sit for a minute. You've been working like a dog."

"Like a horse. My stepdad used to say I worked until I dropped. Mules only work until they're tired, but horses will kill themselves racing or pulling plows."

"I didn't know that." He rubbed his fingers through her slightly damp curls as he pulled her down on the love seat. "I can't help appreciating the use of Jonas's furniture."

"Dolly is generous."

"To a fault." Tom cradled his favorite woman in his arms. He shouldn't encourage her until she knew the truth about his addictive personality. Then he remembered the day's quote, *Pray to God, but continue to row to shore.* He kissed Gina's sweet mouth. Some modes of travel were sweeter than others. "I'm growing awfully fond of you."

"Mother will like hearing that.' Gina laughed.

"I'm serious," Tom said into her ear, feeling her respond to the heat he was experiencing. *Not now,* he told himself. Wait until you know she cares for you, too.

* * *

After a light supper of cold chicken and salad at the kitchen table, Gina invited Tom into the front room. "Do you mind spending a little time with Mother this evening?"

"I really enjoy your mother," Tom said reaching for the coffee pot Gina carried.

Gina hoped he wouldn't comment on how much ground her mother had lost in her fight against the cancer.

"Mrs. Branson," he said as he approached the bed. "I've arrived as your new boarder."

"I told Florence there must be squirrels in the attic, but I guess that was you." Marie positioned a quilted sham to hide her bloated stomach. "Sounds like you moved in an entire town."

"My brother's widow insisted I take away half her house." Tom took her hand and sat down on the padded stool of honor, next to the hospital bed. His elbow knocked into the drip stand. "Sorry, I'm a clumsy giant."

"A grand shape of a man, you are," Marie said. "I've got enough medical equipment in here to start my own emergency room."

Tom nodded, but couldn't seem to think of more to say. He poured Marie and Gina coffee from the pot.

"Mother's been telling me her theories on why God allows suffering," Gina said just to fill the air with words.

Tom answered softly. "I've been taught since childhood all the reasons why Job was chided for complaining. The great Creator of the world is beyond questioning." He shook himself as if to disengage dark thoughts. "Dolly and my nephews needed my brother."

"Who wants to give up this life, even the leaves on trees seem to fight to stay." Marie said. "Who wants to be without sunlight?"

"Maybe--," Gina thought of all the platitudes of heaven as a better place where souls yearn to be, but couldn't recommend anything but life.

"You wouldn't expect a dog to understand Einstein?" Marie said, motioning for Tom to refill her cup.

"But we question," Tom mused.

"Faith is a gift," Marie said. "Life and death still take courage if we believe or not. But faith allows solace. We hope someone greater than ourselves cares."

"My brother, Jonas, went out not knowing." Tom said. "Maybe we should talk about happier subjects."

"Like the poor boy Gina is trying to help?" Marie asked.

"I don't think so," Tom managed as he stepped away from the bed.

Gina mounted the vacated stool. "In the morning, I'm going to see how much Danny has read of Proust."

"Katharine Hepburn read Proust with her evening scotch," Marie said. "Lovely picture, the queen reading away in bed."

Tom paced behind Gina. "How did you really know the lawyer was his uncle?"

Gina kissed her mother's cheek before answering. "Danny said something about finding his uncle 'out.' The word fit with his uncle masquerading as his lawyer."

Marie weakly tugged at Gina's sweat shirt. "Are you going to be Danny's family now that you've banished his uncle?"

"Replace family?" Tom asked.

"I can try to be a friend," Gina said.

* * *

Sunday, October 14th

Sunday night the bathroom sink pipe on the second floor let loose a torrent of water. Gina heard it first and ran up to the attic for a bucket out of Tom's room. "Hot water plumbing disaster." She said and headed for the bathroom.

He was right behind her and shut off the valve under the sink. "Got a towel?" he asked. His hair and shoulders were drenched from the spray. His pajama top revealed a flat stomach, muscles…. Gina reached to touch his warm skin as he dried his face with the towel.

Tom clamped a hand on hers. "All kinds of plumbing problems."

Gina thought she heard a drip. Holding onto Tom's neck, she wanted to ignore the sound, then another drop, then a stream, then a cold spray. She laughed. "Now the cold water has let go."

Tom bent down to turn the off knob for the cold water pipe too. They were both laughing, cleaning up the water, and swatting at each other with the dripping towels.

"What a place for our first tryst." Tom chuckled.

"I'd better check on Mother," Gina said, wrapping her bathrobe more closely around her.

"I'll come too. I can tell her what happened to the pipes."

"Not everything," she cautioned, tugging on the ties of Tom's robe.

In the front room the lights were low. Gina couldn't hear her mother's snores. She switched on the bedside lamp to check on the morphine drip. It was empty. "Mother?" Her mother's eyes were closed but a smile graced her lips.

"Gina," Tom called as if from a long distance.

She didn't want to hear him. She only wanted to look at her mother's smile. "She heard us laughing, Tom," she said, knowing what he would say next.

"Then she's sleeping peacefully, Gina."

Chapter Six

Monday, October 15th

Alone in Gina's attic, Tom couldn't sleep. He punched the pillows of Jonas's bed assailed by the insanity of his twin being accused of aiding thieves. Tom wrestled with his love and loyalty on the one hand and the sure knowledge that Jonas could never get enough money. At three a.m. Tom dressed for work and slipped down the back stairs of the house into the kitchen. He brought a cup of freshly made coffee into Marie in case she was awake.

"You dear," Marie said, spying him as soon as he stepped over the threshold. "How did you know I was dying for a cup of coffee? She popped two pain tablets in her mouth, swallowing them with the hot coffee.

"I could have gotten you a glass of water," he said, wincing at the thought of hot coffee burning her throat.

"One pain kind of blots out the rest." Marie motioned toward the empty morphine drip. "I suspect I'll have to beg Florence to stay through the night." She smiled at him as she touched her hair and then lifted the mirror Gina had given her. "I hear you helped my daughter find this beauty."

Tom nodded. Marie's courage vanquished his voice. He could almost touch the pain radiating from the bed. He sat down quietly on the visitor stool and took her hand. "You're a beautiful woman."

"And you, sirrah, are a beautiful liar. But thank you." Marie rested for a moment as the first wave of narcotics eased the war in her body. "You two had a good time. . . ." She winked at him. "Fixing the plumbing last night."

"We did," he had to admit.

"And, you're up early even for your awful sunrise job." Marie smoothed the sheet fold over the blanket.

"Worrying about my brother," Tom said, inclined to talk about it. "That kid Gina hopes to get out of jail told the authorities it was an inside job."

"Never happened," Marie said.

Tom smiled at her blind faith.

"Don't look at me like I'm a drooling idiot. I knew both your parents, remember. Along with those tempers, they each possessed enough integrity for the two of you to inherit. By the way, I'd appreciate a wedding ceremony before my daughter talks you into having sex."

"Ma'am, I don't think Gina--."

"Nonsense, I know my own daughter, don't I?"

"Of course, but I'm not the kind of man you're looking for."

"Why not?" Marie had stopped smiling. "Don't you love my daughter?"

"I'm very fond of Gina. She let me move in because Dolly was selling the house. I hope we didn't give you the wrong impression last night." Tom's rump stayed glued to the chair. Nevertheless it was an effort not to hightail it out of the Branson household. "She hardly knows me."

Marie sat up straighter. "Tell me all your secrets."

Tom considered the pain pills Marie swallowed were causing this aggressive conversation, but only briefly. Marie wanted answers and was straight-forward enough, like her daughter, not to wait a polite interval to request them. Time was short for Marie.

"I'm a recovering addict."

"From what?" Marie stroked his hand as if to comfort him.

Tom shook his head. He didn't really have an answer. "Food, alcohol, sex, you name it. My brother's addiction could be called greed. Today's program quote was, 'It's better to begin at night than not to begin at all.' I think that's right."

"Makes you a better therapist."

"Hope so." Tom was humbled by her acceptance of a flawed stranger into her home.

Marie rubbed her forehead as if to deny access to any pain. "My sister died of cirrhosis of the liver, not cancer, from drinking. I think

J.C., that's how I've refer to Jesus Christ. We're friends you know. Anyway, I think He told the apostles He would be back down because the one thing He couldn't figure out was addiction. That's why He kept hanging around the 'wine bibbers.' Remember."

Tom nodded.

Marie continued, "I think AA has it straight, just don't indulge. But the overeaters, compulsive shoppers and workaholics can't practice abstinence. I think addicts have a larger hole in their bucket than the rest of us."

"I don't understand."

"You know, it's like addicts can only carry a lighter load of happiness than the rest of us. If their bucket overflows, they spill some life force out or kick a bigger hole in themselves, as if they didn't deserve all of God's gifts."

Tom understood. "We therapists call that self-hate."

"How do you cure it?" Marie tipped her head with interest.

"First we get the patient, or myself, to stop the negativity. Then another activity has to be undertaken: anything: a walk, a conversation, like ours right now, painting, gardening, and cooking. Anything to break the negative ruminations persons impose on themselves. After a decent interval when emotions are stable, we look at what caused the upset. Some delusion about our own importance to the universe usually reveals itself. With humility enhancement, fancy words for 'get real,' fewer and fewer opportunities exist to cause an addict to lose control."

Marie smiled, "I think you've got it." She started to set her cup down on the window sill, but it was quite a stretch.

Tom got up and placed it on the ledge for her. "I could make you a wider shelf here."

"Could you?" Marie clapped her hands. "After work, you go down to the basement. My husband loved to work with wood. He paneled that entire attic."

Tom didn't want to encourage Marie's match-making tendencies but he wanted to give her something nice, so he said, "When I first kissed Gina, I smelled the cedar under her lilac perfume. I'd seen Jonas killed earlier that day and thought I was losing my mind."

"It was my husband's work," Marie smiled. "You are a sweet boy. Thank you."

They both turned as Florence Kerner came in.

Tom's watch said it was 5:30 in the morning.

"Florence," Marie greeted her. "You were right. I need you to stay through the evenings."

"And I think you were right," Florence took off her winter coat and busied herself replacing the empty morphine bag with a new one. "I don't see any reason for you to feel pain before we decide to stop it."

"Florence, that's good news, Mother." Gina was standing in the doorway.

Tom could see the tears in her eyes.

She kissed her mother good-bye. "Tom and I have to fly or we'll be late. See you tonight."

* * *

On the ten-minute ride to the school bus yard, Gina drilled Tom. "What did Mother say about last night?"

He laughed, and then laughed again as if his body delighted in the task. "She's serious. She wants me to marry you and we're not to have sex until after the ceremony."

Gina considered. Had he laughed at the idea of no sex or at the idea of wanting to marry her at all? "Which part was so funny?"

"None," he said as if surprised. "I'm just happy, I guess."

If he could be happy, she could too. "Me too." Her mind leapt to the possibilities of time spent with Tom. She knew he thought she was attractive even seductive. Time would will out the truth. But could they learn to love each other enough to sustain a marriage?

* * *

After work, as they returned through the front door of Gina's home, she slapped away Tom's hand on her waist. "Not now."

Tom ignored his momentarily hurt feelings. The last half hour had been spent kissing and holding each other as if they'd wanted their bones to mesh. Propriety in front of her mother was certainly acceptable to Tom. "I have class tonight."

The hall mirror provided a canvas for Gina to arrange her face for her mother. She turned to him. "Are hot dogs okay for supper?"

"I'll make them." He stepped into the front room and pulled her in after him, as if she was reluctant to enter.

"Mother," she said.

Menasha and Florence were playing double solitaire on a card table set up behind the couch.

Marie held out her arms for her daughter. "There you are, bright and beautiful."

"Two calls," Menasha reminded Marie.

"Oh yes," Marie said. "Muller says you have an appointment Saturday morning at the jail with Danny's therapist." She looked at Menasha to see if she'd missed anything.

"Dolly," Menasha said.

Marie nodded, ". . .called about Tom and we invited her to dinner Saturday night. Menasha is bringing Chinese."

"Do Timothy and Jeffrey eat Chinese?" Gina asked Tom.

"I guess we'll find out," he laughed. It felt good to laugh, to have a reason for merriment in the face of Jonas's death. He almost believed laughter would keep death at bay, away from ending Marie's painful illness.

* * *

Saturday, October 20th

Gina often caught herself laughing at and with Tom. The finals for his degree loomed and his concentration for mundane things, like walking and remembering to shut off the stove took up too much space in his poor brain.

For the fourteenth time on Saturday morning she told him. "I have to leave. I can't help you make a shelf. Everything's in the basement. Have at it."

"Why can't you help?"

"Danny," Gina reminded him. "Danny's therapist asked me to meet with them."

His reaction was always the same, surprise, then a hint of controlled anger. Whether caused by his denial or confusion, their relationship was suffering as far as Gina was concerned. Between her mother's illness, her fixation with Danny's welfare or Tom's need to study for finals, Tom found increasing reasons not to pursue her.

She'd about had enough. "When are we going to spend time together?"

Tom rushed at her, taking her purse away, dropping it on the floor. He ran his hand up and down her back, kissed her neck. As he let go, he said, "Let's see how we feel, after you get home."

Gina pushed him away. "I know how you'll be. Cold."

"I will not." He tried to pull her back into an embrace.

"You'll be mad because I visited Danny."

"I don't like you getting involved with a criminal." Tom let go of her.

Gina could have hit him. "He's a child!" She stormed out of the house, sorry. Sorry that they hadn't made up.

* * *

The rain let loose a minute after Gina slammed the door. Tom spent half the day providing containers for the leaks. Every pot in the kitchen was in use in the attic. At one point he wondered if he could arrange the cacophony of pinging rain into some sort of musical interlude. Crazy.

Gina was driving him mad with her leaky roof and spongy brain. Visiting the boy's therapist. Nothing like playing right into the defense attorney's hands.

The buckets weren't dinging anymore, they were sloshing with water. After emptying them for the third time in the second floor bathroom tub, Tom decided to attack the basement storage in a search of more buckets. Were the heavens mimicking his grief with these torrential outpourings?

Instead of a trove of buckets, Tom found the woodworking shop unrivaled by any he had seen. If Mr. Branson's equipment proved ability, the attic renovation was the accomplishment of an expert. An ideal playroom, the back section of the basement faced the driveway and garage behind the house. Sliding glass doors faced a colonnade holding up the overhead porch. Blue cork-board walls were hung with half-pattern templates, tools, and saws. The floor was laid with red tiles as if to accentuate the cleanliness of the place.

The faint smell of cedar lingered. Gina's stepfather's machines gleamed from careful oiling and vacuuming. Tom ran his hand over the power tools and work benches. A drafting table and stool backed up to the patio doors. Tom recognized a mate to the padded stool positioned next to Marie's hospital bed. The wall-long work bench held a mounted sanding grinder, a disc sander, a variable speed bench drill press, a nine-inch blade table saw and a miter box. Hammer drills hung on sturdy brackets above the bench, each plugged into separate outlets.

No plumbing tools were in evidence and no extra wood to make a shelf.

Three portable drills perched above their displays of bits. Tom pulled out the individual drawers which hid a precision-built router, an electric hand-held belt sander, a portable circular saw and two saber saws. Opposite the work bench another cabinet contained the rest of the man's hand tools and machine parts. The outlay of money for the equipment must have been reached six figures.

Too bad the obviously compulsive Mr. Branson hadn't prepared a fund for his widow's upkeep of the house. The assembly of every man's ideal workshop might soon be on the auction block. An additional elaborate bench and matching cabinet on the opposite wall were no doubt the carpenter's creation.

A lathe had red painted legs, but the fixed headstock, bed and movable tailstock as well as the tool rest were cast iron. Even the motor and v-belt that drove the spindle to turn the wood were objects of art to Tom. The shaper with its vertical spindle for finished smoothness didn't carry the allure of the lathe's virgin products. The machines crowded each other for floor space.

Tom realized the extensive gingerbread on the house had been planned and made right here. He continued to search for buckets for the attic flood. Instead his hunt only produced admiration for a Rockwell uniplane, a Toolkraft joiner, a 15-inch floor standing drill press, and the all-important jig saws for curved and irregular gingerbread shapes. Three saws, each tilted to a different angle, stood ready to fashion any idea. One band saw, a Rockwell radial arm, a small Black and Decker for crosscutting, and a Sears table saw waited with the rest of the army to slice into a carpenter's next sacrifice of wood.

Antique acquisitions were also in evidence. In glass door sections under the drafting table, Tom found the reference books for Victorian architecture: "Rural Residences" with three dimensional views written by Alexander Jackson Davis in 1837, along with books by Davis' friend, Andrew Jackson Downing, "Cottage Residences" from 1842 with great gingerbread, and "The Architecture of Country Houses," 1850.

If Tom ever became a member of Gina's family, he'd want to spend time in this glorious workshop to keep the place up to her stepfather's standard of perfection. He'd come home. Books on Cape May and San Francisco always intrigued Tom, now he paged through pictures of Mark Twain's house in Hartford, Connecticut and the Wedding Cake House in Kennebunkport, Maine.

Tom smoothed his hand over the slick cover of the books. There were more books in this house than he could ever read. Lately books meant work on his degree: research, lab reports, findings couched in Latin terms, publication searches. He wanted to enjoy the printed word again. He wanted to be able to throw a book across the room or right out a window if an author insulted or disgusted him.

He was going to get thrown out if he didn't hurry upstairs to empty the rain catchers. Finding more buckets in the wood- working shop appeared hopeless; but there was enough equipment to make Marie's shelf, as soon as the indoor deluge was dealt with followed by a trip to the lumber yard.

* * *

Stupid therapist. Telling a kid not to trust her, calling Gina a rescuer.

"Danny needs to face reality." The woman had a callous face, scrunched up and mean. Her face was lined and her hands bony, as if she feared being good enough to herself to eat.

Gina concentrated on the brass name plate on her desk. The awful woman couldn't even sit with Danny without hiding behind a mammoth desk. Think sweet thoughts, Gina told herself. "Danny," Gina reached over to his chair and took his surprisingly strong hand. "Have I made you any promises to you?"

"You lent me your books." His smile was genuine.

"How are you progressing with Proust?"

"He certainly puts me to sleep." He laughed and Gina joined in.

They both turned to Miss Hillary Gingrich, who possibly was not capable of smiling. "You won't be there for him, when he needs you."

"Probably not," Gina agreed. "Unless he can get in touch with me."

"Now see, that's wrong," the unpleasant woman said.

"It is not." Danny and Gina said in unison and then laughed in relief.

Miss Gingrich made a note in the file on her desk. "I want Danny to agree to psychiatric drugs to help with his narcolepsy."

"What else is available?" Gina asked. "Could he get a seeing-eye dog to bark when he starts to nod off?"

Danny sat up straight in his chair. "I like dogs."

"Not that I know of," Miss Gingrich's eyebrows rose, increasing the lines in her forehead.

"Will he be remanded to a group home?"

"The jury will decide at the trial." The cold excuse of a woman lifted a stack of papers in front of her tapping the bottom of them on the desk to align all the sheets.

"Can I make recommendations for his sentence?"

"You'd have to see his defense lawyer."

"I'll do that," Gina smiled at Danny who seemed to be shrinking in his chair.

"Can you convince Danny to take the medications I'm prescribing?"

Gina looked at the boy. *No,* she thought, *I can't.* She shook her head and Danny smiled. "Don't take them. Read Proust instead."

Miss Gingrich stood. "The session is ended."

"Good," Gina said. "Don't swallow any pills, Danny."

* * *

Saturday night Gina chose the only blue skirt and shirt she owned, because her mother insisted on dressing in her best blue satin outfit from India, which Menasha loved. Her white hair was fixed in a Gibson Girl bouffant and her favorite long strand of costume pearls graced the dress. The morphine drip stand was wrapped with a garland of yellow roses. Tom wore a blue shirt with a matching blue tie.

Florence and Menasha greeted Dolly and the boys at the door and brought them into the dining room to meet Marie.

"Marie Branson," Menasha nearly bowed to the queen of the evening, "May I present Dolly Woods, Tom's sister-in-law, and her two good knights, Sir Jeffrey and Sir Timothy."

The boys delighted in the play-acting and bowed at the waist before sitting with Menasha at the foot of the table.

"I'll need a spy glass to keep my eye on you two," Marie scolded.

Jeffrey turned to his mother. "Mom, Timothy's been on his best behavior."

"Yes he has." Dolly rubbed Timothy's head of dark hair. "I'm delighted you asked us over. Tom has certainly come up in the world."

"From the basement in your house," Tom explained, "to the attic in this one."

Marie peered at Dolly on her left. "Tom, did you notice your brother's widow looks a lot like my daughter?"

"Especially now that Dolly cut her beautiful hair." Tom dived into a Chinese food container of spicy beef.

"Who did your mother date?" Marie asked.

Dolly blushed and Gina intervened. "Mother, what are you implying?"

"I'll bet you a dime, Lucille dated Montgomery Orr before she married Dolly's father."

"It's true," Dolly whispered nodding in the direction of her children. "He died in Vietnam. My boys love their grandfather."

"Mum's the word," Marie said, a bit drunkenly. "Montgomery loved to sword fight too."

Gina looked at the decorated morphine drip stand. "Florence, maybe you should slow the flow down.

Marie grinned, "In truth there is morphine. No that's wrong."

Florence fiddled with the mechanism among Menasha's roses. "Ouch," she cried and sucked her finger. Menasha got up to inspect the injury, moving closer to Florence than was absolutely necessary.

"My goodness," Gina realized. "Dolly, we're half-sisters? And these boys are my…," she leaned closer to Dolly and whispered, "My nephews?"

"Would friends be okay?" Dolly whispered back, then added. "When you first came to the house I loved your hair cut. That's one of the reasons I cut mine."

"I noticed the similarity that day too," Tom said, "but as I got to know Gina I kind of forgot about the likeness."

The shocking morphine-driven evening progressed on a more even keel through the naming of various Chinese dishes for the boys to pick from. They finally disdained everything except the sweet-and-sour pork.

"It's the pineapple," Dolly explained.

When the satiated boys grew restless, tired of the older people's conversations, Dolly said her goodbyes; but Gina kept her hand in hers at the door, reluctant to let the possibility of a sister in the house leave without acknowledging their bond. "Would you go shopping with me…or something?"

"I'd enjoy spending time with you." Dolly looked at the boys. "Mother loves to babysit. Call me, soon."

Menasha was at his courtly best. Both Marie and Florence seemed completely in love with him. Then Menasha turned his attention on

Gina. "I hope you're not going to return to racing anytime in the near future."

"Oh, I'm not going back to that. I have to fix the roof and find a lawyer."

"I'm a trust lawyer." Menasha laughed. "Does your job at the school have a retirement fund?"

"I'm serious, Menasha. You know about the robbery. Do you know a good defense lawyer for the teenager who was involved?"

"You want to pay for the defense of the boy who held us hostage?" Tom's tone left no doubt about his adverse opinion.

"Just like your mother," Menasha said. "I'll have Harvey Slemmons meet with the boy."

"I can't pay anything immediately," Gina said. "Would tomorrow at one be okay?"

"Harvey occasionally does pro-bono work, when I ask." Menasha was laughing. "She's just like you, Marie."

"That's the best compliment you've paid me all evening," Marie said.

* * *

Sunday, October 21st

Lorna Hale, the Episcopal minister, promised to drop by after the eight o'clock service. Gina agreed to help Florence deal with Marie's choice of clothes for the visit.

"I am not appearing in bed clothes," Marie stated.

"Perfectly proper, since you are in bed," Florence tried to reason with her.

Gina proposed, "The dark purplish-blue Indian outfit is comfortable."

Marie agreed, "I won't have to the wear the pantaloons and the brass-coin necklace from my Arizona trip will hide half my wrinkled neck."

Florence smiled at Gina until Marie added, "The counterpane has to be changed."

"I'll get it," Gina offered. "Which one should I bring down?"

"Florence," Marie asked. "Am I causing too much trouble?"

"Mrs. Branson, everyone likes to dress up." Florence answered.

Marie winked at Gina. "Florence always calls me Mrs. Branson, when she's ready to throw me out the window."

Florence laughed. "It's our code."

"Would the white chenille be all right?" Gina asked.

"Perfect," Marie clapped her hands.

Tom ducked his head into the front room. "I'm off to walk Mrs. Stiles's dog."

"Stay for Reverend Hale," Gina coaxed.

"Off with you, Tom." Marie waved him out. "Find your own minister."

"I like your mother," Tom said, pecking Gina's cheek. "Be back in an hour. Two at the most."

Gina watched him go, shut the front door after him, and then finished her chore of providing a white bedspread for her mother. Her mother was waiting for her, completely dressed for the minister's visit. "Florence, would you mind bringing in some cups and saucers and a dessert for Reverend Hale?"

"Nooo, Mrs. Branson." Florence headed for the kitchen.

"Gina, come over here," Mother beckoned. Gina knew that tone of voice. She had committed some felony apparently. "Tom is a grown man?"

"What did I do?" Gina felt like pouting.

"He's not a racecar, so keep your hands off his steering wheel." Marie pulled her close for a hug. "You've taken care of yourself and me for so long, you think the whole world will accept your meddling."

"Meddling?" Gina felt unduly chastised. "I found him a job and a place to stay. He likes me."

"That's exactly why you shouldn't push your agenda down his throat."

"Danny."

"Exactly. Tom hasn't take exception to your actions. You best let him control his own life." Marie bit her lip.

"He'll come around." Gina's chin went up in the stubborn way even she recognized.

"And why should he?"

Gina refused to feel quilty about taking care of Danny or Tom. "Tom's stuck in the anger phase of grief. That's where all the vengeance comes from."

"You've got him so busy defending his position." Marie coughed and held her side. "He can't see the kinder side of himself."

The doorbell saved them from further disagreement.

Gina tuned out of the conversation after hellos were exchanged between the minister and herself. Had she been bullying poor Tom? She would take care not to interfere anymore, if she could. She would talk to him about her problem of over-controlling every aspect of her life and everyone's within the three-county area.

"We are encouraging parishioners to ask Congress and the President to establish a living wage as the standard of compensation for workers." Reverend Hale accepted a glazed donut from Florence's tray.

"A living wage?" Gina decided to forego her self-flagellations until the minister left.

Marie explained, "A wage that allows workers to raise their families outside of poverty."

"About time," Florence said.

Florence's face registered pleasure. Menasha could be seen getting out of his car from the front window. When Gina checked to see if Mother had noticed, she was rewarded with a triumphant wink. "Told you."

Gina wondered if her own face showed as much delight when she opened the door to find Tom chatting with Menasha. "Come in, come in. Reverend Hale was just leaving."

"Changing of the guard." Menasha swept into the front room.

Tom lingered in the hall with Gina. "Are you angry with me for walking the dog?" He set his jaw and looked her straight in the eye. "I made a promise to Mrs. Stiles that I would come by each Sunday."

Gina could feel her blush. "I'm sorry I made you think you needed to explain to me. I am way too controlling."

"But sexy," he whispered in her ear, bringing waves of heightened sexual awareness with his warm breath.

She wanted to invite him upstairs, but the front room was quickly filling with people. Instead, she settled for rubbing the inside of his arm as they joined the group.

Menasha consulted his pocket watch. "Gina, you have fifteen minutes to meet Harvey at the jail." Gina hugged Menasha, Tom and her mother before grabbing her keys and purse.

* * *

Home Depot
Sunday, October 21st

After lunch, Tom intended to fulfill a promise to Marie and build her the shelf for the windowsill. Menasha thought it was a great project and insisted on visiting the lumber supplier with him. Menasha stopped at a display of sliding doors of mirror and wood-laced bamboo. "Should I build Marie sliding doors for the front room?"

"Excellent idea," the greedy salesman said. "We have easy-to-install tracks for the floor and ceiling."

"Marie's ceilings are awfully tall," Tom cautioned.

"Right," Menasha gave the idea up. "One thing at a time."

"We have free standing screens," the salesman ventured.

"Might make her feel we think she should hide herself away," Menasha ran his fingers down the white wood of an oriental screen.

"Her daughter might know if she wants a room divider." Tom was busy measuring redwood for his shelf.

Menasha came over. "Can I believe Marie's illusions; you two are going to marry?"

Tom stopped at his task. "I frankly don't know."

"You like the girl?"

"Absolutely!"

"What's the problem?"

"I don't think you can say we have a problem." Tom's hand held his measuring tape suspended over the wood. "I wish she wasn't so determined to let Danny off without consequences for his involvement in the murder of my brother."

"Understandable. But if Danny was out of the picture would you want her for your wife?"

"I'm not very desirable as a provider, yet." Tom finished measuring the wood. "After I find a position with my degree, I'll probably take a closer look at my feelings."

"Of marriage?"

"Yes," Tom said at the cash register. "If things work out. I'm not sure Gina knows how she feels about me yet."

"Oh, she knows her own mind." Menasha laughed and slapped Tom on the back. "You'll be lucky if you know your own name when she's through with you."

* * *

Dean Street, Geneva

Gina resolved to keep her own counsel about her visit with Harvey and Danny. She brought Menasha and Tom hamburgers and chips to eat as they worked side by side in her stepfather's woodshop. "Dinner."

She wanted to stay and watch Tom flex his muscles around the tools as the shelf took shape, but she'd decided to adopt a hands-off policy for this project. After all, what did it matter if a make-shift shelf for her mother's cup irreparably ruined the windowsill? People were more important than things and Menasha and Tom were having a good time.

Tom waved his thanks, his mouth already busy with the food.

"Good girl," Menasha winked at her for some reason with a knowing look on his face.

When did Menasha find it necessary to comment on her behavior? She was getting crazy around Tom. Every word anyone said to him or any that he uttered without first saying them to her sounded unpleasant to her surprisingly delicate ego. When anything involved Tom, she could feel the ugly power of possessiveness rear its head. Thoughts were acceptable. She wanted his last toenail, but her actions would stay presentable, she hoped.

* * *

After the shelf was nailed in place and Tom had accepted the over-stated praises from his favorite women, Menasha rescued him. "We're off to spend time among men." Menasha laughed as he pushed Tom out the door.

"Thanks," Tom said. "Getting a bit deep in there."

"That's what happens when a man comes courting."

"I'm not courting."

"No?" Menasha drove them to a bar in St. Charles, one block south of Main Street.

Tom reviewed the Twelve Steps as Menasha bought rounds for a large passel of friends.

"Gina Branson's beau." was the only introduction Menasha would offer.

"Tom Woods," Tom corrected maybe seven times only to hear condolences for Jonas's death and debates about the guilt of Danny Bianco.

Pretty soon, Tom smiled along with the beau introduction, listening to the men trade stories about cases, investments, and the futures of various children of the patrons of the bar. The amount of alcohol consumed varied.

Tom could check off the ones in trouble with addiction. They never ordered mixed drinks and answered in monosyllables after their third drink. Easier it was not to slur words like yep and nope. The fumes of the flowing liquor started to permeate the air and his sobriety.

He didn't want to leave and he knew he was in trouble. He liked Menasha and didn't want to hurt his feelings. But Tom knew the excuse was a cunning ploy of his addiction. Nevertheless, he stayed as if to push the powers above to keep him sane.

Someone had to pay: for his brother's murder, for his parents' death, for the two apple trees. Tom felt like a frog he'd seen on a National Geographic cover. Inside the magazine they explained the huge size of the frog was directly related to the fact he could absorb moisture and nutrients through his skin from the humidity in the marshes of the Amazon. Was he getting drunk on the alcohol-perfumed air as well as from the friendly, competitive atmosphere around him?

Tom accepted his first drink of the evening. Menasha seemed overly pleased.

* * *

On Sunday evening Gina lay in her bed on the second floor, counting her blessings. Harvey Slemmons seemed more than capable.

In the afternoon, Harvey had asked Danny to cooperate with the police giving all the details he could think of about his Uncle Passantino and his associates. "Acting under threats or coercion can't be used for a defense in the robbery unless your uncle is arrested for the murder," Harvey had explained. "Narcolepsy isn't considered grounds for an insanity plea, unless you've been having hallucinations."

"Uncle Alan says I made up memories of my mother." Danny shook himself to remain awake.

"I'll get a more competent therapist for you too." Harvey wrote himself a note. "Now, I want you to allow the new expert to hypnotize you."

Danny reached for Gina's arm. "Only if Miss Branson can be with me."

"We'll both be there, Danny," he said.

Gina could see this bald lawyer go up in Danny's estimation.

"Okay," Danny said. "I'll do it."

Gina wished she had shared how proud she was of the kid's courage, with Tom.

But, Tom wasn't home yet. He and Menasha had been gone for hours. It was nearly one in the morning. The St. Charles library had to be closed. He couldn't be studying. She and Tom had to be at the school bus yard at six a.m.

Finally she heard the latch, but he didn't come upstairs.

She wouldn't be able to sleep anyway, so Gina decided to confront him downstairs. As she stepped out into the hall she smacked right into his chest. "Ow," she said and thumped his chest with her fist.

"Now that's not very welcoming." His speech was slurred.

"Drunk?"

"Yep."

She stepped aside and he swayed over to her bed and fell on it, dead asleep, snoring. Gina took off his shoes and climbed into her side of the bed. Nice thing about living together. Tomorrow would be another day of at least proximity.

"Formidable," Tom said in his sleep. "I love a form...formidable woman."

"Well, you aren't all bad." Gina scooted next to him and kissed Tom's tousled head. "And the formidable fool loves you," she whispered to the man asleep in her bed.

CHAPTER SEVEN

Monday, October 22nd

Tom's head throbbed. Had it ever hurt this bad? His leg twisted around the sheet as he rolled to a less heated side of his head. He yanked at the covers and put Gina's pillow over his eyes.

Fully awake in Gina's empty bed, he grabbed the pillow and stumbled up the attic stairs to his bedroom. The pillow's enduring lilac perfume nagged at him. Gina was turning him inside out. He loved her, but how could he throw his feelings for his lost twin to the winds.

It was Menasha's fault. If Menasha hadn't invited him out for a nightcap last night none of this would have happened. His aching head reminded him Menasha probably didn't have a drinking problem. To change the things he could and accept the things he couldn't change, didn't inform Tom what to hang onto when the changes came faster than he could take them in. He knew one thing: alcohol had been the wrong choice, again.

The noise in his head increased. Danny. But, a definite rhythm of noise outside of his brain kept the pain from decreasing. He swung his long legs over the edge of the bed to peer at the digital clock. Noon. Gina probably called in sick for him.

The sturdy poster at the foot of the bed saved him from falling over, as dizziness engulfed his senses. Someone was banging on the roof. Tom could see a ladder against the attic's gable window. He opened the matching dormer window across the room. "Hello," he called to the devil with a hammer.

The hammering stopped. "Aye?"

Tom couldn't think of what to say. "Will you be long? I have a blister of a headache."

"Best head downstairs, mate," the voice advised. "Mrs. Branson's friend, Menasha, gave us two days to take care of your roof."

"Right," Tom said.

Did God order this racket as punishment for being hung-over? He pinched his nose to see if he could alleviate any pain. He didn't have a nose bleed. He lurched down to the second floor bath. As the shower eased the muscles in his neck the painful throbbing lessened.

In the attic again, Tom hurriedly pulled on his clothes wishing he'd remembered to take them down to the bathroom where there was less noise. He grabbed his Twelve-Step book and headed for the kitchen for coffee to take the edge off his self-imposed illness.

The fumes of the drip pot eased his dry throat as he read the quote, "How unhappy is he who cannot forgive himself."

That's me, he thought. His Higher Power had his number, knew his weaknesses and the guilt sewn into the act of drinking. As he poured his second cup, even the phone conspired to torment his aching head.

"Sergeant Muller," answered to his unfriendly hello.

"You found the kid's uncle?"

"No, but Judge Wilcox wanted you... both to know jury selection starts tomorrow."

"Thanks." Tom hung up without chatting. Something wasn't right. Judge Wilcox probably told Muller to inform Gina. Muller didn't know how to get out of telling Tom, when he answered the phone.

Jury selection. The coffee in Tom's cup smelled like heaven. Twelve jurists, akin to twelve apostles and the twelve tribes of Israel, would decide Danny's fate. Twelve indifferent persons would dilute the responsibility and reinforce the justice of a decision to put Danny away for his entire adult life without causing more of a rift between Gina and himself. Tom had to be there, but finals for his degree were Tuesday night. Tom had studied all he could. He and Gina needed to take a leave of absence from bus driving to attend the trial.

Tom made another pot of coffee to share with Marie and Florence. When he walked into the living room, they stopped whispering.

"Fell off the wagon," Marie said.

"I did," he admitted. "How's Menasha?"

"Now that's a real problem for me." Florence, a mere wren of a woman, had her hands on her hips. "You could have killed him."

Tom smelled danger. He sat the pot and cups on the night-stand, waiting for the worst of it. "Is he in the hospital?"

"Florence," Marie scolded her helper, "you're scaring the kid."

"Could have been," Florence mumbled.

"What happened?" Tom patiently asked Marie again. "He did get drunk."

"How do you know?" Marie asked and Florence focused her angry attention on him.

"The waitress knocked over a pitcher of beer. Most of it landed in Menasha's lap. All of us jumped up and ran around like chickens with our heads cut off."

"Did you ever see that?" Marie interrupted.

"What?" Tom asked trying to hold on to the flow of his story.

"Chickens." Marie said. "With their heads off, flopping around in the dirt?"

"Yeah," Tom scratched his tender scalp. "On my grandfather's farm. Anyway, Menasha just sat there with beer in his lap and a silly grin on his face."

Florence and Marie nodded at each other.

"He's on drugs for high blood pressure, you idiot." Florence stayed irate.

"He can't drink any alcohol," Marie explained.

Tom held his head with both hands. "Is he going to be okay?"

Marie patted the stool. "Sit down. He didn't go to the hospital. He just called to say he couldn't get out of bed to bring me my roses and donuts."

"I'll go get them." Tom jumped up immediately. His headache reminded him all was not well.

"Good," Marie said.

Tom tended to the chores, yellow roses and glazed donuts, and then he telephoned Dolly. "Gina might be mad at me. I need you to be there for the jury selection."

"I'm not going."

"Why not? That kid should see the widow of the man he shot!"

"Tom, you know Danny's uncle shot Jonas."

Tom hung up, not angry, but nearly defeated. If Jonas's own wife couldn't get riled up enough to see justice carried out, he was on his own. Except for Gina.

The headache was letting go of his eyeballs.

Tom opened the refrigerator door after starting another pot of coffee. The reek of spoiled food filled the kitchen. Moldy leftovers presented themselves on each tray of the refrigerator. Without breathing deeply, he took three steaks out of the freezer and popped them into the microwave to thaw.

Tonight would be his last chance to prove his love to Gina, before they got into guaranteed disputes about which juror should be excused for cause. She'd be home at 4:30. That wasn't too early for a supper, if they drank a bottle of wine first. Tom's head reminded him Merlot was the furthest thing from his body's appetite.

Tom pushed up all the windows which increased the level of racket from the roof. He dispensed with the rotted food and waved at the torturers on the roof. They were still pounding away on the shingles.

"I'm fixing steak for supper, Florence." Tom walked over to Marie's bed. "My head is lagging behind my intentions."

"Want a hit of this?" Marie tapped the morphine stand.

"You are an irreligious dame." He laughed.

"I'll take my chances with my Maker." Marie grinned.

"Mind if I move this philodendron to the fireplace grate?" Tom asked.

Florence frowned at him. But Marie waved her approval. "Sprucing up the place are you?"

Tom lit the candles along the mantel to get rid of the mild smell of medicines. "Is it all right if I set the table in here, Florence?"

"Give the lad a hand, Florence," Marie directed. "Always encourage the male of the species to cook."

Florence removed an unfinished hand of solitaire from the card table. "I'll bring in another chair from the dining room."

"What are you fixing," Marie asked.

"Steak, asparagus, frozen corn steamed with more sugar than salt and strawberry cobbler." Tom spread a snowy cloth over the card table.

"Setting the mood for a romantic dinner." Marie approved.

Tom found a box of Bisquick and followed the easy directions for drop biscuits. He flavored them with orange peel spices and ground-up walnuts. The house smelled of fresh baked bread, a Christmas aroma in chilly October.

* * *

Gina couldn't break the habit of checking in on her mother as soon as she stepped in the door. Marie was asleep. On the fireplace candles sputtered in their holders, burnt down to mere nubs. Tom had forgiven her. She rushed into the kitchen to find him balancing two plates of food.

"Is it too early to eat?" Florence asked, holding a bottle of wine and a third plate.

"I'm game," she said, meaning a whole lot more.

At the table behind the couch Tom poured Gina and Florence a full glass of wine and poured ice water into his own. Gina didn't comment on his shenanigans on Sunday, but couldn't hide her smile.

"The roofers woke me at noon," he said.

"Oh good!" She put a bite of steak in her mouth.

Tom didn't eat. He was watching her. Waiting for her answer? "Very good," she said of the fried tenderloin. Then she understood the implied question. "Mother said Menasha wanted to pay for the roof."

"I thought your loan came through." Tom hadn't stopped himself in time. He studied the food in his plate.

Gina could tell he didn't want to think about Jonas being shot, or that they might not have met, or befriended Danny, if she hadn't been in the bank for a loan. He was so beautiful. She looked forward to a lovely evening and didn't want to ruin the mood.

"Muller called," Tom said before choosing an especially big bite of steak.

She saw his satisfaction in making her wait for him to swallow. "His uncle?"

"That's why I thought he called, too." Tom smiled at her. Gina willed herself with considerable effort to stay on the safe side of any subject. Tom continued, "Judge Wilcox wanted you to know jury selection starts tomorrow." Gina nodded. Tom poured himself a large dose of water, took another large bite of steak and mimicked her noncommittal nod.

"Are you two mad at each other?" Florence asked.

They both glared at her.

Florence gathered the dishes and disappeared toward the kitchen. "I'll fix the dessert," she called from the hall.

Marie spoke up, ""I'm getting agitated. You are both waiting for the other one to get upset."

"Sorry." Gina ducked her head like a chastised child after downing most of her wine.

Tom poured her another glass. "State-appointed defense teams are usually low on funds."

"I thought so, too." Gina smiled at her mother. "Menasha's friend is a hit with Danny."

* * *

Gina's eyes got bigger the more she tried to get around the contentious subject of Danny's punishment. He refused to care if she'd arranged for a high-class defense attorney. They needed to understand each other's affection tonight.

Marie coughed before saying quietly, "You two should try to get along now. The jury might take a month for the selection process."

Tom doubted Gina would let him keep living in her house if they couldn't share emotional intimacy. "I only know I need this beautiful loving creature to belong to me."

"I want you too," Gina said.

"Then stop standing in the way of your own happiness!" Marie demanded.

"What happened?" Florence had returned with a tray and four warm strawberry cobbler desserts complete with ice cream.

Tom breathed deeply and reached for Gina's hand. "My finals are tomorrow night too."

"We should take a leave of absence for the trial," she said, holding onto his thumb as if he might fly away.

"We're agreed on that." Tom smiled. "We can do this."

* * *

Gina didn't want to split hairs or get near any disagreeable subjects. Men were like hummingbirds. You had to feed them sweetened information so they wouldn't back off. "Absolutely," she said. "We have all the time in the world."

Tom stood and pulled her up from her chair, gently touching her curls with his fingers. "You have the best face I've ever seen."

"You're supposed to tell me I'm beautiful."

"You are. Your eyes can make my day, or break my heart."

"Shh," Florence said.

"Don't talk about your differences," Marie prompted from her bed.

"I'm always going to be next to you," Gina said. "Do you know I love you?"

"Yes," Tom said.

Gina was already past the point of being able to rationalize their relationship. "I've loved you from the first day I met you."

"In high school?"

"Yes," she lied, not wanting to bring up the horror of the bank. Gina stood on her tiptoes and kissed Tom lightly on the lips. "Your eyes are like black pools I want to dive into and never come out."

"Which one," Tom kidded, winking at her, "my left or my right?" He kissed her, long on her mouth, short on her cheeks, eyelids and nose.

Marie and Florence broke into their private world, clapping enthusiastically.

"We should never let anyone or anything come between us." Tom wrapped his heavy arms around her.

"Let's promise," she said kissing his mouth.

* * *

Kane County Court House, Geneva
Tuesday, October 23rd

They drove separate cars, because Tom's last exam would be at seven o'clock that evening. Gina wore her black short skirt and white blouse. She promised herself to buy a blue silk suit before the next day of jury selection. Maybe charge two or three. Tom Woods loved her, but when would he get over his vengeance illness? Maybe it was like a virus, two weeks and gone. *One could pray'* she thought. *Right, Lord'*

When she stepped into the court room, her worst fears were realized. Tom sat behind the prosecutor next to Sergeant Muller.

Menasha arrived and Gina kissed him on the cheek, before sitting behind the divider on the defense side of the court room. Harvey Slemmons turned around and smiled at her. "Gina Branson, I want you to meet my helper with the jury selection. Dr. Pheiffer, this is one of the hostages and a new friend of Danny's."

They nodded to each other. Danny wore a new shirt. He reached out his hand to her and she took the cold, strong hand in both of hers. "Mr. Slemmons knows what he's about. I'm going to be hypnotized after we're through here."

"I'll come too," Gina said. She couldn't help turning to look at Tom. His smile was faint, his eyes shut down. *No pools for me,* she thought and then became distracted by the forty adults, all sizes and ages, entering the court room's audience section.

The clerk called off twelve names alphabetically to fill the jury box.

Gina tried to identify anyone who might have been in high school with Tom, Jonas, Dolly or herself. Four of the women could have been about their age. One was skinny as a rail, too skinny to show off bony legs under a short red skirt. The other three were over weight by five, ten or fifteen pounds, respectively. She didn't recognize any of them. Of course, they could have moved into the county in the twelve years since she'd graduated.

Only one of the men seemed close to their age group. He limped slightly, but seemed happy. A grin, she might have remembered. Jimmy. It was Jimmy Pierce. She wished she would have thought to give her yearbook to Mr. Slemmons. Would having a classmate of the deceased be a good or bad thing for Danny?

Judge Wilcox asked the first questions of the prospective jurors. "Do any of you have medical conditions that would cause a problem or inhibit your ability to serve on this jury?"

The skinny juror said, "Kidney problems."

The judge didn't excuse her.

Another said, "My son was arrested for drunk driving Saturday night."

A third claimed, "My obstetrics practice demands I ask for a pass."

They both were excused and two other jurors filled their places.

The judge instructed the remaining jurors to keep track of the questions asked by the prosecuting and defense attorneys. They were to inform the judge if they had any reason to be excused before they took their place as a juror.

The thin prosecutor, Ms. Krisch, asked each woman, no matter her age, a prescribed set of questions. Ten were excused when they answered 'no' to, "Were your parents divorced?"

The fifteen pound over weight woman Gina had considered as a possible high school classmate was not one of them. The woman's blue blouse gapped at the button between her breasts. Anyone could see her brassiere if they looked at the opening.

Five more potential women jurors exited for having teenage children, two for doing volunteer work, one who lived near the St. Charles Boys' Home, and four who had witnessed crimes. Twenty-two women marched out of the court room, excused for cause by the prosecutor. Six stayed seated in the decision box after answering '*no*' to "Have you heard about this case in the media?" or "Have you discussed this case with anyone to date?"

Gina questioned their honesty.

At five o'clock Judge Wilcox called for adjournment, asking everyone to return the next day.

Tom came over to her side of the aisle. "See you at home."

"Couldn't Dolly find a sitter for the kids?" Gina asked just to keep him, who she deemed her personal giant, close for a moment more.

"She refused to come," he said.

Gina wished she hadn't asked. "I'll call her. Good luck on your finals."

Mr. Slemmons tipped his chair back after he watched Tom leave. "You live together."

"Yes," Gina said, refusing to elaborate. "Do you want to know if Tom or his brother, Jonas, or I went to school with any of the prospective jurors?" Mr. Slemmons nodded. "I'll bring you my yearbook. But I can tell you the man with a limp, Jimmy Pierce, was in our class. Does it make a difference?"

"Yes," Mr. Slemmons said. "He knew the victim and should excuse himself. I'll explain to the judge tomorrow."

CHAPTER EIGHT

In St. Charles above Burger's drug store, Dr. Pheiffer's upholstered office furniture welcomed Gina. The blue walls exactly matched the denim outfit she had hurried home to change into. The room was bordered at the height of normal wainscoting with a strip of Sweet William flowered wallpaper and its horizontal red trim drew the walls of the room together into a safe package. Gina breathed in the manufactured heated air and sat next to Danny.

He seemed all elbows and knees in his shy awkwardness.

However, Dr. Pheiffer re-directed Gina to sit across from Danny on the soft couch next to Harvey Slemmons. The prosecutor's representative, sitting on Harvey's right, was introduced to Dr. Pheiffer as Ms. Krisch.

"Uncle Alan said you were all on television." Danny tugged at the white hair behind his ear. "He knows where you all live."

The four adults stared at each other, until they said in unison, "When?"

"He called me at the jail. You know, after the jury questioning."

Harvey spoke up, his voice calculating in its deliberate, casual tone, "Did he like your new shirt?"

Danny squirmed in his chair. "He said he knew when he quit, Miss Branson would provide a good lawyer." He smiled at Gina. "But he said this hypnotism stuff won't help." Danny tried to apologize by repeating his uncle's words in a quickening staccato, "Cause I already know why my hair is white—from the Boys' Home."

Dr. Pheiffer spoke quietly disputing the boy's uncle as kindly as she could, "If that were true, Danny, you wouldn't have had an attack at the bank."

"Is that right?" Danny asked Gina.

"We'll have to try Dr. Pheiffer's method to find out," Gina said.

"Did you talk to Sergeant Muller after your uncle called?" Harvey asked.

"Yeah," Danny said in the elongated way of his. "I'd promised to tell him everything." Danny was frowning. "I never break my word." Danny's arm fell to the side of the chair. He coughed to keep himself awake. "Except, Sergeant Muller says murderers like my uncle don't deserve loyalty."

Dr. Pheiffer interrupted. "Let's concentrate on the session. On you, Danny. The ongoing investigation is not part of your therapy."

Danny gladly gave her his full attention.

To Gina, Harvey said quietly, "I'll telephone Muller."

Dr. Pheiffer ignored him. "Danny, I'm recording this session for the court."

"That's good," he said. "Then I can hear it too?"

"If you want to."

"Probably be boring stuff." He winked at Gina.

Dr. Pheiffer explained, "Not necessarily. Your unconscious knows the seat of your narcolepsy problem. Because of all the recent trouble, part of you will be motivated to reveal what happened in the past for you to arrive at this point, juncture in your life."

"Yeah," Danny agreed.

Gina's mind was chewing on the fact that Danny's uncle said he knew where they all lived. She'd heard Danny's tone and wanted to say something about the word 'yeah' being a trigger for the sleeping events but Dr. Pheiffer was engrossed in her methodology.

"This isn't going to take long, Danny." Dr. Pheiffer began to relax him. "If you feel at all threatened, I want you to drop or throw this ball. I'll bring you back here safe and sound, feeling refreshed and none the worse for wear."

Danny laughed and threw the ball at Gina.

She worried Muller had not asked if Danny's Uncle Passantino knew the color of Danny's shirt was light yellow. Maybe the uncle had not seen them on television and did not know where they all lived. Gina tossed the ball back, underhand.

"You throw like a woman," Danny said.

Dr. Pheiffer resumed her directions, "Concentrate on the center of this spinning wheel while you go to sleep."

Danny watched the black-and-white circular cardboard for less than three minutes. "Am I sleeping?"

"Sort of." Dr. Pheiffer turned off the mechanism. "You're back to a peaceful time with your mother."

Danny smiled, then giggled childishly.

"How old are you, Danny?"

"Almost seven. My birthday party is on Monday. That's tomorrow!"

"Is there anyone besides your mother in the room?" Dr. Pheiffer read from a list of questions Gina had seen Harvey hand the doctor.

"My uncle," Danny smiled. "But he can't stay. He gave Mom money for the birthday cake." Danny blew a kiss. "She'll be right back."

"What's wrong, Danny?"

"Nothing." Danny relaxed more. "Uncle Alan's tired. We're watching TV in the bedroom." He frowned and squirmed.

"What's happening now?"

"Uncle Alan took a shower. He forgot to put his clothes on." Danny was definitely not happy. "If I don't like looking at it, it's big, I can sit behind him."

Gina moved to tap Dr. Pheiffer on her shoulder, but Harvey patted her knee. "He's not being hurt."

'Yes, he is,' Gina disputed silently. Danny is being abused, injury enough for any child.

"Danny," Dr. Pheiffer called to her charge. "What is Uncle Alan doing? You're safe now and nothing can hurt you. Don't forget to throw the ball if you want us to stop."

Danny squeezed the ball, but didn't throw it. "We're playing cho-cho and I'm supposed to pull the throttle. For the steam whistle to blow." The ball in his hand disappeared in his firm grip. "I don't like this game."

"Where are you?"

"Behind Uncle Alan. His back is all sweaty. He's using my hand on his thing. Oh, oh."

"Now what?" Dr. Pheiffer asked.

"Mom's in the doorway. She's mad. Uncle Alan doesn't see her. She's real mad!"

Danny relaxed.

"Danny? Is everything okay?"

"Mom's gone. Uncle Alan fell asleep. I'm going to go wash my hand." Danny soaped and rinsed his hands thoroughly under imaginary water. Suddenly his head twitched and he shut off the non-existent spigot.

"What Danny? What do you hear?"

"Mom's screaming." He peered around an obstacle or a door frame existing only in his memory. "She's got a big knife!"

"Danny?" Dr. Pheiffer asked. "Are you safe?"

Tears ran down his face. "No. Uncle Alan woke up when she stuck the knife in his back. He's got the knife now." The tears didn't let up and Danny was sobbing uncontrollably.

Gina stood up, but Harvey pulled her back down. "Wait."

"Danny, remember you have a ball you can throw when you want to leave."

"Yes," he said, "but Mother's not moving." Danny's voice rose in anger. "He did it. He stopped her from screaming and kicking. He used the knife all over her." Danny stopped breathing and his body stiffened. "Now he's putting the red knife in my hand. He smeared it on my pajamas!" Danny threw the ball so hard it broke a window and sailed into the street.

Gina was helping him wipe his face dry with the hem of her long skirt. "Danny, Danny," she cried.

Dr. Pheiffer motioned for her to return to the couch. "Danny," she said to the blank-faced boy. "Do you want to know what happened now that you're safe with us?"

"Yes," he said, turning to Gina and holding out his hand which she rushed to hold.

Dr. Pheiffer led him through the scenes in his memory from the tape with all the hurt repeated.

At the end, Danny recalled. "That's when I threw the ball at your window."

Gina wished Tom had witnessed Danny's agony and courage. Her watch said it was only 6:30.

The prosecutor's assistant was sobbing. "Eight years," Miss Krisch hiccupped. "They imprisoned him for eight years and he's innocent!"

Harvey blew his nose twice.

Gina felt cold, shivering instead of crying. The seven-year-old Danny had known scant warmth.

"Does this mean I won't fall asleep anymore?" Danny asked.

"I think so, Danny." Dr. Pheiffer said. "We're all proud of you. You went to a place very few of us will ever have to see in our lifetime. And you survived a terrible crime."

"Yes," he said, releasing Gina's hand. He smiled faintly and touched Gina's face as she knelt at his side. "My mother loved me."

Gina embraced the teenager.

Harvey drew her away. "Come, come, Gina. Dr. Pheiffer and I will talk to Judge Wilcox. We'll see to this. I'll call you as soon as I have news."

Danny brushed off his jeans. As he stood, Gina imagined he'd grown an inch or two.

After thanking Dr. Pheiffer profusely, Gina still found it difficult to leave. She remembered a black-and-white film on the Turner Classic channel, where a comedian from long ago sang a ditty which she repeated for Dr. Pheiffer and Harvey, "Did ya ever feel like you wanted to stay, when you wanted to go, but still you wanted to stay?"

"Jimmy Durante's song," Harvey said as he pushed her into the hall. "Go home, Gina. Say hello to Marie for me."

Dr. Pheiffer opened the door, poking her head into the hall. "Gina, you are to be commended for your perception and loyalty to this innocent lad. I don't know if you realize children need to tell more than eight people if they have experienced sexual abuse before someone believes them."

"That's horrible," Gina said, finally able to leave the next steps for Danny's release in the lawyers' hands.

* * *

Reluctant to face the continuing tragedy of her mother's illness at home, Gina drove into Geneva. She dialed Dolly's number on her cell phone. "I need some clothes for the trial tomorrow. Will you meet me at the Little Traveler's? We could shop after we have a pot of tea."

"That would be fun. I'll be there as soon as I drop the boys off at Mother's. I've been looking forward to your call."

Tucked away at a small table among floor-to-ceiling merchandise, all attractively displayed, Gina and Dolly were surprised to find little to discuss. Dolly expressed Gina's thoughts perfectly. "We both have tragedy to share and the rest of our lives to begin our fresh sisterhood."

"Maybe I should wait to shop. The police might catch Danny's uncle. The therapy session revealed Danny was innocent of his mother's murder, too."

"I'm happy the boy isn't going to suffer imprisonment again."

Gina wanted to hug her newly found half-sister, instead she said, "Would you come home with me, just to get me in the door? I'm horrified to find I'm avoiding going home."

"Facing death, you mean."

* * *

Florence was busy checking Marie's morphine drip and pulse when they arrived.

"I can't tell if she's asleep when she doesn't snore," Gina said. "I'll take Dolly upstairs."

"Gee whiz," Marie answered. "I was just resting my eyes. It's a good thing I've arranged to be cremated or I'd wake up in a box."

"Mother," Gina scolded. "Don't say horrid things in front of Dolly."

"I'm sure Dolly Woods is well aware of the issue of death," Marie answered somewhat testily. "Besides I want to visit with Dolly too."

"Sorry, Mother." Gina kissed her mother's forehead gently. "I'm nervous about getting to know my half-sister."

"Better half than none." Marie closed her eyes again. Florence and Gina exchanged glances. "Dolly, maybe you can talk one of these two into finding my yearbook. I think Montgomery is in there."

"Mother said he went to a private school, Mrs. Branson," Dolly answered. "You were all sixteen years old, weren't you?"

"You better call me Marie while you still have a chance."

"I hope you like day-old donuts," Florence said as she brought in a coffee tray for the card table behind the couch. "I think I'll head up for a nap." Florence stroked Marie's hand. "Try to be sociable, Marie. Gina will wake me when Dolly leaves."

Gina poured coffee for her mother and Dolly. "Where do half-sisters start?"

"We can't gossip about our cousins," Dolly laughed.

"Do we have any?" Gina asked.

"If we did, I doubt they would want to hear about their uncle's peccadilloes."

"But he wasn't married to anyone," Gina defended their non-existent father.

"Never offered," Marie said. "Better just be thankful for each other."

"Is my mother your aunt?"

"Of course not," Marie said. "I think it's called 'once-removed.' But you share the same blood. His family held onto their wealth for three-generations. Maybe you two should hire a detective. You could be in line for inheritances."

Dolly changed the subject. "When Tom called, he said you were unhappy with him."

"He came in drunk Sunday night," Marie said.

"I've forgiven that," Gina said. "He's been under a lot of pressure. Tonight he's taking his final exam."

"Don't be an enabler," Dolly said. "If I hadn't accepted my parents' help, Jonas might not have had the mistaken idea that money impressed me."

"Tom doesn't have a drinking problem." Gina didn't feel as confident as she sounded.

"Better ask him," Marie said.

"Both the brothers have addictive personalities," Dolly said. "I think you should talk to Tom about going back to his AA meetings."

"He went to meetings?"

"Watch yourself," Marie said. "That is not any of your business."

Dolly looked at Marie's bed and then patted Gina's hand. "Your mother is right. Tom's attendance at meetings is his own responsibility, as is his drinking."

Gina had known drunks on the racing circuit. Losers all. "I love him," she said quietly. "The thing about AA I never really approved of was the anonymous part. Not only should friends know if someone they meet has a problem, but I think the liquor companies are getting a free ride. Tobacco companies got their comeuppance. Why should liquor dealers get off?"

"Prohibition didn't work," Marie reminded her.

"Yes, but alcohol does so much physical damage and the addiction element is the same as smoking." Gina was plowing a new field. The words coming out of her mouth had little time for reflection in her defensive confusion.

"It's still Tom's problem," Dolly insisted.

"I'll ask him if I should schedule an Al-Anon meeting."

"Go anyway," Marie said. "It helped me understand my sister."

"I'll call Florence to come down, Mother." Gina kissed her. "Dolly and I will be back shortly. I want to buy some clothes for Danny."

* * *

The mall parking lot was full of cars; so Gina asked Dolly, "Do you ever pray to St. Anthony for a parking space?"

"Does it work?"

"Watch this." Gina drove down a fresh aisle of cars and an empty space appeared after the fifth car. "St. Anthony finds things for you, parking spaces, car keys, anything; but you have to give him credit or he won't help you again."

Dolly held the outside entrance door open to Macy's department store. "Have you tried to tell the police to pray to St. Anthony in their search for Passantino?"

Gina got too involved in shopping to worry about Passantino. She tried on a peach wool suit which fit perfectly. On her way to the cashier, she picked all the size eight suits off the rack. One was light blue, one a soft tan, one black, one white, and one pale yellow. The pale yellow might never be worn but she liked the fit.

Dolly, a fellow shopper, and the clerk gaped at her as if she'd lost her mind.

Dolly followed her into the men's department, where Gina charged Danny two suits by guess and by golly. She described the teenager by comparing him to the salesman. "Your height, fifteen, big shoulders, no fat."

"Slim waist?" The salesman licked his lips. He laid two outfits on the counter. "Shirts and ties?"

"Yes," she said heading for tee-shirts and underwear. "Dolly, could you pick some out with socks to match."

A woman, who had already witnessed Gina's shopping spree, had a shoe box under her arm as she canvassed a tie rack.

'Shoes.' Gina hadn't thought of shoes. She'd call the jail and ask for Danny's size. "Could I use your phone?"

The salesman's dark eyebrows lifted nearly to his hairline as she asked information for the number of the Kane County jail.

"Size twelve," she announced to Dolly and couldn't buy just one pair, so she charged two.

Dolly cautioned her, "Are you a compulsive shopper?"

"Money is only fun when you use it." Gina couldn't go home empty-handed for Tom. So, she bought the most expensive tie she could find.

The rack of ties was abandoned by the less than enthusiastic buyer, who was busy on her cell phone.

"It doesn't go with the suits," Dolly pointed out.

"Different person," Gina explained. "This tie is for Tom."

"Way different person," Dolly told the salesman.

In the parking lot as Gina unlocked Dolly's door, she noticed the other shopper in the same lane of cars no longer carried the box of shoes which had triggered Gina's memory to buy them for Danny.

Dolly seemed particularly quiet. "If Tom mentions going to a meeting, you might ask to go with him."

"My shopping only goes out of control when I'm in a store," Gina said. "You didn't buy anything."

Dolly shook her head. "I just wanted to spend time with you."

"Weren't you bored?"

Dolly pushed her shoulder. "No. I feel as if I'm watching myself. Do you think we have the same way of walking?"

"Yikes," Gina slowed the car and turned into her mother's drive. "I hadn't paid attention."

"Looks like Tom is home," Dolly noted.

Gina checked her watch. Eight-fifteen. "I'll leave the packages in the trunk,"

"Why do that?"

"I want to talk to Tom about Danny without any distractions." Gina turned toward Dolly. "I didn't mean you. I'll be glad when this trial is over so I can continue a normal life."

Dolly laughed. "Call me when you can arrange to come out and meet my mother."

"Thanks, I will."

* * *

When Tom got home before eight after his final exams, the phone rang as he came in the front door. He was closest to the receiver and picked it up after waving hello to Marie and Florence.

Sergeant Muller explained about the implied threat from Danny's uncle. "Harvey Slemmons was quite concerned. Could be nothing but I have my people keeping an eye on all of you." He coughed as if his lie about the surety of their safety stuck in his throat. "Be careful. If you see anything suspicious, give us a call."

"Gina isn't home."

Muller laughed. "She's shopping with your sister-in-law, Dolly. My detective is with her. And, Miss Branson called the jail to ask for Danny's shoe size half an hour ago."

"Thanks." Tom stepped into the living room where he kissed Marie on the forehead. "How's my favorite girl?"

"Two-timer," Marie said. "And with my only daughter."

"When do you expect Gina?"

"Any minute," Florence said. "She's shopping with Dolly. They should be back soon. I set the table for us, but Marie has already eaten."

"How about a pork roast and fixings for supper?" Tom walked into the hall. "I left it in the oven with timer set." He heard Gina's key in the lock and opened the door for her. "Dolly, stay for supper."

"I shouldn't," she said.

"He's a good cook," Gina said, hugging him.

He kissed Gina. "My finals were easier than I had hoped."

"Jonas would be proud of you," Dolly said.

Sadness descended on Tom. The rage and guilt had disappeared. *Oh, third stage of grief,* he counseled himself.

Both Gina and Dolly were staring at his obvious distress.

Tom escaped into the kitchen.

Jonas would never again share a triumph or failure. Their parents had been sticklers for perfection. Neither of the grown men felt they measured up to their parental expectations. When Jonas found Dolly, the only daughter of one of the richest families in Wayne, their mother told Jonas he could have done better. Poor Jonas tried to keep up with his wife's family. His only goal was to earn more money. Not even his two sons satisfied him.

Tom had once heard Jonas scold the oldest, after the boy asked for a toy advertised on television, "It costs me money for you to wake up in the morning." Dolly had struck her husband as hard as she could with her fist on his shoulder. Jonas had only laughed at her attack. "You've never hurt me, so far."

'I should have counseled him,' Tom tormented himself. 'Talked him out of his avariciousness. He might not have died if he hadn't danced after all that money falling from the balcony of the bank.'

Tom tried to recall if Jonas was already in the bank, when he had unlocked the door. If Jonas was in on the caper, he would have had to be there. Tom's memory failed. If that was denial, so be it. But, Jonas would have controlled himself if he'd been guilty. Jonas's spontaneous actions proved his innocence.

Dialing Sergeant Muller's cell phone, Tom wondered if Dolly had been questioned about Danny's claims. What if Danny was the source of the lie and the threat to them? "We didn't tell you Jonas went crazy when the money started falling?"

"No. Miss Branson observed this too?"

"Everyone in the bank. That's when he stuffed the money into his pockets."

Muller's end of the line was quiet as he reflected on the information. Finally he said, "You're right. He would have played his cards closer to his chest if he'd been involved."

"Danny could have made up today's phone call from his uncle, too."

"I'll check the phone records from the jail." Muller coughed. "I'm not sure I told you how sorry I am for your loss."

"Yes," Tom said. "We miss him."

After he cradled the phone, Tom turned on the outside lights. While locking the storm door to the back porch, Tom discovered a small visitor. A bedraggled calico kitten sat trying to wash its nose. When she caught sight of him, she renewed her efforts to be presentable by washing both ears at the same time, one paw on each ear. The resulting imbalance toppled her.

Tom carefully unlocked and slowly opened the door. "Sweets," he called, grabbing her by the scruff of the neck. "Poor baby, are you too hungry to run?" Now he had a pleasant surprise for Gina.

* * *

As Gina crossed the room with her mother's coffee cup, Tom came in with the kitten. "Supper is almost ready. Look who crashed the party." Tom held up the kitten, which he'd nestled in a dish-towel.

Gina set the cup down and cuddled the kitten next to her neck. "Tom, are we going to keep her?"

"We have to." He came closer to Gina careful to stroke the kitten's back. "I've already named her. She was washing her ears so hard with both of her front paws. She fell right over; so I named her Sweets."

Sweets knocked her small head against Gina's chin, demanding attention.

"Perfect," Dolly said and they all listened to Sweet's loud contented purr.

"Muller called," Tom said.

"About Danny's uncle knowing where we lived?"

"Said he'd have his people watch out for us."

Gina laughed. "I wondered why the woman in Macy's didn't buy anything. He's having us tailed?"

"Until they catch Passantino." Then Tom asked, gently, "How is Danny?"

"Do you really want to know? How were your finals?"

"Passed." he said. *Man, he wouldn't be asking about the kid if he didn't have the guts to hear about the session.* "I'm feeling sad about Jonas. Tell me something cheerful about Danny."

Gina lit up. "Really?" then without stopping, "I wish you could have been there. Danny was so brave. He remembered his mother coming after his uncle with a knife." She stopped for a breath, handed him the kitten. "His uncle was abusing Danny and she caught him."

Tom tucked the snuggling kitten back into the dish-towel. Then he invited them into the dining room. Flowers and candles graced the table.

"Marie's right, we should make things special." Florence blushed.

After the kitten and the towel were safely under the table, Tom lit the candles. How could he mention the possibility of Danny making up the threats and slandering Jonas?

Gina sat down next to Dolly's place, still talking. "His uncle managed to take the knife away from his mother and killed her. Right in front of Danny. Then he put the knife in Danny's hand and smeared blood from his mother all over his pajamas."

Tom pulled out his chair. "It explains the narcolepsy."

"You know what he said?" Tom shook his head "Danny said, 'My mother loved me.' Isn't that great?"

"The most healing thing I've heard in days."

Gina broke down.

Tom knelt beside her chair. She participated in the hug wetting his neck with her tears. He kissed her and she clung to him the way she had during their first kiss.

"You listened." She kissed his cheek. "I was so afraid you wouldn't want to hear about Danny."

"I love you," Tom said. Even if Danny lied about Jonas and his uncle's menacing call, he could have been prey to earlier horrors. "Time to eat." Tom got up to bring in the food. He heaped everyone's plate with pork, potatoes, onions and carrots.

Then he asked Gina, "Have you heard of the therapy term 'screening'?"

"Tell me," she said. Her eyes were wet from her tears and the flickering candles made them sparkle.

He loved to watch her mouth when she ate. How could he insert doubt into her sweet mind? *Brutal truths,* he thought before he continued. "Therapists use screening as a technique, like hypnotism, to bring out memories from troubled patients. They introduce the idea of a movie theatre with a blank screen. The patient projects his thoughts onto the surface, with guidance from the therapists."

The line between Gina's eyebrows surfaced.

Tom bent his head, unable to continue his scenario while under her critical gaze.

"You mean Dr. Pheiffer led Danny into making up a lie?" Dolly asked.

"No," he could say truthfully. "I believe Danny did go through hell. But the possibility of therapists influencing stories occurs."

Gina stood up. "I went shopping."

"Finish your meal," he ordered softly. "We'll get to that."

She obediently sat back down. "The roast is awfully good."

"Not too dry?" They ate in silence until Tom got up the nerve to continue. "I called Muller about Jonas dancing. He thought Jonas would have acted less crazy, if he'd been in on the heist."

"When was Jonas dancing?" Dolly asked.

"Tom," Gina was on her feet again.

Tom tried to change the subject without answering Dolly. "Muller said when you were shopping, you called the jail for Danny's shoe size."

Gina sat down again but held her fork in midair. "Muller thinks Danny fabricated the claims about Jonas, instead of his uncle?"

Tom nodded. God she was beautiful. How could he bear to injure her?

"But he believed the threats." Her eyes widened taking it all in. "He had us followed."

"He's reviewing the jail's phone records. In the meantime, he has to be sure we're all safe."

Gina let go of her fork. She played with her lower lip, biting it while trying to assimilate the conflicting information.

What if she would leave him? Imagining her sweet lips, Tom's mind had leapt upstairs. He thought about all the things he hadn't seen, like her toes. He hadn't even kissed her toes.

Gina finished the last carrot on her plate. "What did you think of the prosecutor excusing twenty-two women from the jury?"

Smash went his dream. "So what?" he said without thinking, angry about the interruption in his erotic plans.

Gina sat mute.

He'd destroyed the mood. "I don't think I'm up to talking about the trial," he said as softly as he could.

She blushed.

But, Tom reasoned the blush stemmed from repressed anger.

* * *

Wednesday, October 24rd

Tom was up with coffee made and the kitten fed. He'd filled Jonas's bed with the packages from Gina's trunk while she was in the shower.

She came into the kitchen wearing a peach colored suit which made her pale skin bloom. "You're beautiful," he said. He turned on the dishwasher before kissing her.

Gina held out a slim box for him. "We left the kitten downstairs last night?"

"Tie?" Tom opened the box and ran his finger over the silkiness. "For today?"

"If you want," she said.

Sweets tried to climb up Gina's nylons, but Tom rescued the situation by picking up the monstrous kitten.

Gina sat her empty cup on the counter. "The clothes I bought for Danny to wear to court are out in the trunk. Do you mind going early?"

"I put all the packages upstairs. Do you like my new tie?"

"You're the most handsome man in town." She kissed his mouth, tantalizing him. "I'll run up and retrieve Danny's clothes."

Tom hadn't let go of her hand. "I'll drive too. I need to stop for groceries and a paper." He turned and sprinkled milk over toast crumbs for the kitten.

Gina still stood in the doorway of the kitchen, smiling at him.

He kept talking just to keep here there, happy with him. "While I wait for court to start, I can comb the want ads now that I have a degree under my belt. When court's over, if you need to talk to Harvey, I'll start on supper."

Gina left the room. Could he keep Gina's mood right where it was? Trying to control others wasn't encouraged in the AA program.

CHAPTER NINE

After handing over Danny's new clothes to the county jail's desk sergeant, Gina made her way to the second floor of the courthouse. The quiet court room was empty except for her favorite giant. She tugged Tom to the defense side of the aisle. "You're on my side aren't you?"

"I certainly am!" Tom leaned over to kiss the bridge of her nose. "There's a want ad in the Courier for a driving instructor for Geneva's high school."

"Where?" She read the details after he pointed out the black-bordered ad. "Are you going to apply for it?"

Tom winked at her. "It's all yours."

"Probably should. I seem to get along with teenagers."

"Because you are one." Tom put his arm around her. "Dolly asked me to stop by after court. Jeffrey and Timothy have been asking about me. I'll get groceries before I go over. Maybe we'll have cold cuts and potato salad for supper."

"Sounds fine." Gina watched as he folded the newspaper. "Did you find any jobs with your qualifications?"

"Maybe," he said. "I'll tell you later."

The remains of the original jury pool marched in. Seven women and five men lined up in the jury box. Harvey Slemmons, Dr. Pheiffer, and the prosecutor seated themselves. Hillary Gingrich, the original therapist, was missing from the adversarial side of the room.

Danny was brought in from the side door. He started to strut, but changed his mind and walked in a dignified manner to their table. His white hair reflected the courtroom's fluorescent lighting and the dark blue suit accentuated the fine figure of a young man.

Gina turned to Tom for confirmation.

He gave her a faint smile.

Then Sergeant Muller came in, right up to Tom. "Judge Wilcox has Dr. Pheiffer's statement." He leaned past Tom to Gina. "We've added the murder of Danny's mother to the arrest warrant."

"Any leads," Gina asked.

"Some," he said smiling at a stone faced Tom. "Some."

Judge Wilcox arrived and the business of jury selection continued. "Jimmy Pierce, did you attend high school with the victim, Jonas Woods?"

Jimmy stood. "Yes, your Honor."

"You're excused. If any of you knew the deceased, please excuse yourselves at this time."

The woman who was fifteen pounds overweight, the one Gina thought she recognized from high school in a slimmer incarnation, left the jury box. At least the woman had worn a vest over her white blouse, which had the good grace to stay buttoned at the crucial juncture.

The clerk approached the judge who nodded in agreement to whatever was requested. "One moment, Mr. Slemmons," Judge Wilcox said. "We have to replenish the troops."

They waited until the clerk ushered in the next group of forty prospective jurors.

Harvey Slemmons asked two of the older men to be excused after they answered *'yes'* to, "Do you have college plans in place for your children?"

One middle age man left when asked if he worked for the legal system. He had worked as a parole officer, but recently retired. Tom moved in the seat next to her. Did he want the man on Danny's jury?

"Any military associations?" Harvey asked. Two young men rose and left their seats on the jury. Harvey then asked, "Do any of you own membership in the NRA?"

"National Rifleman's' Association," Judge Wilcox decoded the alphabet soup. No one admitted to being a member.

One older man was asked, "Do you know the statute of limitations on murder?" He did not and was excused.

Another senior gentleman left after answering *'yes'* to, "Do you have a checking or savings account in Geneva's City Bank?"

By then it was lunch time and the Judge called a recess.

* * *

Tom and Gina ate in the ugly basement cafeteria of the courthouse. None of the lawyers joined them probably because the food was worse than the surroundings. The bread in the vending-machine sandwiches was soggy, the lettuce wilted, and the thin slice of bologna tough. Gina crunched potato chips and a shriveled apple. The coffee held no aroma, mere rotgut.

"Slemmons is getting rid of all the older men," Tom knew he was complaining to the wrong person.

Gina frowned at him. "Well, the prosecutor got rid of twenty-two women when he was choosing."

Tom couldn't help grinning. "Only the hale and hearty men." He wished he'd thought before beginning the subject.

Gina's frown line entrenched itself in her brow. "I wish Muller could tell us where they're looking for Danny's Uncle Passantino."

"That's like asking where a bear can sit." Tom tried to take her hand. If she would just give him a small smile, some sign that she hadn't forgotten she loved him. "Anywhere," he said when she didn't respond. "Muller's looking anywhere and everywhere."

"I hope so." Finally, a smile. "Didn't Danny look fine?"

Tom nodded, disappointed at the direction the conversation was taking. "A young gentleman," he said; but thought irreverently, *can't make a silk purse out of a sow's ear.*

* * *

Back in the court room, Gina was thinking about applying for the driver's education job when Harvey asked a past-middle-age man, "Is there any reason you would not be fair to the defendant?"

"Too pretty." The man said.

The court erupted in laughter. Even Danny joined in until Judge Wilcox banged his gavel.

"Silence!" Judge Wilcox allowed a slight smile to play with the corner of his mouth.

"Excused," Harvey intoned dramatically. Harvey had warned Gina jury selection would take hours. They'd been at it for two days with no end in sight.

A young man barely over Danny's age was asked, "Will sitting as a juror cause you any undue hardship?"

"I'm writing a screenplay."

"Excused," Judge Wilcox interrupted; then explained to Harvey, "His mind won't be on the trial."

At four in the afternoon, the seated jury finally consisted of two women, and ten men. The prosecutor had used his peremptory challenges against ten more women. Harvey had accepted no man over thirty.

Danny's trial would begin the next week on Monday.

* * *

Sergeant Muller and a plainclothes detective waited for Tom and Gina in the hall. "Miss Branson, Tom Woods, I'd like you to meet Detective Jerry Hoffman."

The red-headed man shook hands with Tom. He slightly bowed to Gina. "Ma'am, we'd like to discuss the case with you all."

Tom grinned at Gina because of the detective's southern accent.

Back in Muller's office Gina described why she agreed with Tom. Jonas was not involved in the bank robbery. "I know he wasn't."

Tom said, "I can't remember if he was in the bank when I unlocked the place."

"I remember," Gina said. "Because I had to wait for him. I sat for a half-hour before he arrived."

Relief touched Tom, for a moment.

But Jerry wasn't convinced. "Getting to work late to throw off suspicion doesn't prove a thing."

Sergeant Muller interrupted. "You weren't there, Jerry. These two and the other women in the bank told me Jonas Woods was dancing with his hands above his head to catch the money before he was shot."

Jerry considered the information. "Yep, you all are right. Why did you ask these two here?"

"We checked the phone Danny used." Muller faced Gina's chair. "His uncle has called and we're tracing the billing address of the cell phone. I wanted you both to know, as far as we can tell, the threats against you are real. Jonas was falsely accused as an accomplice but we need to caution you two. Alan Passantino is a violent man, intent on *not* being locked up."

"He's armed?" Jerry asked.

"I know he has a big automatic and Tom's gun." Gina said.

"Your gun?" Jerry asked.

"I was a guard at the bank." Tom lowered his head. "I've never shot a gun. I threw it at the window hoping to break the glass."

"How'd ya get the job in the first place?" Jerry asked.

"My brother, Jonas, was the loan officer," Tom admitted. "He put in a good word for me."

Muller added, "Tom lives in the basement of his sister-in-law, Dolly Woods."

Tom and Gina both looked at Muller. Something in his tone when he said Dolly's name alerted Tom. Muller's face turned nearly purple under their stares.

"What's going on?" Jerry asked.

"Nothing," Muller said, then waved his hand in exasperation. "She's as beautiful as Gina, here."

"Bachelors," Gina said.

* * *

On the way to their cars, Gina said, "Let's eat out tonight."

Tom was relieved he couldn't think of anything he wanted to cook and cold cuts sounded grim after their unsavory lunch. "I have to see Dolly's kids and we need to feed the kitten."

"I'll follow you home to feed Sweets. Could I go with you to Dolly's parents?" Gina pulled on his lapels.

"We don't have to mention the questions about Jonas."

"I wish Dolly hadn't heard about his actions at the bank."

"Maybe Dolly will let us take the kids to Johnson's Mound." Tom felt better, as if a case of the flue had passed. "Did you ever walk around Johnson's Mound? Mom used to take Jonas and me out to the Mound when she had a fight with our dad." The word 'our' flipped off the cheerful switch in his head. He blushed when he noticed Gina registered the change in his mood.

"I've heard of it. Is it out west of Randall Road? I know a place on 47 that serves fresh fish. I used to race my stepdad's Oldsmobile up and down the hills on Baker Road. Got it up to a hundred. Course he'd asked me where I'd driven, because I'd emptied the tank from speeding."

"It's still gravel." Tom shook off a cloak of sadness. "I wonder if they'd let the kids fish for their own dinner?"

"I bet the boys would like seeing Sweets. We've got to feed her anyway." Gina smiled. "Let's go pick her up."

Tom gently pulled on her curls. "I love you, midget."

Gina swatted at his hand, but said, "Me too you, you giant."

Gina lowered herself into her car. Could this be the start of the rest of their lives: kids, pets? Tom stayed in his car when Gina went in to fetch the kitten. She hadn't spent much time with Jeffrey or Timothy yet. What did it matter if Danny Bianco got a second chance in life? How else could the two of them, Tom and Gina; ever be able to live together? Would he need to step up and help Danny's return to society, especially because Danny's uncle lied about both murders?

* * *

Tom looked at the open door of the repainted and re-roofed, two story house where he might live out the rest of his life. Gina was taking her time. Maybe she was changing out of her suit.

Had he heard a cry? The cat had probably ruined a drape or knocked something important over. Tom locked the car and pocketed the keys, before a coldness crept into his chest.

"Gina?" he called from the front door into the empty hall.

Gina had stopped to check on her mother. Marie took her hand. "Such a beautiful bride." Marie smiled.

Tom sensed a crisis. Marie's breaths were short bursts of air. "Florence, run call Dr. Wiggns."

"Yellow doesn't become you, dear." Marie waved at the space behind Gina's head. "Change into a white veil."

Tom moved to the other side of the bed.

"I'm sure Tom will agree." Marie squinted. "Oh it was the light behind you. I." Marie waved both arms as if having difficulty breathing.

Florence clamped an oxygen mask over her nose and mouth. "Dr. Wiggins's on her way."

Marie nodded then pushed the device away. "Thank you, Florence."

Gina cried out, "Mother, wait."

Marie's eyes didn't focus when she turned to her daughter. "Yes, dear. I'm not going anywhere. But, Tom, could you turn the lights back on?"

Then Marie rested.

Florence took her pulse. "Gina." was all she needed to say.

Tom embraced Gina. Her mother was gone.

* * *

Saturday, October 27th

So this is grief, Gina thought on Saturday morning. The shower felt good. 'Too good,' her mind reprimanded her. Mother had said she missed her daily shower after she was bedridden.

Ever since Thursday evening when her mother died, Gina's mind contained a stop. Every memory, every step into her next hour carried pain. Her mother hadn't needed any help, smiling to meet the next world. Maybe Mother would still be living, if she hadn't believed she'd seen Gina as Tom's bride. Gina did think of Tom as the best man on earth, but her mother may have waited for the ceremony, if she hadn't been hallucinating from the pain medication.

The water falling on Gina's shoulders turned cold. How long had she been standing there with suds in her hair? Well the cold water would make her curls shiny at least. What do you wear as an orphan?

'I've got to be gentle with myself to get through the day.' She dried her face and then convulsed into sobs. Would she ever have a dry face again? Would her tear ducts finally dry out?

"Gina," Tom was calling her.

"Yes," she answered, happy to let her mind alone for a second.

"Are you all right?"

"No," she sobbed.

Tom pushed the door open and held her, wrapped in soft clean-smelling towels, close to his chest. "It will get easier."

"Promise?"

"I'm an expert, remember." He didn't let go. "Hours and days heal the void."

"Why does her death hurt so much? I knew she was ill. We expected her time was less than long? Why am I so surprised?"

"You're not surprised. You just wanted her to stay longer."

"I need her." Her sobs were never going to cease.

"She knew you had me." Tom kissed her wet face and began rubbing feeling back into her chilled back. "Better get dressed. Florence is here and Menasha."

When Tom left, Gina opened her closet and drew out the black wool suit she'd bought with Dolly.

* * *

Saturday's memorial service proceeded while visitors to the house told Gina all the reasons why her grief would pass. Tom felt like shaking each new arrival. He wanted to yell at them, "Let her be sad." Now was the time to feel the depth of grief. "Don't tell her to put it off." The guests who made Tom weep along with Gina were those who merely showed up, being there silently for her.

He wanted to remember everyone's name. He concentrated on alphabetizing them in the moment between their self-introductions and their condolences to Gina. There were St. Charles names he had heard in Catholic grade school and Geneva names from high school: Armenoff, Buell, Chapski, Cornell, Dewitz, Ellis, Hart, Hibbler, Kelly, Klick, Knutzen, Manuel, McKiness, Pearson, Salter, Schelstreet, Shepard, Spradlin, Spriet, Staples, and Umathum. Vander Meer, Wolfe, and Zimmerman.

Marie Branson had a boatload of friends, more than on Noah's ark. They explained themselves to Tom as he sat next to Gina on the couch which they had backed up to the flower-strewn bed: There was no grave-side funeral service, because Marie arranged to be cremated.

"Worked with her twenty years ago at DuKane." The couple, twenty years older than the woman they were paying their respects to, clung to each other.

"I was her favorite butcher," a rotund redhead about Tom's age claimed.

Surprised at the number of young people attending, at first Tom assumed they were friends of Gina's. But they enlightened him. "She knew my mother," would be said. Or even more interesting for their sheer numbers, "She dated my father."

A perfectly groomed, size five contemporary of Marie's said, "Before she was bedridden, Marie cheated at bridge with me every Friday."

Twenty pounds heavier than she ought to be, one beautiful young woman explained her presence. "Marie let me fix her hair."

The Episcopal minister, Lorna Hale, bowed. "A long-time parishioner, Marie, was one of God's polished souls."

"Stood with her on peace pickets during the Vietnam War. Robert Koelz." The dapper man with tears in his eyes introduced himself. Apparently he knew Menasha and Harvey Slemmons, too.

Another man dressed in his fire department uniform insisted they know, "After Marie graduated with a degree in Human Resources, she wrote my resume." When neither Gina nor Tom could respond, the man added, "I'd been out of work with a back injury."

They both nodded as if now they understood and he moved on.

"Neighbors," Gina explained after a couple told them, "Marie always brought in our mail when we traveled."

"Physics," two men Gina's age answered about their doctorates. "Marie told us a person with any brains shouldn't smoke."

A hulking, ugly man Tom's size with faded green eyes and a shock of white hair said, "Marie listened to me during my divorce, when I was suicidal." Tom noticed he wore snake skin cowboy boots when he walked to the other side of the front room.

"Marie was there for me," many said.

"She went to court with me," a flamboyant divorcee bragged before adding, "but she wouldn't attend my custody hearing."

More than one young and old acquaintance of Marie's said, "She told me to see a therapist. To use them as rent-a-friends."

As a fledgling therapist himself, Tom took particular note of these guests, who one and all seemed well-adjusted and friendly to other strangers gathered in the room.

Five or six women admitted that they had stayed under Marie's roof to escape abusive husbands. One slight woman said, "She advised me to wait until my husband fell asleep and then to beat him with my cast-iron skillet. I divorced him instead."

At one point Gina turned to Tom. "I think the house is going to explode with people."

She even smiled faintly when Tom whispered back, "We would lose the new roof."

People brought food and wine. Florence arranged the offerings on the dining room table, setting out all the dishes and eating utensils in the house. Luckily one guest had the forethought to bring plastic wine glasses.

Gina wouldn't accept a bite, but everyone else in the house ate as if it were their last meal. Tom felt nauseous as food disappeared into different shaped mouths. Fat and lean alike seemed determined to prove they were alive by eating themselves into oblivion.

The wine flowed just as freely without any gaiety seeping into the somber proceedings. The attendees walked Gina around the house, out into the small back garden, touching her black curls, telling her stories about her mother, patting her back or hugging her before they left.

Florence came to Tom to complain, "The kitchen is filling up with food."

"They're all eating," Tom pointed out, sweeping the room with his arm to show her the filled plates, the moving jaws.

Gina appeared at his elbow. "Remember the loaves and fishes in the Bible. Everything seems to be multiplying, no matter how much they eat."

"Florence," Tom suggested after the three of them assembled in the burgeoning kitchen, where smells of various meat sauces vied with baked goods. "...send as much home as you can with each guest when they leave."

"That would be rude," Florence said. "I can't remember who brought what."

"We'll take it to the homeless shelter." Gina said.

"They'll want their dishes back," Florence added to the conundrum.

"Pack the food in Mother's Tupperware." Gina said as she left to return to her duties as the bereaved.

Florence reluctantly pulled out all the plastic wear from the cupboards. "I hate leftovers."

Jonas's funeral didn't resemble Marie's. Jonas was more interested in the influx of money rather than the people who crossed his path. Tom sucked in his breath from the pain.

A hefty man with a plate piled high looked over his shoulder as he left through the garden gate. 'Guilty of his haul,' Tom thought.

"Where's Gina?" Dolly met Tom in the crowded front hall.

"She's not in the kitchen or the front room," Tom said.

"Marie was well loved."

Tom nodded his head. "Marie's the reason Gina gave up racing. When her friends were killed, she stopped making new acquaintances, afraid they would die. After she came home, she decided she wanted people in her life, the way Marie had them in hers."

Marching up the stairs through the rooms with Dolly in search of Gina, Tom started counting the people who claimed Marie dated their fathers. "A lot of divorced people live in Geneva."

"And St. Charles." Dolly said.

"Marie couldn't have dated all the men whose children showed up today."

"Why not?"

Tom led the way back downstairs. "I counted sixty."

Dolly stopped at the bottom of the steps. "Divided by 36 months is how many?"

"About two a month. Tom pondered the numbers and the names: Zimmerman, Warner, Walker, Williams, VerDuin, Smrt, Prettinhoffer, Pierce, McNamer, Leonard, Harmening, Dunn, Chaban. He could only remember a dozen names. Gina would remember the other four dozen. Maybe there were more men in Marie's life, who had never married, never had children.

Without finding Gina, he surveyed the downstairs rooms from the central hall.

"Let's try the garden," Dolly said.

Then Tom remembered the heavy man with his heaping plate. The thought froze his insides. The words 'girth' and 'heavy' played havoc with his mind.

"Gina," he called loudly, startling the quiet visitors.

Dolly rushed back into the house with him. Florence dropped a full dish of Jell-O when she saw Tom's face.

"Please, God," Tom prayed as he dialed Muller's number.

CHAPTER TEN

Gina's memory of her old habit kicked in. She looked into the front room, but this time she was hunting for a lively kitten instead of watching the swift decline of her mother's health.

After searching the ground floor, Gina spied Sweets pawing at the garden gate to the alley. Gina swiftly opened the gate and stooped to pick up the calico kitten.

The shoes outside on the gravel path were not on Tom's feet.

She straightened up as Alan Passantino pulled her into the alley. He clamped one dirty hand over her mouth and held her with the other arm against his huge stomach. Gina only had time to drop Sweets before he pushed her into the passenger side of the car, then he climbed in after her ramming her behind the steering wheel.

"You drive," he barked.

Standard shift, handy emergency brake between the seats. A top-heavy four-wheel drive. Gina buckled her seat belt. *This joker is going to get the ride of his life,* she thought unafraid.

"Find side roads up to Rockford."

Without a word of contradiction, Gina headed west.

Passantino didn't smell pleasant.

She opened her window for fresh air. Not much time to shower or change clothes when you're on the run.

Passantino held Tom's gun from the bank in his right hand, low so that no one could see it through the window. He had hidden the car behind the garage in the alley used to pick up rubbish.

Tom wouldn't have seen them leave.

* * *

Sweets was staring out the back gate, still interested in the shenanigans that must have gone on when Gina was abducted. Tom stuffed the kitten under his shirt. Her fur smelled like Gina's lilac perfume with the faint hint of cedar.

Tom knew Gina had been abducted when he dialed Muller. "He's taken her."

Dolly and Florence clung to each other near the kitchen sink.

Tom could hear the static as Muller picked up another phone. "Where the hell is Hoffman? I told that blimey redhead to stay on their tail." Muller came back on. "He's in the alley. Get out there. He's seen them leave."

Tom handed the phone to Dolly and ran. When he got in Jerry's car he remembered he still had Sweets under his shirt. Sweets meowed.

The car swerved as Jerry looked over at him. "What was that?"

"My cat," Tom comforted the kitten as he buckled his seat belt around her. "What kind of car?"

"I thought you were crying." Jerry shrugged his shoulder in apology. "Black Ford Taurus. She's driving. Where would she take him?"

"She's a professional race-car driver. Baker Road, gravel, heads north. Take Randall and turn west on Dean Street. First road on the right."

The detective nodded. When they hit Randall Road, he turned on his siren and the lights.

Tom's thoughts rushed faster than the speeding police car. Gina. She couldn't be gone. He wouldn't think of losing her.

Sweets clawed his chest wanting freedom. He slipped her farther up on his chest, where his shirt allowed her to stick her head out. She didn't like the noise or the flashing scenery and ducked her head back under his shirt.

Please Lord, he prayed silently, *don't let one curl be touched on Gina head.*

He remembered Marie's acceptance of God's painful tyranny. Marie still loved her God. Could he continue to love God if anything happened to the only woman he had ever loved. Maybe not, after the deaths of both his parents and his twin.

Not now, Lord. Don't chastise me now'

With the police car careening onto the dirt of Baker Road, with his fears for Gina's safety racing his heart, the kitten's tongue licked his neck.

Hope leapt in his heart.

If a stray kitten could show him affection, when she was terrorized, surely the Lord would love him enough to save his future wife.

Thank you Lord, he prayed without any rational reason.

Jerry jolted him back to earth. "They're headed toward us!"

The police car stopped, immediately parallel to the oncoming dust cloud.

* * *

Originally Gina had turned north on Randall Road.

"Get off this main road." Her kidnapper's voice resembled a dog's growl or bark.

"I'll take Dean Street one block west to Baker. It's a gravel road all the way to Rockford." She hoped he didn't know that rural road stopped not five miles north of St. Charles. No reply. *Good,* she thought. Too bad they couldn't talk about Danny.

"Danny thinks you're his savior." Even that was a hostile grumble. "He's been blabbering like an idiot."

Think, she demanded of herself. *Present a conundrum.* "He'll want to hear from me."

Passantino laughed. It was worse than the barks. "We'll call him in Rockford, and Canada."

"Sergeant Muller has my house watched," she tried to appear frightened, lowering her forehead and staring up at him. "Should I go faster?"

"Yeah," he said. "Floor it."

Now he was talking.

Passantino tried putting the seat belt around his big middle but it must have been stuck in the door.

Gina gunned the Ford. *Go ahead,* she thought, *reach for the door. Try to open it to get your belt uncaught. You'll be sailing into the ditch.*

The speedometer read eighty mph.

The narrow road, steep hills, and deep ditches on Baker Road were perfect. She remembered the first time she drove her dad's Buick out here, beeping the horn at the crest of each hill to warn oncoming cars. Thank the Lord, she knew what she was doing. Racing cars had it advantages.

Ninety-five miles per hour.

Each hill sent them sailing free style only to bump down hard.

Passantino hit his head, but he kept hold of the gun. "Slow it down," he ordered.

She did.

Gina pulled on the hand-brake with all her might and the car fishtailed into a boot-leg turn, reversing the direction of the car.

Passantino grabbed for the handle of the door, dropping his gun.

The centrifugal force slammed him into the door. He'd flown out of the car, rolling into a ditch.

Gina clamped her foot down on the gas pedal. A right back tire blew but she turned left away from the tipping momentum and righted the impending roll over. The rearview mirror showed the gravel and dust cloud she was leaving for Passantino.

The wheel's going to be wrecked, she thought heading for home. She saw the police lights before she heard the siren. Thank God she had mentioned Baker Road to Tom.

The stupid cop had stopped his car in the middle of the road.

Blockade, she reasoned, as she brought the Ford to a screeching halt, not two feet from the side of the car.

When Tom leapt out of the police car, Gina opened the Ford's door and jumped out.

Relief from the danger buckled her knees and she went face down into the dusty gravel road.

* * *

"Please God, please God," Tom shouted. He held her in his lap with his face turned to the sky.

"Quit yelling," Gina managed, spitting out a pebble.

He stared down at her. Sweets peeked out from the neck of his shirt.

She knew her face was a mess, because it hurt when she tried to laugh.

The medical team rescued her from Tom's firm grip.

"Did you get him?" she asked.

Tom nodded.

Jerry Hoffman said next to Tom's shoulder, "You're a mess."

"Did he hit you?" Tom asked.

"No," she whispered. "I fell out of the car."

"We'll have to stitch your lip at the hospital," one of the team said.

"I'll come with," Tom said.

Jerry Hoffman pulled him back. "We'll meet you at the hospital. I'll need a statement."

"Call Dolly, Tom." Gina yelled as they shut the ambulance doors. "He would have forgotten," she whispered to the attendants.

* * *

Jerry dropped Tom and Sweets at home. Dolly and Florence were still cleaning up after the memorial service.

Florence managed to extract the kitten from his shirt. "Poor baby needs to eat."

"I've got to get to the hospital," Tom said, wondering if he could take some of the flowers from the service to Gina.

"How badly is she hurt?" Dolly asked.

"Her face is messed up."

"Oh, my God, Tom."

"No. It's not that bad." He grabbed a fist full of yellow roses. "Florence, can you find me an empty vase?" then he answered Dolly, "She fell and her lip got cut, a few pieces of gravel scraped her cheek."

"You made it sound like bones were broken and plastic surgeons would be called in."

"Nothing like that. Bad swelling, bruising."

"Still, she's lucky. Wait for me." Dolly gathered up an armload of flowers too. "If she doesn't want them, other patients will be glad to have something cheerful in their rooms."

"I'll bring the rest," Florence said, "after I call your parents, Dolly."

Dolly settled into his Escort. "Do you still walk Mikey for Mrs. Stiles?"

"Sure, on Sundays. I prayed for Gina," Tom admitted.

"Been a long time?" Dolly asked, not mocking him.

"You bet," he said. "I guess the old Guy came through."

"Bout time," Dolly giggled.

He laughed, finally free of the fear. "I feel so good, Dolly."

When he parked the car at the hospital, Tom told his sister-in-law the rest of the truth. "You know I love the girl."

"You bet you do." Dolly was quiet, not opening the car door. "Jonas would have been proud of you."

Then Tom couldn't talk. He coughed and laughed to get away from the cloud of grief closing in on him. "I miss him so much."

Dolly let him cry.

He shook as he laid his head on the steering wheel, grasping it with all his might. "I'm sorry, Dolly." Tom apologized. "Don't get upset."

"Hey, didn't you tell me to let the grief happen, 'not try to dam it up'?"

Control resurfaced. "I hate it when you use my own words against me."

"I can't wait to see Gina." Dolly said. "She's a brave one and lucky to snag you."

* * *

October 28th, Sunday
Delnor Hospital

Gina threw a paper cup filled with water at the closing door of her room. "I want out."

"Temper, temper," Dolly kidded.

Muller wiped up the spilled water with a towel from the bathroom. "The doctors want to see if you have any other injuries." He nervously paced at the foot of her bed.

"I look like Frankenstein's bride, but I'm not dying."

"Did Hoffman already take your statement?" Tom wondered why Muller was still around.

Muller answered for her. "I did it. Jerry was busy making sure Passantino got his rights."

"How is he?" Gina asked.

"Who cares," Tom said, then thought better of it. "Did he survive?"

Muller shook his head. "Well enough to stand trial. Mad as a wet hen, I'll say that for him."

"Good," Gina said.

The door swung open and Judge Joe Wilcox stormed in.

Without the raised platform and robes of office, Tom barely recognized the judge. His small stature and his rumpled suit left the impression of a hyperactive teddy bear.

"Very unusual," the judge said, taking off his jacket and aiming it at a chair.

Muller picked up the discarded coat, folding it neatly on the back of a chair. "Judge, this is Mrs. Jonas Woods, the victim's widow."

Judge Wilcox nodded to Dolly. "I'm not supposed to get involved, but I heard what happened." He continued nonstop to Gina, "I'll recuse myself from sitting on Passantino's trial. Are you all right?"

"Look bad, don't I?"

"Yep," the judge said. "You drove racecars?"

"Until her mother got sick," Dolly answered for her half-sister.

"Someone must have been praying for you." Judge Wilcox looked at Tom.

"Guilty," Tom said. He couldn't figure out why the judge would visit Gina.

Muller spoke up. "Judge, about Danny Bianco?"

"We'll meet with the lawyers and a probation officer in my chambers, but I might as well tell you. I'm stopping his trial. After I heard Dr. Pheiffer's tape and listened to... What's her name?"

"Hillary Gingrich." Gina offered.

Tom touched her short curls, finding them gritty with road dirt from her fall.

"That's her." The judge continued. "You know the jails are full. The kid already served eight years for something he didn't do. The probation officer will interview you, Mr. Woods."

Tom jumped to attention. What did they need to hear from him about Danny Bianco?

"And you, Mrs. Woods."

"Dolly," she said. "I'm afraid I don't know what the boy looks like."

Muller explained. "Victims have to be consulted in these cases."

Judge Wilcox stared at Gina. "You've gone out of your way to fight for this boy."

"Mitigating circumstances," Gina said.

"That's it entirely; but I want to keep tabs on the young man, too. Make sure no one else decides to take advantage of him."

"No jail time," Tom said mostly to himself.

"Three to five years' probation," Judge Wilcox said, "depending on what I hear about the child." Judge Wilcox used the hospital foot rest to climb up and sit right on Gina's bed.

Pushy Napoleonic tendencies, Tom rehearsed his assessment of the man.

Dolly busily arranged the flowers she'd brought. The funeral blooms gave off their normal scents but they mixed with the disinfectant smells or the anger rising with Tom's frustration. He walked around the bed and tried to open the hospital's window.

The judge tapped the bed, as if he missed having a gavel in his hand. "I woke up thinking about an adopted son of an acquaintance I knew in Ann Arbor. The boy was four when he was adopted. His own mother beat him senseless. That's why he was taken away from her."

With his back turned away from them Tom wondered if the judge thought he and Gina were going to adopt Danny. *Not in this lifetime.* Tom turned to see if Dolly agreed with his assessment.

Muller was patting Dolly's hand on Gina's bed tray.

Dolly didn't notice because she was intently watchng Gina, whose eyes showed her interest in the story, maybe even an interest in adopting Danny?

The judge extolled them further, "Without his knowing about it, my friend's wife beat the kid too. They divorced and I met the boy when he was about fourteen, just briefly, about a year later. I'd heard the kid was in a detention home in Waterloo. I visited him there. His counselor took me aside and told me not to waste my time. I was outraged at the time, but I didn't go back."

This is a set up' Tom thought. *How stupid do these people think I am? They want me to adopt the kid who helped kill my brother?*

Dolly began to comb the gravel out of Gina's hair.

Muller moved toward the door, as if to allow them the judge's undivided attention. He waved at Tom or Dolly and left.

Judge rubbed his finger across his forehead as if to bring out more of the memory. "Then Michael showed up on my doorstep with a buddy, hungry. I fed them and asked about the boy's father. Harold, I think. The kid didn't know where his father had moved, but he knew where I lived. He said they swiped a car to drive into Detroit. I told them to leave, that I wouldn't call the police. The detention home wasn't going to cure what ailed the boy. He was a little miffed that I wouldn't let him stay, even made a half-hearted threat. I explained I didn't want someone around who stole cars."

"How did he take the rejection?" Tom asked.

Dolly noticed he was angry. She shook her head, *'no,'* pointing to his balled up fists.

The judge answered Gina, as if she'd asked the question. "He told me it wasn't wrong unless he was caught."

Gina was oblivious to Tom's discomfort as she took the judge's hand. "You're wondering if Danny's life has convinced him of similar morals."

"I want to be sure that is not the case," Judge Wilcox said.

"Are you able to mandate education?" Gina asked.

"He's already sixteen." Tom had gained control of himself to speak in a normal tone.

"If private funds were available?" Gina had thought this out, Tom could tell.

"Not legally," Judge Wilcox said. "But it would be a factor in his early release from probation."

"I'll talk to Menasha, he's my mother's trust attorney," Gina said.

Sure, talk to Menasha. Tom's rage was growing. *Talk to everybody and anybody but me about everything.*

He did remain silent when the judge wished Gina a quick recovery and left.

Why hadn't Gina told him about her plans to educate Danny? Tom tried to understand his growing frustration. He wasn't going to adopt the kid. Was Danny going to be invited to move into Gina's house? Obviously, Gina didn't trust him with that bit of news, even after all the time they'd spent together.

* * *

Gina understood Tom was upset even before Dolly left. He'd started to answer her questions with monosyllables. "I'll be home in the morning."

"Should I be?"

"Why are you upset?"

He turned too quickly toward her, angry words on the tip of his tongue. But he relaxed and sat in a plastic armchair next to the windows.

She watched him breathe in and out, controlling himself. "Peace, Love, and Harmony?"

"That's what I thought we were doing, but apparently I was wrong." He crossed his legs and folded his arms.

"What did I do wrong?" Gina watched as he clenched his jaw.

"Nothing." Tom shook his head. "You're a saint."

"Don't get sarcastic with me." She brushed the gravel from her pillow. "I'm trying to talk here."

"About time," Tom was on his feet pacing.

Gina racked her brain. When had his mood changed? Her head was hurting and her bottom teeth throbbed from the jolt they'd taken. The flowers were starting to nauseate her. "Danny's schooling!"

"Bingo."

"What's the big deal?" Gina couldn't believe he was serious.

"There isn't any." Tom sat back down in the crummy armchair. ". . .for you."

"Tom, give me a break." She tried to smile at him, but her mouth, everything hurt. "Spell it out for me."

Tom got up again. "It doesn't matter."

"Yes, it does." Gina was surprised to find tears welling up. "But I don't know why."

He shouted his answer, each word spaced with anger, "You. . .don't. . .trust. . .me!"

"I do." Her tears ran down her face with a mind of their own.

"If you trusted me, I'd be the first to know." His voice had lowered but not his rage. "Not the last. You think I still hate Danny, but I'm over my anger about Jonas's death, and my guilt in not shooting Passantino for him, I'm just humanly sad now. And I may never forgive Passantino or want to, but I can see why a young man should not be held responsible for actions he didn't commit. But no! I'm the bad guy. You can't trust me with your plans for Danny."

"Wait a minute," Gina started, but he was on a roll.

"You're not interested in me. You don't care that I've filed with the State's Civil Service exam for probation officers."

"You didn't tell me," Gina got out of bed in her shameless hospital gown. "How was I supposed to comment?"

"Exactly," he said, pointing at her.

"Tom," Gina explained, climbing back under the covers. "I love you. I'm sorry I hurt your feelings. I trust you. I knew you would tell Muller or someone about Baker Road. I depend on you. Weren't Judge Wilcox and Muller great?"

"I'm exhausted," Tom said, coming over to the bed.

She made room for him on the hospital bed. "Hold me."

With a superhuman, or sub-human, effort Tom instead forced himself to leave. "I love you," he said.

CHAPTER ELEVEN

Saturday, October 27th

South of Delnor Hospital back in Geneva, Tom had fallen asleep unhappily on top of the covers on Jonas's bed in Gina's attic. Sweets woke him by sitting on his head and purring.

"Hungry?"

Tom headed downstairs. He needed coffee before showering. The big house echoed with each foot step. Tom wished Marie was still alive. *Selfish*, he thought, remembering her Herculean fight against the painful cancer. Tom asked the kitten on his shoulder, "Did she know her daughter doesn't understand the first thing about trust?"

He was always going to miss Gina no matter where he lived. He had felt at home here. "Who wouldn't," he asked Sweets.

The marble fireplace in the living room, the cedar paneling in the attic, the kitchen where he'd cooked most of their meals since he met Gina; it was a house to be proud of. As he opened the cupboard for coffee, he remembered his plans for the workshop in the basement: new kitchen cabinets with stained glass doors, the bathroom shelves he'd drawn, the hall chest and clothes tree were all lost to him.

Now he would need to find new digs to live in and maybe land a different job, if the Lord helped him take advantage of his degree.

The empty workshop in the basement haunted him. Kids on probation would find the woodworking tools ideal instruments for learning a new craft. The parole officer who'd been excused from Danny jury because of his court affiliation had given Tom the impetus to follow up on the civil service examination he'd read about, before he'd found Gina the advertisement for a driver's education teacher.

His own children who he'd dreamed would fill the bedrooms in the house could have become friends with his nephews. Tom had imagined the Christmas parties with Dolly and her family. A substitute family, a substitute life for reality; all his plans were a delusion.

First two people had to love, respect and trust each other.

Not happening.

"Do you want to live in this beautiful house or do you want to rent a room with me?" The kitten eyed him and her milk-soaked food. "Understandable," Tom said. "Feast with Gina or famine with me. Hard choice."

Sweets tasted the soy milk and concentrated on eating.

Tom carried his coffee cup upstairs. Gina would have to store Jonas's furniture for him until he found a place to live. He'd be able to think straight with coffee in his stomach.

Call Dolly, he told himself after the cup was empty and the shower had his body's full attention. With both his duffel bag and suitcase in his car, to forgo any possibility Dolly might find the words to talk him out of leaving, Tom dialed his sister-in-law's number in Wayne.

"I've lost her," he said.

"She's dead?" Dolly drew in a sharp breath.

"She's alive," Tom hurried to say. "She doesn't trust me. I'm moving out."

"Nonsense. I'll be right over. Don't move." Dolly hung up before he could protest.

He was glad he'd had the foresight to pack. But Tom stalled, wanting to be stopped. His recovery book of daily quotes was the last thing he put in the duffel bag. He didn't relish coming back to retrieve the kitten once he'd moved out. He put the kitty litter on the floor of the back seat.

'I'm a thief,' he told himself as he secured Gina's dish-towel drawer with the passenger's seat belt.

"Sit," he said to Sweets who ignored him and crawled out of her box into his lap.

Tom slid her under his jacket where she snuggled down purring and pawing at his tee-shirt. "Happy now?"

He found the handbook for AA and read the day's quote, "Defeat is a school in which truth always grows strong."

"She never loved me," he told the kitten. "There's the truth of it."

When could he ever be happy again? The most loving, beautiful woman he had ever known couldn't trust him. No wonder people decide to live alone. He gave his heart without any restrictions. She gave hers, to a point. Too independent to rely on him. Someone else could drive her home from the hospital, or she could call a cab.

Tom parked his car in front of Wisniewski's, bought a paper and ordered coffee. The waitress was a knockout. At 18, her looks placed her somewhere between the redheaded actress, Ann Margret and the gyrating blonde in Coke commercials.

Sweets stuck her head out from under his shirt as he turned the paper to the rental page.

"Aww, what's her name?" the Venus asked.

"Sweets," he said trying to concentrate on the newsprint.

"Do you need a place to stay?" Her eyes were bigger than her pouting mouth.

"I do," he said, starting to forget his resolve of living single.

"My grandmother has a place behind the park in St. Charles. You know, the one across 64 from the library."

Tom smiled at his recollection of walking across town from Dean Street, nearly every Saturday if the weather permitted. Jonas enjoyed other outdoor pursuits, but Tom had found the small brick edifice with Doric columns a respite from boredom.

The librarian knew him by sight.

No televisions blared, no chores were handed out as soon as you sat down with a good book, and no telephone calls from girls who wanted to talk to his twin. The authors demanded his undivided attention and Tom was more than willing to slip into their alternate realities.

"Perfect," Tom said. "Is it expensive?"

"Not at all," Venus smiled. "My parents want someone to live there and take care of the place."

"How much is the rental?"

"I think they'd pay you to stay." She poured him another cup of coffee and sat down. "I'm Alice. What's your profession?"

"I'm taking the civil service exam to become a parole officer. I'm Tom Woods."

Alice seemed to recognize his name. "I just moved out of the apartment. It has one bedroom, a Pullman kitchen and a small television room, but the entrance is through the front door, because we want you to look in on Grandma."

It was too good to be true. "Why did you move out?"

"Well," she crowed, blushing. "I'm getting married on Saturday. I'll be Mrs. Alice Steel."

"Congratulations." Tom folded the paper. "When could I move in?"

"Right now." Alice waved at her boss behind the counter. "One thing, though. It is confidential."

Tom nodded, wondering if the family wanted to keep the diagnosis of their grandmother's illness unknown to their friends. "I should confide in you, too," he said. "I'm a recovering alcoholic."

"Totally fine!" Alice's teeth shone pearly white in the harsh restaurant light. "I was going to tell you there is an AA meeting in the dining room every Sunday evening. Grandpa had a problem, but he died sober. Would you mind making coffee for everyone? They'll pay you for the coffee, not for making it."

Tom couldn't believe it. "I guess my Higher Power wants me to attend an in-house meeting." Here was a family ready to trust a stranger, when the girl he loved couldn't bother to confide in him.

Alice untied her apron, called into the kitchen that she was leaving and opened the door for them. "I think someone is looking out for you."

* * *

Gina had waited an hour after leaving a message for Tom.

She wanted out of the hospital! People, her friends, died in hospitals. No pastel ambiance could change the fact this was a place for the sick and dying.

The taxi took another hour to arrive and Gina actually hoped Tom would appear before the cab. What was he doing? Repainting the kitchen? Building a cat tree in the basement? She knew he was angry, but he'd get over it.

Now she was angry. At least he could have taken her home. It was her home after all!

When the cab hit the stop light at 31 and Main Street in Geneva, she noticed Tom. Gina rolled down her window to holler. He was busy, opening the door of his beat-up car for a high-school beauty. "Oh, no," she said out loud.

The light changed and the cabby agreed, "These lights are long."

Gina tried to stretch her face into a smile for him. Her face was a mess. Her whole world was going down the drain. No wonder Tom had been so spiteful. He was looking for an excuse to break up with her.

Why not? He had this young beauty on the side. No wonder he left her. He had a perfect ten to compare to her swollen face.

Well he could get his things together and get out of her house.

Gina was sure of one true fact; she didn't need to put up with anything!

As the cab drove up to her house. It looked perfect. The paint job, the roof, the new landscaping made the house a show place again. 'Mother would be proud but I wonder what she'd think of that two-timing creep.'

As she walked up to the door, Dolly pulled in the drive in her parents MG.

Gina started to cry.

Dolly was at her side in a second. "I know all about it. He's a jerk. I'll talk some sense into him."

"You knew about the young chippy?"

Dolly shut the front door behind them. "There's nobody else."

"I just saw him helping her into his car. I had to take a cab home from the hospital while he's off gallivanting around with some high-school beauty queen. And my face--."

"Isn't as bad as he--." Dolly stopped.

"See," Gina pointed at her.

"He called to say you were having some trust issues." Dolly strolled into the kitchen and Gina followed. "We need tea."

"Coffee."

"Okay," Dolly looked around. "Where's the coffee pot?"

"He took it," Gina wailed.

"There's a drawer missing." Dolly's confusion heightened Gina's panic.

"And he took the cat!" Gina felt ridiculous sobbing. "He's never coming back. He took the cat!"

"Calm down, Gina." Dolly pushed her into a chair. "Tom called to say he lost you, he was leaving."

Gina waved helplessly at the cruelty.

"Who's this young woman you saw him with?"

"Girl. I bet she's not eighteen."

"Where did you see them?" Dolly's impatience showed.

Gina tried to get a grip. She bit her fingernail. "In front of Wisniewski's."

"I told Tom I'd be right over." Dolly poured them each a half glass of milk and threw the empty carton away. "He's probably grocery shopping."

"Where's the kitten?" Gina was tempted to start wailing again. "Where's Sweets?"

"Let's see if Tom's things are still here."

Gina trudged up the stairs to the attic. "He said I don't trust him because I told Judge Wilcox I would send Danny to college."

"I wondered if you had discussed your plans with Tom." Dolly opened the attic door. "I knew he was ready to throw the judge out the window he tried to open.

"It just came into my head while we were talking." Gina peered into the attic bedroom. Jonas's bed didn't look slept in. She opened the closet. Tom's duffel bag was missing from the top shelf, along with all his clothes.

"He's gone!"

CHAPTER TWELVE

Mrs. Burns, Alice's grandmother, greeted Tom warmly. "I know all about your family, young man. Your father and my husband had coffee every morning at the Log Cabin restaurant for years. Sorry to hear about your loss. How is Lucille's daughter holding up? Dorothy, right?"

"Dolly," Tom leaned forward to pronounce the name distinctly. Mrs. Burns' loud voice indicated the elderly woman was fairly deaf. "We call her Dolly. She's doing fine and the boys."

"Sons." Mrs. Burns heard that. "How many?"

"Two." Tom contrasted Gina's grand house with its gingerbread trim and extensive wrap-around porch, fireplaces in every room, even the attic, grand circular staircase and high ceilings to Mrs. Burns's gabled cottage. The ceilings were high enough. He needn't duck his head but the arched doorway's required added attention.

"Twins?"

"I think they're supposed to skip a generation," Tom lowered his voice.

Mrs. Burns had no problem with her hearing. Her voice was naturally loud. "I have five sons, two daughters." Mrs. Burns bowed her head. "Thank the Lord, they'll all outlive me. How did you meet my granddaughter, Alice?"

"At the restaurant, Grandma." Alice kissed her cheek. "I'll get Tom settled upstairs and then I have to go back to work."

"Yes, dear. You run along. Tom can look after himself. The directions are simple. Up the stairs young man." Mrs. Burns pushed the television's mute button on her soap opera, where two waist-stripped men were arguing. "And make sure I'm alive before you leave for work on Tuesday."

"Grandma," Alice seemed confident there would be no problem. "Tom is in recovery. How long have you been sober, Tom?"

"I was sober for two years, but recently relapsed. I appreciate your confidence inviting me," Tom said sincerely.

"Never known a stranger," Mrs. Burns said as she waved him away. "Perfect place for you."

"I could cook for us," Tom added.

"Can't afford to pay you."

"Room and board is payment enough," Tom said.

Alice shook his hand at the door. "The Lord has, no doubt, sent you to us."

Upstairs, Tom placed Gina's kitchen drawer on the bedside table in his flowery wall-papered bedroom. The bedroom drapes and bedspread were pink. He disengaged Sweets from her warm sleeping place under his shirt. The cat still smelled of cedar.

"Your new home," he said, certain the cat would be out of her box before he left the room.

After unpacking and situating Sweets' litter box under the bathroom sink, he ran the back of his hand over the clean kitchen counter. The refrigerator held an open box of baking soda in one corner. He switched on the large television, careful to keep the sound on CNN civilized. The comfortable couch beckoned but he chose the La-Z-Boy until he could summon the energy to buy groceries. Sweets jumped on Tom's stomach, which growled from dissatisfaction with his flight-imposed diet of coffee.

The apartment couldn't be improved on. Except, Gina wasn't there. He knew her telephone number, but he couldn't think of a reason to call.

He had planned to talk to her about establishing a workshop program for kids on probation. Her stepdad's woodworking tools in the basement stood idle when they could provide a training ground for youngsters, if she would be willing to open her home.

Tom's ire raised its head. Was it easier for Gina to open her wallet than her home?

He disturbed Sweets to reach for his recovery book. He turned to the wrong page. May 24th's first word of the daily quote got his attention. "Angry men are blind and foolish, for reason at such a time takes flight and, in her absence, wrath plunders all the riches of the intellect while the judgment remains the prisoner of its own pride." He didn't need to read further to be chastised for his anger.

I'd have to completely negate who I am. She'd run rough-shod over him without a backward glance.

Tom had been taken in by her kindness to Danny. She had easily empathized with the bullied teenager. Why couldn't she take a moment to consider Tom's grieving personality changes? Of course he had been a monster at the bank, but he knew they loved each other now, didn't he? Why didn't Gina take more pains to understand him than she did Danny?

Any man would wonder why his future wife--' Tom stopped his ruminations.

Did Gina know he intended to ask her to marry him? Maybe she did. Making the decision, without consulting him, to fund Danny's college education, could have been a gentle strategy to inform Tom she preferred to remain single. Then why did she allow him to move in? Tom shifted in the padded chair.

Sweets frowned at him. Gina might love him, but her negative opinion of men in her racing world convinced her to keep her own counsel. Who needed that? Sweets continued to paw him, seeking the comfort of her mother. Tom rested his hand on the warm ball of fur.

Please Lord, Tom prayed. *My life is out of control, Your will, not mine be done.*

His mind let go of the worry and anger. Tom drifted into a nap which re-established Gina in his mind as a lost lover. His mouth watered from hunger for her taste, his body yearned for her warmth. His dream vision did justice to her lithe, supple body. She called his name. When he woke, Tom knew on all levels of consciousness he would never forget Gina Branson.

* * *

Sunday, October 28th

"Mrs. Burns, what time is the meeting tonight?" Tom moved their supper's dirty dishes to the downstairs kitchen where he had already prepared two gigantic pots of coffee, but hadn't plugged them in yet.

"6:00. Don't all AA meetings start at 6:00?" She used her walker to maneuver out into the hall. "Unlock the back door so they can come right in. Your roast chicken was perfect. Why hasn't some young girl bagged you?"

"Trust issue," Tom answered.

"Takes time, my boy, once you've disappointed someone," she spoke more quietly than her usual tone of voice before sliding the doors to her front sitting room closed.

Tom plugged in the coffee and filled the dishwasher with their dishes. Gina had disappointed him. She wouldn't understand why he left. Good thing there was a meeting available.

By 6:30 the dining room chairs were filled, so men and women seated themselves on the floor with their backs against the wall. They also stood in the hall and in the kitchen doorways. Tom considered making more coffee, but one of the members told him not to bother.

"Enough is enough," he whispered.

Tom bowed his head during the Serenity Prayer and prayed for those who were still suffering. He listened closely to the readings of the Preamble, the Twelve Steps, and the Promises.

Three groups arranged themselves. Those at the table read from the Big Book. Tom joined a small group of ten in what was called "Barefooting," talking about any issues, as they stood around the center island in the kitchen. The group in the hall arranged themselves on the stairs, taking turns reading from the Twelve-Step Book.

The first to speak in Tom's group, thanked him for making the coffee. Her first name was June. "I'm doing okay today. Glad you all came. I feel so at home when I'm around drunks, when they're sober that is."

He introduced himself as Tom, saying he had been sober for two years, broke his sobriety in September and now found himself living upstairs as Mrs. Burns' boarder. "I haven't attended an AA meeting since I got drunk, but I haven't used since. I could list reasons why it happened, but I'd rather just listen. I think I'll hang on to AA, get a sponsor, and try to learn something this time around. Obviously, the Lord wants me to stay sober."

An older man, named Stan said, "We're glad you're here. I think you're right to listen for a while. Get to know us and then pick a sponsor you are comfortable around. They might turn you down if they're too busy; but the rewards are worth the wait." He continued, "I've been recovering for twenty-two years now, day-by-day. I woke up this morning feeling anxious."

Several of the people nodded their heads.

Stan said, "I know fear is not trusting my Higher Power enough, so I said my morning prayers and left the worries for the Lord to sort out."

The next to speak, a small older woman in a shocking purple sweater, said her name was Norma. "I keep doing the Third Step turning over my will and my life, only to grab it back when I want something to go my way. When I have enough sense to forget about myself, I'm much happier."

A fidgety young woman with bright eyes nearly hidden by long black bangs and wearing her hair past her shoulders spoke next. "I'm Jan. My husband is still drinking and my mother wants me to leave him."

No one commented.

Stan said, "We're not supposed to cross talk, which means commenting on each other's concerns, but you might want to join Alanon, too. They teach ways of letting go with love."

Jan nodded.

"I'm Judy. I always ask the Lord what to do."

Another middle-aged woman said. "I don't expect Him to answer directly, but at least I feel I bring Him into the situation. I get great comfort, knowing He cares."

"How do you know?" Jan asked.

"I've been sober, through his strength for eight years." Judy clasped and unclasped her purse. "I know I couldn't stay sober on my own."

A lanky boy, probably not twenty, said. "I'm Jimmy. I'm in detox now, but I wanted to see what AA is all about."

Stan said, "I didn't notice your hand up when they asked for newcomers."

"Too embarrassed," he said.

"We've all been there, Jimmy." A man in a red baseball cap said. "I'm Ron. Even though this is a barefoot table we would have had people talk about their first experience trying to stay sober, if we'd known this was your first meeting." Ron pulled out a breakfast stool from under the counter and got comfortable. "At my first meeting, I thought: Sure this is a God thing. I can do that on my own. Five years later I was back, hoping to find whatever it was AA offered. I found a sponsor, immediately for the first three steps, lost him when he tried to help me write my fourth step, found a therapist to hear my fifth step, and then found Andy, my present sponsor. I've been sober for five years now."

Another kid standing next to Jimmy punched him. "Hi, I'm Todd. Jimmy's my friend. I told him AA was the answer. I've been sober for eight months. I have a sponsor and he told me to find someone to sponsor."

"Can you sponsor me, if we're already friends?" Jimmy asked.

Stan said, "Best way to do the program, Jimmy. If you weren't friends before you will be after you learn about the program."

A woman, about thirty, Tom guessed, smiled before hanging her head to say, "My name is Connie. I've been sober for three months, my sponsor told me to speak up, but I'm only going to listen this time."

"Was there anything specific, your sponsor told you to share?" Stan asked.

Connie lifted her head. "I'm a prescription drug addict. I have two small boys in grade school. My husband left me the first month I was sober, because I wouldn't go to the bar with him anymore. My parents stopped speaking to me when I married him. They're Jewish."

"We're here for you, Connie." Stan said. "Keep coming back. You are one of us now. We all have lost family because of this disease."

No one else needed to speak, so they ended holding hands and saying the Lord's Prayer.

The dining room table group had already cleared out. A few stragglers were still talking in the hall, but thanked Tom and left by the back door.

Tom's chest ached and his knees dragged as he went up the stairs to his room. He shook his head and breathed deeply. He showered before laying down relieved more than sleepy. Even if Gina never forgave him for leaving her, or understood why not trusting him had been so painful, Tom knew with the Lord's help at least drinking was not in his future.

* * *

Saturday, November 10th

Two weeks later, Gina wandered around her mother's Victorian house. She felt more alone than before she met Thomas Woods. Memories of years of coldness and the empty thrills of racing threatened to crush her spirit.

She could hear Tom's words in the bank, changing from his growl at the shock of seeing his twin gunned down to reasoning tones. After he gotten a chance to calm down, she remembered touching his shoulder when they were freed, how he covered her grip with his big warm hand and then wouldn't let go.

She summoned up the vision of Tom's muscles flexing as he fashioned a shelf for her mother's windowsill. The workshop would stand idle with Tom out of the house.

Keep busy, Gina told herself, *try not to think.*

Cleaning could serve two purposes. The house should be in tip-top shape before she interviewed for the driver's education job. By then her face would be presentable. Hopefully her mind wouldn't continually dwell on her grief for her mother, or Tom.

In the living room she decided to alphabetize the books by author; but how could she remember the writers' names of the art books. The gift shops of museums Gina visited during her racing travels contributed to her mother's library. The New York Metropolitan and the Modern Art Museum, the Getty in Los Angeles, others in Chicago, Denver, Des Moines, Phoenix, Sante Fe, Seattle, Vancouver, Dublin, London, Florence, Milan, and Mont St. Michel burdened three shelves. She filled the couch with them, dusting the tops away from the spine.

She rubbed the back of her hand over her dry lips. Her first kiss with Tom had been a heated life-line to reality. Tom had acted as if he too never wanted to let go of her, never wanted to face the harshness of life outside their embrace. Perhaps the heightened emotions in the bank robbery caused them to mistake their need for each other.

She hadn't seen Tom for a week.

Keep busy, she insisted.

Her mother's collections of the Kennedy family, histories, photographs, and reminiscences of the president, Jacqueline, Robert and John John should stay together. All the books mentioning Joan of Arc, at least 30 assorted volumes with Abraham Lincoln as their subject, the Titanic collection, and the September 11th horrific publications including a book on the obituaries of each victim, refused to be separated by their authors' names.

When the water-pipe catalyst initiated their first tryst, Gina never imagined her mother's death would keep them separated as long as it had. They had held onto each other without seeking pleasure. The comfort of another human being's closeness sufficed.

That was over. Tom was gone.

Back to work.

Gina decided she needed to box up her stepfather's mathematical texts, the Yiddish and Chinese volumes, which numbered at least two thousand. She thought of giving them to the State's prison library in Peoria.

Harvey Slemmons had informed her of Danny's placement in a halfway house in Elgin, which afforded the young man a chance for a new future. Gina promised to help register Danny for college in the fall.

Judge Wilcox had limited her visits to once a month.

Harvey had explained, "To give the young man a chance to settle in with his new house mates."

Would Tom attend Alan Passantino's jury selection or trial? They would be called as witnesses by the prosecutors if the case went to trial. The evidence against the man was so heavily weighted, Harvey thought a plea bargain would save the state money.

"Fifteen to life," he predicted. "Can't prove premeditation in either murder."

Gina stacked her stepfather's books in the hallway along the walls. When she had the emotional stamina she'd find out which official could accept them for Danny.

The empty workshop came to mind. Maybe Danny and his friends would like to play…work down there with the tools. Getting their hands on beautiful wood and crafting usable items might be a form of play to a young man. She'd talk it over with Harvey, when she got the chance.

In the meantime, the Latin and travel books from Holland and Rome were allotted clean shelving.

But, the sudden memory of Tom's muscular body rocked her.

She slumped into a wing-back chair facing the empty fireplace. Tongues of desire crept through her. How could she survive withdrawal of his loving kindness? He was so stubborn. What was the big deal about providing for Danny's future?

She dragged herself from the chair and started to dust the ancient hardcover reprints of Mark Twain and Dickens. When she surveyed the endless copies of American Heritage, the daunting task undid her good intentions. Three sets of encyclopedias also confronted her. She might need them someday and the outdated maps inside were fascinating. Nevertheless, Google held all the information and was much more accessible. Gina finally admitted she was accomplishing nothing.

No amount of avoiding thoughts of Tom would alleviate her loss. Orphaned she was, except for Dolly. Dolly. What could Dolly accomplish with her stubborn brother-in-law?

Hey, Lord, Gina prayed, *I could use a little help down here. Remember Mother wanted us to marry.*

Gina left the front room in disarray, rescued an Orange Crush from the refrigerator and fled upstairs. Her determination to create a family and a community of friends had been dashed by Tom's rejection.

Tom was right about one thing, Gina wanted children.

She sat on one of the twin beds in the second floor guest room. The windows faced north and the tall oaks kept the room shaded all summer. No sense thinking about a color scheme for a nursery in the future. No sense planning anything. Her destiny seemed fixed, a do-gooder with nowhere to place her affection.

The attic bedroom called to her. She steeled her nerves against the anguish and opened the door. She recalled Dolly standing in the doorway of her master bedroom when she gave Tom the furniture. Jonas's bed had brought heartache to two women.

Gina rushed down to the phone in the kitchen, the one closest to the back door and the possibility of escaping her gloom. "Mrs. Stone, this is Gina Branson. May I speak with Dolly?"

"Of course, dear. I was sorry to hear you were injured, but we're all proud of our local heroine."

"I hardly--."

"Gina," Dolly interrupted. "I was trying to find a polite reason to call. Come over. I'd love to see you. We could meet at the Hunt Club for lunch."

"I couldn't, Dolly." She touched the stitches between her nose and lip. "I look a fright."

"Well, come over here then," Dolly sincerely invited. "You need a respite from that house."

"You can say that again." It still hurt to laugh. "Would fifteen minutes be too soon?"

Gina tore out of the house. She raced her Mustang at the top-allowed speed between Geneva's clogged streets and the open countryside near the Stones' residence. Qualms abruptly slowed her car in the driveway to the house. She lowered her visor and tried to ignore her lip. Her dark curls had decided to resemble an abbreviated Afro, but her clothes caused her the most concern. Worst of all her hands were less than pristine from the dusting frenzy.

"Dolly, let me apologize," she said, looking up from her gray fingernails as soon as the door opened. "I was cleaning, but I had to get out of there."

"Of course you did." Dolly embraced her. "Come out to the patio. The boys are practicing soccer kicks."

Gina wiped her hands on her jeans. "I was sorting books. Would your boys like a set of Mark Twain and Dickens?"

"I'd love them," Dolly said. "I'll bring my little helpers with me to load up my father's van."

"I'm happy to find a good home for them."

She appreciated the Stones' home as they proceeded toward the back patio. The ceilings reached a story and half. Blue oriental carpeting on polished oak flooring nearly outshone the antiques scattered around the comfortable rooms. Gina understood for the first time the glee Jonas demonstrated in the bank when the money rained on his head. But the money represented in these rooms was accumulated over more than one young man's lifetime.

Outside, Lucille Stone, Dolly's mother, crowed every time Jeffrey or Timothy succeeded in kicking the ball. "Aren't they beautiful?"

"Gorgeous," Gina answered.

Jeffrey had the sweet, serious demeanor Gina equated with Tom's personality. Timothy could hardly contain his enthusiasm for the game. At times he would tackle his older brother for the sheer fun of it, laughing when they rolled in the grass.

"They resemble the Woods's side of the family," Gina said.

"Don't they?" Lucille beamed with pride and then stifled a sudden sob. "Jonas never knew how much I adored him."

"Yes, Mother," Dolly said, laying a comforting hand on her mother's arm. "He always talked about how you spoiled him more than his own mother had."

"Did he?" she said sadly. "I wish I'd convinced Jonas we loved him for who he was, not his title at the bank, not what he did. We praised him for his accomplishments, but he acted as if our congratulations contained a false note. In a way Jonas was right. We loved him the most for his love of our Dolly. He appreciated the miracle you are, child."

Dolly inclined her head in Gina's direction. "We hope we don't make the same mistakes with Jeffrey and Timothy's uncle. Thomas Woods is a part of our family forever. We all love him."

Gina avoided releasing her tears.

Mrs. Stone reached for Gina's hand. "I'm going to go in. I don't want the boys to see me break down. Please excuse me. I want you to feel free to visit Dolly whenever you have a chance. You, dear, needn't call. There's always someone home."

Gina thanked her.

The boys noticed their grandmother's distress. Jeffrey walked slowly toward them, but seven year old Timothy pulled the back of his shirt. "Don't stop the game."

"Everything's all right, Jeffrey," Dolly said smiling. "I need to talk to Gina and then we'll have lunch."

After watching his grandmother re-enter the house, Jeffrey went back to kicking the soccer ball up and down the lawn with his little brother.

Gina broached the painful subject. "Maybe Tom was right about my fixation with Danny's future."

"No. He wasn't," Dolly said pouring them second cups of coffee. "You didn't want to adopt the boy."

"Justice did seem a worthy goal," Gina sighed, "until Tom mixed everything up. With his young woman in the picture, there's no hope of getting back together." She was determined not to cry. "I don't know how to compete for a man."

"Not for a true and noble heart?" Dolly sipped her coffee. "I'll find out what's going on, but I can't believe another person is involved."

* * *

Sunday, November 11th

Tom made two pots of coffee for the AA meeting and set out the chocolate-chip cookies he'd purchased with the contributions from the previous meeting.

Stan, the group's treasurer, said the rent for use of the room had been paid to Mrs. Burns through December. "She's giving the house to the county in her will for a half-way house with the stipulation that the dining room is used on Sunday's for an AA meeting."

"Well, I fit right into her plan," Tom said.

"It was your brother who was murdered in the bank robbery, right?" Stan checked to see if the members arriving were far enough away from them for a confidential chat.

Tom nodded. "Not sure I'm able to talk about all the resentments I need to release, yet."

"I can wait," Stan said. "You said you were looking for a sponsor."

"Would you take on the task?"

"Proven way to keep me sober." Stan slapped his shoulder and they joined the group in the dining room for the opening prayers.

* * *

Saturday, November 17th

Tom Woods drove down Dunham Road to Wayne's intersection on the following Saturday. Dunham Castle on the north-west corner had been shipped stone-by-stone from Ireland before income taxes and the depression prevented such lavish outlays of cash. He patted the kitten, safely nesting under his shirt. "I hope I don't have to remind you to be on your best behavior."

Sweets no longer held the familiar odor of cedar from Gina's house.

The lavish estates resembled equestrian breeding farms. They were incorporated into the small village of Wayne to prevent the ugly sprawl of Chicago's suburbs from attacking the quiet fields. Prancing thoroughbreds and high white fences were the predominant landscaping schemes.

Dolly's parents, Lucille and Henry Stone, owned three homes: two in Wayne and Dolly's in St. Charles. The first house in Wayne belonged to Lucille's parents, the Eckridges. The one story cottage edged up to the Riding Club's property. Not imposing, the small home boasted a historical marker as one of Illinois' earliest pioneer homes. Across the road the Stone's house, on the original homestead, sprawled at the crest of a treeless hill with an acre of pristine lawn sloping to the road. The red-brick structure with more white pillars than windows demanded attention.

When Tom called Dolly to tell her about starting work for the Kane County District Court as a Probation Officer, she invited him to dinner at her parents' house in Wayne.

"The boys have almost given up seeing you again." Then Dolly's end of the line went quiet.

Tom could almost hear her thinking up some scheme.

When he drove his rusty Escort up the driveway, he considered buying a new car before he found another apartment. He didn't want his nephews to be embarrassed by his clunker.

When he knocked on the Stones' front door, Dolly came outside and shut the door behind her. "We need to talk, Tom." She walked toward his wreck of a car.

"Dolly, your white slacks will get filthy in my car." He stood between the car and her. "What's the problem?"

She pushed passed him and climbed into his car. ""Let me buy you a cup of cappuccino. Drive to the Club."

Now he was in for it. Jonas said when they were courting, Dolly invited him to lunches when she was upset because then he couldn't raise his voice in public. "Do you think I'm going to yell at you?"

"No," she said, smiling. "I'm afraid I'll raise my voice."

"I've brought my new friend to meet the boys," he said, letting Sweets emerge to calm the troubled waters.

"Leave him in the car while we eat."

Tom succumbed to his fate.

The stunning hostess graciously showed them to a linen-covered table facing the golf course. Tom had been inside the restaurant only twice. Once on a blind date Jonas had set up and once at the wedding reception of his brother. He never liked the place. The gray walls of weathered barn-wood paneling cast a ridiculous backdrop for the elegant dining room. If they were going to sit in a barn they should be served beans in crock ware, not slippery shrimp on ice.

"You're frowning," Dolly smiled. "The waiter thinks you're angry with him."

"Should I explain you're the one who's angry with me?" Tom hoped a grin would ease the tension.

"Do you have a teenage girlfriend?" Dolly hardly paused for an answer. "Is that why you left Gina?"

"Who told you that?" Tom couldn't fathom what she was talking about.

"Gina saw you in front of Wisniewski's."

"Oh for Pete's sake. That was my landlady's granddaughter. She's getting married next Saturday."

"Really?" Dolly patted his hand. "I'm so glad."

"That's not why I left." Tom played with the barbecued salmon. "I told you why I left. Why didn't you enlighten her?" He struck a carrot with his fork and it sailed into to Dolly's lap. "Sorry. You can tell I was right. Gina doesn't trust me. Probably because I told her mother I was an alcoholic."

"Apparently a live picture is worth a thousand words. She thinks you left her for a high-school teenager." Dolly signed the restaurant's tab. "And I'm the one who told Gina you attended meetings in the past, not Marie."

"The odd thing is I'm living upstairs in a house where AA meetings occur every Sunday night."

"When something good is called *odd*, Daddy always says, 'No, that's a God thing.'"

After the ride for coffee, Tom was allowed into the Stones' home to dinner with his nephews.

Jeffrey mimicked Tom, folding his arms whenever Tom did. 'Missing his father,' Tom thought as he let the little one, Timothy, dive at him from the arm of the couch.

Sweets made a big hit. She thought the boys too rambunctious and fled up the brocaded-satin drapes in the living room. No amount of coaxing could disengage her.

Henry Stone brought in a tall ladder and Lucille placed a bowl of soy milk on the grand piano as an inducement.

Dolly refused to participate. "You know, Tom," she cautioned. "You'll have to come up with kittens for the boys now."

"Or dogs," her father said. "My grandboys should own dogs."

"Horses aren't enough?" Lucille asked.

Sweets was rescued and the boys instructed on how to gently approach her. Tom moved his hand toward the cat and pulled it back slowly. "Make her want to come to you. She's very curious."

Jeffrey sat on the floor to do just that; but Timothy grabbed the back of the kitten's neck and dropped him into his brother's lap. "Their mothers carry them like that," Timothy said proudly.

Tom counted all the people not present to share in the room's happiness. The boys' paternal grandparents, their father, and the woman Tom loved, Gina Branson. All were absent.

After dinner, Dolly walked Tom and Sweets to his car. "Tom, you must come for Thanksgiving. We need your marshmallow sweet potatoes. And, Tom," Dolly hitched her arm in his as if he might escape. "I'm inviting Gina, my half-sister, Jerry Hoffman and Steve, Sergeant Muller."

Tom pecked her cheek with a kiss. "I'll make a double batch. You might as well invite Danny and Judge Wilcox, too." He got in his car and then rolled down the window to add, "Tell the boys I'll drive out Saturday after lunch for a tree-by-tree tour of Johnson's Mound."

Dolly put her hand on the window. "We need you, Tom. It will be our first holiday without Jonas."

Tom couldn't move as memories of the bank robbery overcame his senses. Sweets tugged at his tee-shirt for air and Tom remembered his manners. "Dolly, I'll be on my best behavior. You and the boys are all the family I have now."

* * *

Sunday, November 18th

Attending meetings for Tom was no longer an option. He needed to make the coffee and Stan would be waiting for him. He baked a strawberry sheet cake for the group and iced it with chocolate.

June, past middle age, constantly tugged at the back of her wig and made sure the strands near her ears where straightened when she took her glasses on and off as she read the Steps for the group. And, she started the barefoot topic. "I feel like an orphan. My drinking buddies don't avoid me, but I'm not taken into their daily confidences either."

Norma, an even older woman, laughed. "Don't they tell you what color to wear anymore?"

Stan frowned. "That's funny, but we don't cross-talk here. People need to feel free to share without judging."

Norma apologized. "Sorry, June, you know I love you."

"It's okay," June said. "It's an inside joke between women, Stan, not really a comment. Anyway, I miss my friends being closer to me. But drinking isn't worth it. At least I'm not insulting them, or swearing at them, or belittling them. But the truth is when I'm not here, I don't really feel understood."

Tom filled a moment of silence. "And they don't trust you, just because you admit you drink too much."

Stan shook his head. "No. They don't trust you because you've proven to be untrustworthy. Sometimes we get too paranoid about how people treat us when we're sober. Make sure you check out any assumptions you make of your friends' behavior."

Other people shared, but Tom kept going over Stan's words. Gina didn't trust him. Otherwise she would have shared her plans for Danny. Loving couples talked things over before committing themselves to future actions, didn't they?

* * *

Dolly's initial invitation to a fashion show on the Monday before Thanksgiving at the Hunt Club appeared straight forward to Gina. "I'd love to come."

Then Dolly asked, "Would a walk around Johnson's Mound interest you, too?"

"Sure, when?"

"Next Saturday, the 24th?" Dolly laughed. "Would that be all right? I could meet you out there. Do you know where it is? Say about 2:00?"

"Okay?" Then Gina remembered her face, apparently not exactly country-club perfect yet. "I can understand why you like Johnson's Mound." Gina was proud of her gracious tone of acceptance. "Tom told me Jonas's mother drove them out there whenever she wasn't getting along with their father. I would like to tell you all about my new driver's education job."

"And Mother wants you to come for dinner on Thanksgiving."

Gina couldn't help thinking the invitation was an afterthought, but tried to respond as if she were not a race-car driver who rarely cooked. "What should I bring?"

"Oh, just yourself, Gina. I miss you."

"Please. Would a pecan pie be appropriate? I suppose Tom will be invited?"

"You're both adults. Do you mind? The boys miss him. And, Gina, I'm inviting Jerry Hoffman and Steve Muller. Could you ask Judge Wilcox to come and arrange for Danny Bianco to have a supervised visit? Would you like to invite Florence and Menasha, too?"

"I better bring three pies. Could I invite Harvey Slemmons, too?"

Dolly laughed. "Of course, Pecan is my favorite, but maybe a pumpkin and the boys love chocolate."

"Good thing I know where there's a decent bakery."

* * *

Thanksgiving Day

Seated at his right, Gina bowed her head as Mr. Stone surveyed the silenced crowd and prayed, "Lord, your tender mercies have filled us with overflowing love for each other and for you. We have been shown again and again how precious your gift of life and faith are. Please accept our humble thankfulness for our family, friends old and new, and for this abundant meal in your glorious name, Amen."

At the far end of the table, Mrs. Stone wiped a stray tear away before asking the two serving girls to pass heirloom plates of slices from the twenty-five pound, golden turkey which Mr. Stone was skillfully carving.

Tom sat on Mrs. Stone's right. He had only nodded a brief hello to Gina in the crowded foyer as they gave their coats to two young butlers.

The table gleaming with candles and crystal was long enough to seat all fourteen guests. Harvey Slemmons was next to Gina, then Florence chatting with Menasha, Danny Bianco and finally Judge Wilcox, on Mrs. Stone's left.

Jerry Hoffman's red hair and constant chatter across from Gina provided enough diversion not to stare at Tom, too often. But Tom handsome in the black suit he'd worn for the funeral sported the blue-and-white polka-dot silk tie she'd bought for him. Was it a peace offering? Hoffman's gray knit sweater held no real interest for Gina, but she tried to keep her face pointed in his direction, complete with her friendliest smile, as she listened to his rendition of her escape from Alan Passantino.

Steve Muller sitting next Hoffman turned to Dolly on his left. "Your sister's racing experience certainly saved the situation."

Tim, next to his mother, pulled on his brother's shoulder. "They don't let women race cars, do they?"

Judge Wilcox spoke directly to Tom. "Your girlfriend is one in a million."

Tom's face assumed an un-natural grin as he addressed Danny, "Danny knows what a remarkable champion Gina Branson has been for him."

Danny ducked his head and answered, "Yeah," in his characteristic manner before leaning forward to add to Gina, "I brought your books back."

"What did Gina lend you, Danny?" Mrs. Stone asked as if to lessen the tension growing in the conversation.

"Proust and Robinson Crusoe." Danny smiled shyly. "I used Crusoe the way he used the Bible when he was stranded on the island. Every day I picked a page at random to see what I should think about while I was in prison."

"What did you think about today?" Jeffrey asked.

Danny folded his hands in his lap. "One of the boys where I live reads Emily Dickinson. I remember the line he read to us at dinner last night, 'But above all, in order to be, never try to seem.'"

Gina's minor hero made her so proud of his honesty and humility she almost clapped, but restrained herself. Instead, she smiled open-heartedly at Tom, who surprisingly returned her smile.

"You are becoming an upstanding gentleman," Tom said. "We're all proud of you."

Steve started to clap, smiling at Dolly who joined the table in a round of applause.

Timothy pulled on Jeffrey's shoulder again and whispered loudly, "Will they clap for us when we become gentlemen?"

"We certainly will!" Tom said and smiled again in Gina's direction.

* * *

For Tom, Thanksgiving Day ran the gauntlet of his emotions. He hadn't remembered Dolly said she'd invite the entire bank-robbery trial cast. Jerry Hoffman and Muller buzzed around Gina and Dolly like bees to honey. Gina was dressed in a winter white pant suit. Her ivory skin and black curls gave her a movie-star quality of appeal. Dolly was equally attractive to the bachelors. Still wearing black, her short blond bob accented her blue eyes. Pushing through the gaggle of men surrounding Gina, including Harvey Slemmons, Judge Wilcox, Menasha, Mr. Stone and Danny, Tom was barely able to say hello to her before Mr. Stone took him into the den.

"Tom, my boy, we need to talk about Dolly's future." He poured a drink for himself, then let it sit on the sideboard. "Sorry, Tom. That was stupid. Dolly says you're back in AA. Great organization. Plenty of my employees saved their jobs by joining. I'm hoping Dolly will remarry shortly. Better for the boys. Always said a good marriage is proven by the widow quickly retying the knot."

"I don't know anyone she's interested in." Tom found it difficult to follow Mr. Stone's rapid fire conversation.

"Really, thought you knew this Muller chap from the trial."

"Only briefly met him."

"Dolly's been dating him for nearly a month. Can't stop calling here on some excuse. Mother and I finally figured out they were seeing each other, sort of on the sly not to upset the family. Maybe at the house in St. Charles, when the realtors aren't traipsing around in it. What do you think of him?"

"Sir--."

"Nonsense. Don't call me Sir. You're young. How does he strike you? Integrity?"

"We can count on Dolly to pick an honorable man."

"Quite right. Jonas was a good chap. Worried me that he was trying to match Lucille's family three-generational accumulation of wealth before income taxes in the first few years of his marriage. But that's over now and Dolly needs a husband. Beautiful daughter, she is. Proud of her as you can tell."

"We all think the world of Dolly. How can I help?"

"Be friendly to Muller. I noticed a bit of strain when you arrived."

"It's me Mr. Stone."

"Call me Henry."

"Henry, I've had a misunderstanding with Gina."

"Now there is a looker, resembles my daughter. Step-daughter if the truth be told; but my heart only considers her my daughter. I plan to settle the estate on the boys, but a need a younger trustee. Will you serve."

"Honored, s. . ., Henry."

"Good chap. Knew I could count on you. Let's go eat."

Tom hoped Gina would remember she'd given him the tie he wore. Surely they would have a minute to talk together. Instead he was seated at the opposite end of the table, next to Mrs. Stone.

Jeffery smiled up to him and Tom gave the boy another hug.

He really wanted to slide his heavy chair away from the table and sweep Gina into his arms and out the door. Why were all these people here?

"Tom," Mrs. Stone touched his arm to get his attention. "Did my husband ask you to be the trustee."

"Yes, ma'am."

"Good heavens, Tom. Could you call me Lucille? We're family and I intend to keep you close to us. Talk to me. Does Henry seem all right to you?"

Tom paid attention to the question. "Right as rain. Any concerns?"

"He keeps losing his hat. And he's been telling people he doesn't deserve all the attention he's getting now that he's retiring. Tells everybody the only brilliant thing he did was marry a rich woman."

"I can see why you would be upset."

"I knew you would understand. Could you talk to him, I've tried."

"Lucille, Henry's about as malleable as his steel mill. I doubt he'd listen to any suggestion from me."

"Oh, you're probably right. I guess I can bear the burden." She smiled at him. "Being rich isn't all it's cracked up to be. No one ever thinks you give away enough and the money only goes so far each month."

Tom pushed the pieces of turkey and cranberries around his plate as the conversation turned from Gina's accomplishments to Danny's. When he had complimented Danny along with the others, Muller began clapping with Dolly.

Muller was seated next to Dolly. Now Tom knew why. Tom smiled at Gina who returned his warmth, but why was Hoffman sitting across from her. Had they gotten to know each other, too?

He excused himself as soon as dinner was over to Mrs. Stone. Without more than a nod in Dolly's direction who waved to him over Muller's back, Tom blew a kiss to Gina and fled. What he really needed was a drink.

Please, Lord, he prayed in his tired Escort, *Let me stay sober today.*

* * *

Saturday November 24th

When Tom picked up the boys on the propitious Saturday, Dolly insisted he take her father's van. "I really think it's safer. You know all these seat belt restrictions make me crazy."

"No, that's fine." Tom agreed to drive the van.

She called Jeffrey and Timothy away from their soccer practice.

Lucille opened the front door. "Dolly, they weren't hurting anything."

"Mother, Tom is here." Dolly defended herself.

"Guys," Tom said as he hugged his somewhat over-heated nephews

Lucille joined the group and reached up to touch Tom's face. "Tom, promise to visit us more often. And bring Gina."

"Mother," Dolly cautioned.

Tom spied the mischievous exchange between mother and daughter.

Timothy tugged on his shirt. "Mommy said not to mention Piss and Tino," he said proudly.

"He's a baby," Jeffrey explained after pounding his brother's head.

Dolly shook her head. "Try to behave. You want Uncle Tom to visit again, don't you?"

"They're fine," Tom laughed. He had never liked being called an Uncle Tom. "I'll bring them back by four o'clock."

"You're not going anywhere besides Johnson's Mound are you?"

"Not without checking first," Tom had no intentions of worrying his brother's widow. He wanted to ask her about Gina and Hoffman and about Muller's attendance at the dinner; but the boys needn't hear his grown up craziness.

Chapter Thirteen

On the circular walking path through Johnson's Mound, the clamor of the boys drew Tom's thoughts away from Gina. In sheltered areas, bright-colored, crunching leaves carpeted the trail and an umbrella of dazzling unfallen leaves contrasted sharply to the robin's egg blue of the boys' sweat shirts.

"It's an oak," Jeffrey stated for more than the second time.

"You don't know anything." Timothy grumbled.

Tom intervened. "The old oak will keep its promise to the earth."

"What promise?" Jeffrey asked in a hushed tone.

"To remain stalwart against all odds." Tom thought about his wavering affection for Gina. Maybe he should have stayed in her house, made his plans of marriage known to her. Perhaps then he would have seemed a part of her life, someone she could confide in.

Timothy stood with his hands on his hips, glaring at the dark black trunk of the oak. "Scaredy Cat!" he yelled. "Afraid of a little snow." Timothy kicked the gravel of the path and stomped off.

Jeffrey trudged after him, forgetting entirely that he'd won the argument about the name of the tree.

Tom followed the pair. Timothy's words, afraid of a little snow, ate at him. Marriage wouldn't be easy with Gina. There would be reclining moments of happiness, of vivid ecstasies touching the pulse of creation, sublime and unforgettable. Then the hours of distractions: cooking and driving to and from work. Now the days separating them had stretched into weeks. Dangerous times when the ego erupted, negatives existed that could wreck a twosome, unless they had agreed not to budge from the anchoring position of commitment. Marriage was like a tethered hot air balloon, safe but up among the clouds.

The gloom lifted from Tom's shoulders. The cavorting children before him added to his good spirits. "Have you ever heard of an Indian mound?" he called to his nephews.

Timothy ran back to him, but Jeffrey stopped in his tracks as if he were asking his brain to provide the answer. "I remember a picture of a snake on the hills, somewhere," Jeffrey kept at his ponderous subject. "I don't know where it was, but it was long, like two city blocks and the Indians used it to bury their fathers."

Timothy's face fell as he exchanged glances with his brother.

They missed their father, Jonas, too.

"Sometimes the natives made mounds as a church to their gods, or ancestors." Tom wanted to hug away their grief but keeping them active seemed a better choice.

"They couldn't sit down in a church under a mound of grass." Timothy's face showed his relief in thinking of something other than his father, who was no longer with them. "It's nice you look like Dad," he said, wrapping his fingers around Tom's belt.

Tom swung the young boy up, hugging him swiftly before placing him back on his feet. "I'm glad I've got two nephews in my life."

Jeffrey approached calmly.

Timothy was boxing at the air as Tom held him at arm's length.

"Mom says when we have sons, they might be twins." Jeffrey tipped his head, asking for confirmation.

Tom laughed. "Well now, that's a long time off. How many trees besides the oak do you know?" He motioned for Timothy to come back to the trail. "This is a forest preserve. Everyone needs to stay on the footpaths to respect the roots of the trees."

Jeffrey still concentrated. "Are we walking on dead Indians?"

Timothy jumped in the air. "Creepy." He laughed at his own antics.

"Nobody knows," Tom laughed, too. "Someday maybe you two could get a permit to excavate any relics."

"Relics?" Timothy repeated the unknown word.

"Bones," Jeffrey explained, proud to give the information.

Timothy turned to his big brother. "Let's dig now!"

"You need the government to give you permission," Tom explained.

"Heck," Timothy kicked at the gravel, then smiled at his brother. "Would you want to dig for bones?"

"Yes," Jeffrey said. "Should we make a pact?"

Timothy nodded. "How old do we have to be, Uncle Tom?"

"Twenty-one, at least."

"That's twelve years for you," Timothy counted, "And fourteen for me."

"Boys?" Tom considered the weight of his question. Uncle Tom was a concept they hadn't encountered in their generation. "The word, uncle, reminds me of a really mean man when I was little. He would scare us by pushing his false teeth partly out of his mouth and sliding his wig down on his forehead."

Jeffrey and Timothy paid rapt attention.

"If your mother agrees, would it be all right if you just called me Tom?" Their earnest faces showed their affection for him. "I'm still family, even if you don't use the uncle word."

"Okay," Timothy said immediately and nudged Jeffrey. "Tom."

"If Mom says it's okay," Jeffrey smiled. "We call the sergeant, Steve, now."

Tom thumped Jeffrey gently on the back. "Steve?"

He couldn't very well question the boys about Steve, so his mind turned to another troubling subject. Poor Danny had an uncle worse than any Uncle Tom. Someone who killed Danny's mother, the man's own sister; not to mention abusing the innocent child and then pinning the murder on him. Tom would cut off his hand rather than offend the sensibilities of these youngsters.

How could Gina find Tom the least bit trustworthy after denying Danny the benefit of doubt in his complicity in the bank robbery? Gina was right on the money. Danny's narcolepsy and white hair testified to the facts. The boy had been horribly injured. Gina had the wherewithal to help the lad, and he, Tom, had acted like an idiot, making an obstacle to their happiness out of the minor issue of not being informed of her plans.

"Boys," Tom called. "Would you like to meet a friend of mine? She's kind of mad at me for a dumb thing I did."

Their reactions were predictable: Jeffrey cocked his head wondering if it was a good idea and Timothy ran past them toward the car.

"Come on," Timothy yelled. "Let's go."

On his stroll back to the parking lot, Tom remembered Gina had not been to Johnson's Mound. Gina had no family now that her mother was gone. How could he have been so cruel to leave her, after she'd lost so much?

Had she asked him about the highest point in three counties? He hadn't been to the place. Gina Branson was his highest aspiration, to marry her and start a life with children and contentment beckoning, if she'd have him. The warm breeze from the field of corn next to the parking area blew his way. He missed her cedar smell, those loose dark curls, her sweet mouth. Tom yearned for the sound of her voice.

* * *

In Wayne, Dolly embraced Gina before she crossed the threshold. "Thanks for coming out to pick me up. You will have driven twice as far as Johnson's Mound by the time we get there."

"I thought I misunderstood, when you called me this morning." Gina straightened her silk scarf. She'd taken care to dress properly after arriving in such a dusty, disheveled state on her last visit before the Thanksgiving dinner. She wanted to show off for Dolly's mother. "Is your mother home?"

"Gardening," Dolly said, hurriedly as if she wanted to start the trip.

"Could I say hello, before we leave?"

"Of course," Dolly said, remembering her manners. "She'd love to see you and you look great."

Gina straightened her shoulders. "My mouth is still a mess."

"With the stitches gone, it's only a thin red line. I didn't even notice it on Thursday." Dolly led the way around the side of the house.

"Mother," Dolly called.

Gina's heart fell into her stomach. She halted on the walkway.

Dolly noticed. "What's wrong?" She motioned to a marble bench under an arch of bare lilac branches. "Sit a minute. You're as pale as a ghost."

Gina nodded. "I miss my mother." Her tears wouldn't stop. She was proud she wasn't sobbing uncontrollably, but the tears ran down her face. She fished in her purse for a handkerchief. Then thoughts of Tom assailed her and she pressed the handkerchief against her leaking eyes.

"Dolly, I'm all right." She patted her worried friend's hand. "Your kindness affected me."

Dolly's mother appeared around the corner, but Dolly waved her off as she put her arm around Gina.

Lucille sized up the situation and went back to work with her pruning shears.

"You're processing a lot of changes in your life. Vulnerability means you're a good person. If you weren't upset, it would mean something was dreadfully wrong with you."

Somehow Dolly's words, maybe any words, helped to calm Gina's nerves. "I miss Tom more than my mother. He hardly said hello on Thursday."

"I've talked to Tom and there isn't anyone." Dolly slipped a newspaper article out of her purse. "You saw him with his landlady's granddaughter."

Gina didn't believe that! Apparently her face showed the doubt.

"Here's proof." Dolly handed over the newspaper with Alice Burns-Steel's smiling engagement picture.

"Oh," Gina said as the truth seeped into her brain. She smiled so big she had to hold her hand over her injured lip. "That hurts. Do you have Tom's new phone number?"

Gina's mounting excitement wasn't calmed by the drive through the sylvan beauty of Army Trail Road out to Randall. A possibility existed that Tom might see her again. At least, there was no other woman in the picture.

"He's living upstairs in Mrs. Burns' home in St. Charles." Dolly laughed. "I'll write the number down for you."

"My house is a wreck," Gina thought of asking Dolly over after their walk through Johnson's Mound. "After work, I tried to go through my parents' books, but all I accomplished was a colossal mess."

"Well, the boys will love the collections you mentioned."

"Hey," Gina looked at Dolly for a split second. "I thought Jeffrey and Timothy were coming with us."

Dolly snickered politely. "They're busy this afternoon, but we'll pick the books up shortly."

The stoplights down Randall Road delayed their approach to Johnson's Mound. Gina's mind wandered to Danny Bianco's plight. "Do you think Tom will ever be able to understand my involvement with Danny?" She made another swift glance in Dolly's direction. "As Jonas' widow, do you?"

"Seeking justice doesn't mean you wanted a criminal, or his offspring, in your family." Dolly spoke quietly.

"I'd like a family," Gina said, trying to keep her eyes from misting over from the extent of her loneliness. Tears and driving didn't mix. "I really love being around the kids in the driver's education class."

"I bet you are a favorite." Dolly patted Gina's hand on the steering wheel. "Female racecar drivers are rare, aren't they?

As they passed the intersection of Dean Street, Dolly asked, "Isn't this the road you were on when Passantino kidnapped you?"

Gina pointed to the west. "I drove to Baker Road." She touched her lip injury resulting from the dangerous ride. "Lucky, I was."

"And braver than most women." Dolly wrung her hands. "Steve was really impressed. He thinks I have as much courage as you."

"Competing with speeding cars helped." Gina sighed. "I shouldn't have mentioned Danny."

"Nonsense," Dolly said. "There are times when I forget I'll never see Jonas again. At least you and Tom have the opportunity to reunite. You're both walking on the earth."

"Danny will continue to be a problem, if we do get back together."

"Everything will work out for you," Dolly's smile widened. "Think about how much you and Tom have learned about each other in the last few months. I'd like to talk to you soon about someone I'm becoming acquainted with."

"Who is that?" Gina slowed the car to a crawl when they turned into Johnson's Mound. Had she glimpsed a bit of a blue jacket? A child was running loose, without a parents' hand. Gina stopped before she turned into a parking place. The lot was empty except for a white van.

Dolly said, "Steve Muller," and jumped out of the car.

Timothy?

Gina recognized Dolly's son, but felt confused and then suspicious.

He talked loudly, a mile a minute to his mother, "And there could be Indian bones under us right now and Jeffrey promised to dig for them. We need a permit."

Gina let the car roll into the parking space and joined the pair. "Is your brother here," she asked.

"Sure," Timothy said, as if the question went way beyond stupid. "Mom, Mom, Tom says we don't have to use the uncle word, if it's all right with you?"

"Tom?" Gina asked Dolly.

"He wanted the boys to see Johnson's Mound."

"You wear your innocence at a rakish angle." Gina faced the paths. "Where is Jeffrey?"

"Rakish angle?" Dolly laughed at her. "Sounds like a quote."

145

"Christopher Fry," Gina's thoughts shut all the books in the world. Reality's pleasures beckoned.

Dolly and Gina followed Timothy, who called out to his brother. "Mom's here."

Jeffrey rounded a tree just off the path. "What did she say about uncle?" Tom stopped mid-stride.

Gina held her breath. He'd unbuttoned his coat which accentuated the breadth of his shoulders. His height contrasted with the boys'. A mountain of a man, he was. His mouth held a tentative smile, his black eyes stayed fixed on her. She couldn't cease her approach. Gina wanted to touch those lips, see his eyes welcome her, feel his arms around her, his body pressed to his.

Would he step away from her?

* * *

Tom had quickened his steps to catch Timothy before he got to the parking lot, but the boy had shot out away from him. When he spotted Dolly, his anxiety lessened until he saw the red Mustang.

Gina's black curls and milky complexion complemented an outfit of sky blue. His first thought was of the cedar aroma he missed smelling in Sweet's fur. When passion claimed him, he couldn't take another step.

Dolly was embarrassing him. No, bless Dolly. He needed to see the woman who meant his world could be happy.

"Gina," he called, softly.

She had halted her approach.

He held his arms out wide and advanced on her. He wrapped himself around her small body, lifting her to kiss her sweet mouth. "Gina." He breathed life back into his soul. Tom set her back down on the path, regaining his politeness. "How do you like Johnson's Mound?"

She brushed her mouth with a fingertip as if missing his kiss. "Welcoming," she said as she straightened her jacket. "Of what I've seen of it." Her eyes sparkled. "Welcoming."

Dolly excused herself. "Tom, the boys don't have to use uncle, if that's what you want."

"Thanks, Dolly," he said, meaning more than permission to be a playmate of the boys.

"If you give me my keys, I'll drive the boys to your house, Gina." Dolly hugged Gina. "Then they can haul out your books."

"Oh, yeah," Gina laughed. "Great idea." She hugged the matchmaker. "Thank you, Dolly. You're a real friend."

"Family," Dolly corrected. "I'm your family, even if this big lunk doesn't do something about it shortly. Take your time. I've already promised the boys I'd take them to McDonald's in St. Charles before we pick up the books."

Tom clasped Gina to his side as they watched Dolly and the boys drive off in the van. "Remember the highest point in three counties?"

Gina moved closer. "I think so."

"After I show you all the highlights of Johnson's Mound," Tom ran his huge hand through her curls, "we could drive out there?" From her complicit reaction, Tom knew he could ask her for the moon and she'd climb up the outside of tallest building to pluck it for him.

"Sure," she said, as if competing with Sweets' purr.

* * *

Control yourself, Gina demanded of herself. "I'll drive."

They walked around Johnson's Mound in record time, according to Tom. Gina remembered a blur of trees beyond his face, concentrating hard at leaves he pointed out, and listening spellbound to his recitation of the boys' antics. But all Gina really thought about was Tom. Those eyes of his were more than welcoming, they were downright demanding for a closeness her nerves matched. His voice reverberated through her body, as if every cell knew how important he was to her life. This was going to be the fastest trip out to the county's high-point she'd ever made.

She peeled out of the deserted gravel parking lot, fish-tailing onto the blacktop.

"We have time," Tom reminded her.

Gina gripped the wheel. "I know. I love to drive fast."

They hit route 47, a two-lane road in less than five minutes. The northbound traffic traveled at the 65 mph speed limit. Gina knew the cross roads, where a cop with radar might plan a stake-out for high-flying cruisers like her, so she floored the poor Mustang. A heavy car, it hit 90 mph without a quiver. Passing wasn't a problem. On-coming traffic could be avoided easily with her quick, sure handling of the car. In 15 minutes, Gina recognized the slight rise of the fields to the left of the road. She spied the crossroads, slowing to turn off onto the gravel.

"Some ride," Tom said without much approval.

"I wanted to get here fast." Then she looked at him. He really was not pleased. "Sorry," she said. The trip was ruined.

They got out of the car and Gina walked past a generating station's fence to the field behind it. She spun around without much enthusiasm to show him the landscape which fell away on all sides at a very slight angle.

"This is the highest point?"

"You expected a cliff or something, didn't you?"

Tom could have been a statue. His legs were spread as if to regain his balance after the ride she'd given him. His hair lifted with the wind.

"People say the wind hits you from all four directions here," she said, testing his mood.

"I've lived here all my life and I never been out here." He smiled slightly. "I wasn't sure I'd live to see it."

"You weren't in any danger, Tom," she said, knowing that wasn't what was important. "I live my life the way I drive."

"Avoiding head-on collisions?"

"No," she said turning her back to him so he wouldn't see her tears starting. "I forget there are others, close to me. I should have warned you earlier, I try to control everyone and everything in my life." She spread her arms out expecting to be embraced from Tom still standing behind her. "...within the range of three counties."

Gina admired the colors of the harvested fields at her feet: green winter wheat against black Illinois plowed fields, acres of dried sweet-smelling clover. A red and gold pheasant took flight. She didn't turn around until she heard the car start on the road in front of the power station.

Tom had left her. Stranded.

She sat on the stone step of the brick building, pressing her hands to her temples. "Idiot," she chided herself. She'd left the keys in the car. No reason not to. The man she loved wanted to share a secret place with her, and she'd ruined it.

Chapter Fourteen

Happiness had a way of avoiding Gina. "Just be yourself," everyone advised. *Take on a more acceptable persona,* she chided herself. *You are going to rattle around your old house at 80 without a conversation between another living soul until then if you don't learn how to reach out to another human being successfully.*

He didn't love her. Tom couldn't put up with her for more than 15 minutes without wanting to jump out of the car. Gina smiled to herself. She'd been driving conservatively. She could have really scared the pants off of him. There was no hope for it; she'd never be able to conform to someone else's idea of who she should be.

Gina stood up to start walking back to route 47. Farmers weren't going to come along for a day or two on the side road she was on. At least she could hitchhike once she got to the main road, if anyone would slow down long enough to stop.

Her Mustang was coming back up the gravel road, slowly.

Tom rolled down the window as he got abreast of her. "You scared me."

"I didn't mean to," she said.

"I know," he said. "It's hard to be a man, at the mercy of a beautiful woman."

"Me?"

"You."

* * *

Tom hadn't planned anything, but he couldn't let Gina just drive him home to Mrs. Burns' house. "I should show you my grandfather's farm. He didn't own it, just managed it for the Rosmores."

Gina jumped into the passenger seat. "You drive. I'd love to see it."

Tom drove at a modest speed so as not to miss the McDonald Road sign off Route 47. "From here to Randall Road, about two miles north and one mile south to that tree line, Grandpa Stiles farmed 360 acres for the Rosmores. He was taken out of eighth grade to farm for his father in southern Illinois. Grandma said he was dyslexic. Back then they didn't understand. Poor Grandpa. He knew he was intelligent, but normal things baffled him. He wasn't good with people. Grandma told my mother she would have divorced him in a minute if the kids wouldn't have starved."

Gina seemed happy to listen and he wanted her to know everything about him.

Tom pointed to the fallow field on his left. "I remember seeing this peat bog on fire at night. Probably the closest I can imagine of hell. You could see the fire in cracks between clods of earth. Scary. But I don't believe in hell. Probably not the way to think, but if the Lord loved me enough to save me from drinking, I suspect there are not many crimes He can't forgive."

"If He's asked," Gina said.

Tom didn't want to get into any differences they might develop in religion. He changed the subject. "Grandma's father was the drinker. They say alcoholism might be genetic, or at least the thinking patterns and biological reactions. Her brother died of liver disease. Her father made his own wine. Grandma never took a drink. One time when she still lived at home, she unplugged all the wine barrels in the basement."

"Did she get caught?"

"Grandma said her face looked so innocent, she should have had the courage to rob banks. She was that sure of getting away with it."

Tom pulled into the driveway. "The barn was built when I was ten."

"Well-built then." Gina said. "Did you and Jonas spend summers out here?"

"We did." Tom realized besides loving the girl, he liked her. "Behind those grain bins there used to be a pasture for the cows and horses, but now it's damned up to be a fishery. Grandpa had a sheepdog named Bob."

"Do you think Sweets would tolerate a dog?" Gina stared out at the old house.

"She might need to be top dog." Tom pointed to the left side of the house. "Grandma said there was a pig pen right up next to the house when they moved in. Grandpa moved it out to a back pasture and Grandma used the plot for a garden. I've eaten the sweetest strawberries from there."

"Did you make pets of all the farm animals?"

"No. Grandpa wouldn't allow it. The calves are the hardest not to love. They suck your fingers when they're weaned from their mothers. The turkeys were the dumbest. They died when airplanes flew over."

"Really? And do chickens drown in the rain."

"They do. You have to put them in the chicken coops or they die standing there with their mouths open to the sky."

"I love you," Gina said.

"I'm glad of that," he said. "Me too you. Want to chase the sun down like Grandpa used to do in the summer?"

"It is the opposite direction from home."

"Nevertheless. You can drive."

Gina quickly got out to change seats with him. "I'll be careful. Should we turn around when it's dark?"

"Not until then."

The sky was almost a salmon sky of oranges, aqua and light blues until the darker clouds overcame the light as the sun dipped below the horizon on the first evening of their life together.

"We're not orphans if we have each other," Gina said.

"I'm glad Danny tied us together."

* * *

Sunday, November 25th

Stan was in rare form during the AA meeting, clapping Tom on the shoulder when he handed over the Fourth Step moral inventory he'd worked on until two in the morning. "I'll come upstairs with you after the meeting and then you can read this to me."

Tom mentally reviewed the lack of housekeeping he'd accomplished in his apartment before the meeting. Dirty banana-and-nut muffin tins were still in the sink, but at least his bed was made. Gina was taking up all of his time, now that they were reconciled.

The young married woman, Jan, monopolized the group by sharing the gyrations her drinking husband had been undergoing when he failed at a brief attempt at sobriety. She wore her black hair piled attractively high on her head. Her bangs now allowed her expressive eyebrows to show. She concluded her ten-minute stint with, "He says he enjoys drinking, doesn't drive when he's drunk and sees no reason to stop."

"Have you been attending Alanon meetings?" Tom asked. "My girlfriend should be going too."

"There is one this evening in the Methodist church basement," Jan said. "But I needed fellow drinkers tonight. But, you know, the last time I went to Alanon there were seven alcoholics at my table, all dealing with still drinking friends. I'm planning to alternate between the two meetings; at least until I've found a sponsor to help me with the steps."

Both Norma and June spoke up. They were willing to act as co-sponsors for her.

Stan helped Tom clean up after the meeting. "Why don't you sit down on that stool and read me your Fourth Step."

Tom did as he was told. "You did say to include the positive character traits."

Stan laughed. "Oh, did they outnumber your negatives."

Tom hoped he could one day laugh at himself. "Well I followed the Big Book. First I wrote down all the people I was angry with when I drank: Alan Passantino for killing Jonas, Danny Bianco for ingratiating himself with my girlfriend, Gina; Gina for not trusting me enough to tell me she was going to educate Danny and me for being such a lunk head."

Stan rinsed out the final giant coffee pot. "No reason to make amends to Passantino or Bianco; but shouldn't you talk to your girlfriend about your problem with trust issues?"

"I've been avoiding touching that subject."

"That's what we call denial," Stan said. "Have at it young man, or you will be drinking again. And by the way when you are outlining your part in the misunderstanding explain to the young woman that you will never graduate from AA meetings. This is a lifetime disease."

* * *

Monday, November 26th

Gina had moved her oval free-standing mirror back up into the attic bedroom along with her clothes. Her hair was getting a bit shaggy, but she wanted to wait until she was sure about a wedding date to schedule an appointment to have it styled. Married. Her mother would have been so proud. Surely, she knew even now.

"Please, Lord," she prayed aloud, "Help me be a good wife to Tom."

She was jumping the gun, putting the horse before the cart. But he loved her. Marriage was just around the corner, wasn't it?

Since her first day on job as a driver's education teacher at St. Charles High School, she'd wanted to share her stories with Tom. Harvey said he was doing a good job with two young first-time offenders as their parole officer. She wanted to hear his stories, too. Both of them were ideal for their professions with young people. Tom's therapy training would make him a good listener and the boys she taught respected her race-car experience. She missed his home cooking, too.

When Tom arrived, she was surprised that he hadn't brought Sweets, or his suitcases.

She followed him into the kitchen. "I ordered pizza for us."

He made them a pot of coffee before saying. "I have a sponsor in the AA program now."

Gina sat down as he brought milk and cream for her coffee. Would he kneel down beside her now? She didn't see any ring-box bulge in his shirt or pants pockets.

"Tell me about the young men you're in charge of."

Tom sipped at his coffee. "Even though they both were caught shoplifting, I can't help thinking the young girl they were both courting put them up to it."

"Was she in school with them?"

"I changed schools for both of them. They go to Burlington, now. I kept them together to make it easier."

"I was just mulling over the fact, before you arrived, that you are trained to be a good listener. How are they doing in their new school?"

"The best thing is they have someone to share the experience with, talking about all the new kids, bouncing ideas off each other and me on how to handle the ever-present bullies. They're going to be fine. They both have parents who were horrified by the crime, stealing cheap necklaces for the girl. The parents get out of bed to drive them to their community service jobs at 6:00 in the morning, washing dishes at St. Patrick's breakfast program."

"Are they bright boys?"

"They are, but you know how the young let emotions rule."

"Not like us grown-ups?" Gina knocked Tom's elbow off the table and he nearly spilled the rest of his coffee.

"Watch it. You're still a kid, yourself. So are you speeding down Baker Road to give the kids a thrill at your job?"

"Nooo. But I did make a bookroom cry the other day. She was chatting away to the girls as she was driving. Mary Alice doesn't have many friends and I guess she got high on interacting with her captive audience. Anyway, I raised my voice when she frightened me by crossing the yellow line."

"Was she crying while she was driving?"

"She didn't breakdown until the other girls were out of the car. I just sat with her for a while. Then I commented that I bet her parents never yelled at her at home. She said when they got mad at her or each other, they didn't speak. She hasn't spoken to her father for a year. He'd back-handed her when she smarted off."

"Have you taken therapy classes? I still marvel at the way you handled Danny."

The pizza boy arrived and they ate most of the anchovy and vegetarian pizza before continuing their talk.

"I probably should enroll in a teaching program to get properly certified," Gina said. "The school board would be happier. I'd be better-off if they'd pay for my education."

"Have you asked?"

"Not yet. I've been waiting to see what will develop here." Gina punched his chest hard.

"Stan says, that's my sponsor's name, I need to make amends."

"We're okay, aren't we?"

"We are. Nevertheless, I need to do this or I might start drinking again."

Gina nodded, the poor guy. This AA business was certainly difficult on its adherents.

Tom gripped her hand, as if she might run off. "I thought you didn't trust me enough to tell me you planned to educate Danny."

Gina stopped him. "I didn't think of educating Danny before Judge Wilcox sat on my bed."

"Really?" Stan said "I should have checked out the facts. I was so angry."

"Remember I told you I trusted you to call Muller, when Passantino kidnapped me?"

"I do remember. I'm such a lunk head."

"Why didn't you talk to me on Thanksgiving?"

"Another bad decision, I was too jealous of all those men hanging on your every word."

"What men? I think Steve Muller was there to see Dolly. She mentioned him when we arrived at Johnson's Mound, but I forgot to ask more about him."

Tom laughed. "Mr. Stone said they've been seeing each other. I'm to be the trustee of the boys' accounts. You did notice I wore the tie you gave me." Gina nodded and he seemed to rush his next words together. "Would you attend Alanon on Sunday nights when I go to AA meetings?"

"Do you think I should? Mother did when her sister was drinking. She told me to go because I have a tendency to control the universe."

"We could be on the same spiritual page, so to speak."

"I don't know where to find a meeting. Would I need a sponsor, too?"

"They meet in the basement of the Methodist church. A sponsor does help to explain the steps."

"Of course, I'll go. We'll be exploring the program together."

Tom gathered up their dishes. After he put the pizza box under the sink with the rest of the trash, he turned around to stare at her. "You realize this is a program where I don't graduate?"

Gina nodded. "I can see where not controlling others might be my lifetime goal, too. Is it all right if I invite Dolly?"

"Of course." Tom moved her cup away from her. "Let's visit Metzger's jewelry shop."

Gina looked at the clock over the sink. "They're still open."

"I need a ring before I ask you to marry me."

"I think you just did."

"Yes." Tom finally knelt down. "Will you?"

She wanted to swallow all of him right there. "I will."

Tom lunged for her. "Mine!" To both their amazement he broke out in racking sobs. He put his elbows on his knees and held his head. "Sorry," he gulped. "I don't know what's come over me. Just like a therapist not to know what's going on."

"You've been sad for so long." Gina put her arms around him. "Happiness had to find a way through. Unless you're disappointed because I said yes."

"Not me," Tom laughed wrapping his arms around his wife-to-be.

CHAPTER FIFTEEN

Sunday, December 2nd

Sergeant Muller wasn't in uniform but Dolly looked concerned, when Gina opened the door for them. "Is he dead?"

"No, no." Muller waved his hands. "I wanted to come to the Alanon meeting."

"I'm sure Tom is fine." Dolly wrapped her arms around Gina. "I told Steve I should have warned you. I never thought we'd frighten you, because Steve's not on duty and I drove the van."

Gina took in deep breaths searching for calm. "Of course, of course. Tom told me I wouldn't suffer from PTS; but here I am reliving the nightmare of the robbery."

Muller looked at his watch. "Maybe we shouldn't go to Alanon. It's already quarter to six and traffic might be heavy."

"Nonsense," Gina collected her purse. "I promised Tom we'd go."

"I could drive you there and stay in the van," Muller said.

"Oh, come with us," Dolly said, "for moral support."

The Methodist Church lot was full and it was ten after six when they slid into the packed hall. Tables were jammed together and every chair appeared occupied by a motley crowd.

A greeter whispered a smiling hello and pointed to a less crowded table in a corner.

The entire crowd repeated several prayers and creeds aloud before the speaker asked if there were any newcomers. Muller looked at Dolly, who raised her hand in concert with Gina's.

"Just give us your first names, so we can welcome you properly," the leader said.

"I'm Gina. Thanks for having us. This is my sister, Dolly and s, s, Steve."

Everyone clapped and the speaker went on to other business about needing someone to make coffee and clean up the place for the church.

"I'm really not comfortable," Muller whispered to Gina. "I know half the faces here and I might be breaking their anonymity."

Gina nodded. "It's okay, Dolly. He can wait for us in the van."

Dolly moved closer to Gina. "He's probably right. But I'm glad I came. We are powerless over alcohol."

To Gina the place was a sea of happy faces, a friendly atmosphere, but did people really bare their souls to strangers? "Let's go, too."

Dolly shook her head. "No. Tom might stop going to AA. We should see it through."

Gina dug her fingernails into palm, trying not to break for the door. She smiled at the woman on her right, who smiled right back.

"First time is always the hardest, Gina." She extended her hand. "My name is Helen. Wait just a minute and others will join our table."

Sure enough the speaker sat down at their table and two other women joined him. He patted his chest, as if they didn't know English. "I'm David. We should do a First Step."

The three women nodded.

It's a cult, Gina concluded with its own language and group think. This was not going to work. She was too independent for most people, let alone become a part of a situation where your words had to conform to a set pattern. Was Tom worth it? Maybe she should try one of those on-line dating services. Maybe Menasha or Harvey Slemmons knew some single men for her to date. Maybe Muller knew some men. Not Hoffman though. Only Tom, her heart gave a beat as she thought of his name. She could sit here til the cows came home if that's what Tom wanted. In the meantime, she decided to tune back into the conversation.

Helen was speaking, "My sons make their own wine and their wives party right along with them. My own father was an alcoholic as was my brother. My husband doesn't drink and really looks down on me because of all the craziness in my family. I first came to Alanon to find out how to fix everybody; but instead I found how to live a happy life. I've been coming for four years and these friends and the Lord have gently taught me how to not make my family's problems my top priority. The

Lord has worked wonders with me." She laughed at her own joke. "My husband says to keep coming because it is helping even though he can't figure out how. We attend church together, too; something I never would have considered before joining Alanon and getting to know how personally involved, how caring, the Lord is."

Listening intently, Gina admitted the woman was sincere in her beliefs.

No one spoke and Gina wondered if she was supposed to take her turn, now. *What could she say?* Of course, she believed God loved them, otherwise why had he taken the trouble to create them. She didn't attend church, Mother hadn't. She prayed when she needed help. Wasn't that enough? It wasn't as if she could understand God. Who could? Why make her mother suffer and allow Dolly's husband to be summarily dispatched by a scum like Danny's uncle? They weren't supposed to understand God, were they? As mere mortals thinking like God would be a stretch.

David asked, "Could I bring you two a cup of coffee? You didn't have a chance to get any before the meeting."

Dolly said, "I would love a cup, sugar and no cream. Gina wants hers black."

David, a much older slim man, nodded and went off toward the towering coffee pots.

Gina noticed the basket in the middle of the table with a few dollar bills in it. "Is this for the coffee?"

"Hello, Gina, I'm Jan. We support Alanon with our donations, the coffee is free. I'm a recovering alcoholic, but my husband still drinks and I'm hoping Alanon will help me treat him with respect. I do know alcoholism is a disease over which we have no control. That's the First Step. This in-group jargon can seem a little off putting, but they know what they're talking about. I've only been coming for a few months. But I feel calmer, because I came to believe that a power greater than myself has restored me to sanity. That's the Second Step. And, I wake up every morning with the Third Step prayer, turning my will and my life over to my Higher Power. In AA I have two sponsors who tell me to take it easy. I'm just starting Step Four with them, making a thorough and searching moral inventory of my character defects; but they said I should round out the list with my character strengths. One is knowing when to stop talking."

Gina hoped she could end her part of the conversation with a joke, too. She contributed a five-dollar bill to the basket. "My name is Gina. My boyfriend is an alcoholic and his sponsor thought it was a good idea if I came to Alanon. Dolly is my sister."

David placed paper cups of coffee in front of Gina and Dolly, before sharing, "When I first came, six years ago, I thought, 'All this gaggle of women is going to do is complain about their drunken husbands.' But I was wrong. They've taught me how to let go of my ex-wife with love and how to manage a realationship with my grown children, a daughter and a son, who both drink to access." He looked at Gina then Dolly. "I don't have all the answers. I turned my will and my life over to the care of the Lord and he has rewarded me with life lessons I would have missed if I hadn't found Alanon. We don't expect ourselves to be perfect, just to progress in our spiritual lives."

"I'm Dolly. I'm excited to learn the program. I've heard about your group for years and read your daily devotionals. A lot of what I find there, at times, seems awfully selfish; but then I hear about people whose complete lives are taken over by their children or by emercing themselves in caring for invalids and I can see where there must be a dividing line between acceptable caring and unacceptable meddling. As a mother of grade-school boys, I want to learn the difference more thoroughly before they leave me for the wider world."

Gina closed her mouth. Her new sister had a universe of self, she'd never explored. Tears came to her eyes. The Lord had been gracious in presenting her with this precious soul in her life when she needed people so badly, not to replace her mother. No one could. Nevertheless, here was Dolly…and Tom, too.

A woman slightly older than Jan, Dolly and Gina spoke next. "I'm Beverly. I'm not sure I'm going to keep coming back. This is my third time. My belief system doesn't really fit with the program."

David said. "Alanon is similar to AA in that we let people define their own Higher Power. For a time I told myself the organization would serve. But I have been lucky to receive the gift of faith. The program teaches that we should take what works and leave the rest."

Heather closer to Helen's age was the last to speak. "I've been coming for three years, but I only want to listen tonight. I'm glad you came, Dolly and Gina, you are both so beautiful. And Beverly, we will miss you, if you decide not to come back."

Different tables stood and prayed before dispersing. David led their group in the Serenity Prayer, "Lord, give us the serenity to accept the things we cannot change, the courage to change the things we can, and the wisdom to know the difference."

Gina waited for Dolly to put her coat on before saying, "Let's buy some of their books before we leave."

Muller jumped out of the van when he saw them coming with their arms loaded down with books. He opened Dolly's passenger door before sliding open the side door for Gina to climb in. "Did you buy out their bookstore?"

"Almost," Dolly said. "It wasn't bad."

"They seem like nice people," Gina said. "Are we going to go every Sunday night?"

"Tom does," Dolly said.

* * *

Tom's meeting was becoming more comfortable for him. He smiled at the women, repeating their names in his head: June, Norma still wearing purple, Judy, and Connie. Jan was missing, but she could have chosen Alanon for the night. Would she meet Dolly and Gina? He wondered out loud, "Jimmy and Todd no longer attend. Does anyone know what happened to them after their first meeting?"

Stan set Tom straight, "Stay out of other people's business. Work on yourself for a while and you'll be able to help others."

Ron was a regular but he rarely talked to the women away from the table. In private Tom had asked Stan about it. "We don't encourage men and women to give each other confidences, except during the meeting. Sponsors only sponsor their own sex. Of course, with these new-fangled sexual rights we sometimes encounter difficulties; but the program works for any persuasion."

After the meeting Stan stayed to hear about how Gina had accepted Tom's apology.

"She didn't even plan to educate Danny ahead of time, as I thought she had. She spoke right off the top of her head. She hadn't held anything back from me. I felt like an idiot. Then I lost my temper when she drove too fast and had to apologize all over. I asked her to marry me."

"Whoa," Stan said. "Did she accept?"

Tom nodded. Suddenly qualms hit his stomach. "We haven't set a date. She is going to her first Alanon meeting tonight with her sister."

After pouring himself another cup of coffee, Stan pulled out a stool from the center island in the kitchen. He didn't look happy.

"Aren't you going to congratulate me?"

"Oh, of course. I'm happy for you, but concerned too. You've experienced so many changes in the last few months. You're a therapist, right? Wouldn't you advise caution to a person who has been through so much grief?"

Tom surveyed the man he called his sponsor. His hair was thinning, almost non-existent. He probably never even felt passion anymore.

Stan laughed at him. "My wife is still the apple of my eye, and don't get any ideas about our love life. We do just fine. I still say you should slow down."

"Sorry," Tom said.

"And I forbid you to use that word again. Change your behavior so that you never need to mouth an apology. And I don't want you to say the word 'worry' either. Every time you catch yourself worrying, pray instead. I'll pray about you and you pray, too. Deal?"

"Deal," Tom said, glad the evening was ending.

"Oh, and find a church to attend. You want a church wedding don't you?"

* * *

Friday, December 7th

"The trouble with including people in your life is they all have opinions." Henry Stone, Dolly's father, filled in a long gap in the conversation at the Hunt Club restaurant in Wayne.

"About everything." Dolly agreed.

Her arm felt fine on Gina's stooped shoulders. "No," Gina said, swallowing the lump in her throat. "It isn't that I don't appreciate all your ideas. I didn't intend to ruin the party. I was thinking of Mother."

"She knew we'd be together," Tom's voice held no sadness when he added, "Jonas would have given me a sizzling bachelor party."

"I can come up with that!" Henry laughed and then gasped as Lucille jabbed him gently with her elbow.

"Life is for the living," Lucille said. "We're the survivors and we're going to do them proud."

Gina admitted to herself the preparations were getting way out of hand. A church wedding was the only thing Lucille and Dolly would stand for. Gina wanted Lorna Hale at St. Patrick's to perform the ceremony.

Henry insisted he be allowed to pay for everything, because Jonas would have wanted it that way. Every person the Stones had known for their 40 years of marriage obviously had to be invited to the wedding. Tom had friends and professors from school and Gina wanted all of her mother's friends to witness her happiness. Her new job as a driver instructor for the Geneva school district inspired her to think about inviting the entire junior class. She hoped Tom's new job as a probation officer would mean all the people in his department, maybe even some of his parolees would be included.

Within the safety of the assembled restaurant guests, Gina brought up the instigator of her happiness as diplomatically as she could, "Danny--?"

"Should be my best man," Tom said in a heartbeat. "He's the one who originally tied us together."

"That's what I'm talking about." Gina lifted her up-turned hand to Dolly, and started to weep again.

Tom stared at Henry, who also couldn't understand the fresh motivation for tears.

Dolly explained to Tom, "That you're perfect, you idiot."

"Well," Henry coughed. "Danny obviously needs something in his life now to hang onto. Nothing like being called a best man to increase your self-worth."

* * *

Was he on a train he couldn't stop? Fumes from the wine glasses reached Tom. He fished in his pocket for the 24-hour coin, Stan had given him. "About a date--," he started to speak. "Stan says--."

The cheerful conversation came to an abrupt halt.

Gina sipped from her water glass. Her cheeks were bright, her low cut electric-blue dress, her luscious mouth only further confused his intentions. She had turned down a refill of wine. Dolly just stared at him then turned to Muller who must have touched her below the table.

Mr. Stone asked politely, "What did your sponsor say?"

"He's concerned about the quick succession of changes in my life, my job, my family, my affection, my new program--." What was he talking about, delay?

Gina never to be named a coward asked? "How long does he want you to wait?"

"He didn't give a time. He just wants me to be sure, to consider everything, to understand I may not be thinking straight."

Gina abruptly left the table.

Tom knocked over his chair as he hurried to follow her.

Dolly beat him to the restroom door. "Go call your sponsor, Tom. Do you have his number? Tell him what just happened."

Tom walked outside the club, then down toward the stables. He felt like walking all the way back to Mrs. Burns' house. Instead, he pulled out his cell phone and called Stan. "Can you talk? I messed up."

"You took a drink?" Stan's voice wasn't as upset as Tom thought it would be if he needed to confess he'd been drinking.

"You thought I might?"

"This program only works one day at a time, Tom. I'm glad you're sober. I am too, for today. What happened?"

"Gina thinks I want to postpone the wedding."

"I didn't know you had set a date."

"We haven't."

"I'm sorry. I don't understand. Start at the beginning."

"I told them my sponsor, you, said I should wait."

"I did *not* tell you to wait. I told you a lot of changes have been happening in your life and I wanted you to think about what you are planning. Take responsibility for believing you should wait. Gina's angry because there is someone in your life controlling you, not her?"

"I don't want to wait. I was just talking. How do I fix this?"

"Set the date, you stupid--. Sorry, Tom, I apologize. Remember I told you not to do or say things you need to apologize for...and listen to me. I have a quick temper, not perfect but making progress. Did you pray about your decision?"

"I thought about it. I think the Lord has given me Gina."

"I think she has to consent to the gifting." Stan laughed. "Get back in there kid, and keep your chin up. Maybe keep your chin down and your eyes up."

"Thanks, Stan." Tom turned back toward the restaurant. His feet almost danced down the gravel path. "I know the Lord is with me, but it helps to have another man routing for me."

"Don't forget. You keep me sober by calling. Never hesitate."

Tom hurried to the Stone's table. No Gina or Dolly. Thankfully, Muller was still sitting with them. "Would December 15th fit with everyone's schedule?"

Mr. and Mrs. Stone nodded.

Muller asked, "Has Gina agreed?"

"Not yet," Tom admitted and headed back to the women's lounge.

* * *

"I hate him," Gina told Dolly as she tried to wash off smeared eye make-up.

"No you don't." Dolly sat down on one of the upholstered couches.

"Why does he want to put off the wedding? I thought he loved me."

"He loves you and does want to marry you. He was just blabbering. Jonas said stupid things all the time. They were brothers, remember. I would get so upset. Then I realized I had the freedom to react differently. Jonas usually thought better of things after a while and returned to some sort of sanity. All my raw emotions were just wasted time. I decided if I wanted to be the sort of mother for my boys that my mother taught me to be, I needed to change."

Gina sat down to listen. "I'm so glad I found you."

Dolly leaned into Gina's shoulder. "The Lord giveth and the Lord taketh away, blessed be the name of the Lord."

"How do you learn not to react?"

"Everyone reacts. I choose what I want to happen. You want to marry Tom, so you need to keep the goal in mind. When he's wrong, ignore it if you can. If something happens in the future, keep the goal of a happy married life a priority in your mind and act accordingly. You can't run out of the house when the baby needs to be changed and the cake is almost ready to take out of the oven."

Gina laughed. It surprised her to be so devastated one moment and joyful the next. She hugged Dolly. "In racing, we called it: 'taking the hit.'"

"I told Tom to go call his sponsor. I haven't had a chance to tell you about Steve, yet."

"It will do Tom good to cool his heels. He told me your father knows you two are dating."

"We've been meeting at my old house, when the boys are in school. He wants to marry me."

"Do you love him, then?"

"In a way. Steve's kind and I don't want to lose him. I am going to marry him even though he's not a believer."

"Does that matter so much?"

"It does, in a way." Dolly turned away for a minute, then said. "It says somewhere in the Bible that if a nonbeliever gives a cup of water to a believer, they are saved. I don't know how to live alone and with the boys, needing a male around--."

Gina relaxed waiting to hear more.

"I need to explain the gift Steve wants to give you and Tom for your wedding. It's a book about how the histories of Roman and Greek civilizations was destroyed by Christianity's censure and destruction of their historical documents. Steve says he wants to know what you two think of the book, it's called 'Swerve.' He thought it would impact my faith, but it hasn't really. I've read parts of "On the Nature of Things,' one of the documents mentioned in 'Swerve.'"

"Don't worry, Dolly. I'm sure Tom and I will both read the books without losing our faith. When people talk about the Lord wanting us to hate people who don't think the way they do, I sing a little ditty in my head to keep me from saying controversial things back to them. I don't think we should blaspheme or look down on other people's ideas. In India some people believe snakes are gods. Others imagine there is a monkey god. And still others summon up a being bigger than themselves like an elephant. But the Lord is the entire universe, all things, in every rock and cloud, everywhere and everything and perhaps our soul's awareness of glory, so I sing, 'My God's bigger than your God."

Dolly grinned and then poked Gina. "Steve and I are going to marry on Valentine's Day in St. Patrick's. Now, what are you going to do?"

"I'm going to set my wedding date. How does December 15th sound?" Gina turned away from the mirror. "As sisters now we'll have the same last name."

"Only until Valentine's Day. Let's go tell Mother and Dad," Dolly said.

As they opened the door, Tom greeted them. Gina and he asked in unison, "December 15th?"

They embraced, but Gina thought she heard Dolly say to herself as she walked back to the table. "Was he listening at the door?"

CHAPTER SIXTEEN

Saturday, December 8th

Lucille Stone and Dolly insisted they needed to help Gina decide on the appropriate wedding dress. A trip to Chicago, however, was more than Gina could cope with.

"Macy's in Schaumburg will either have a dress to fit me, or they can alter it." Gina needed to keep her hands tight on the wheel of the Mustang. The two women in the car, Dolly and Lucille, could have melted her resolve to keep control of something.

"Are you going to choose a veil or a hat?" Lucille asked. "I love shopping for wedding clothes."

"A hat would be awesome," Dolly said to her mother.

Lucille nodded her head in agreement.

In a mood to test the waters of their friendship, Gina said. "I was thinking of a long veil flowing with the train of the dress."

Both women bobbed their heads with visions of glory.

The first presentation by the sales lady in Macy's resembled a business suit with a long skirt. "I don't think so," Gina said.

"No magic," Lucille sighed. "But maybe for the aunt of the bride? I am sort of your aunt, aren't I, Gina? Do you sell it in blue or grey?"

Gina didn't want to decipher if Lucille was or was not her aunt. "Sounds good to me. I need an Aunt."

The saleslady was frowning. "If you two are sisters, isn't she your--."

"Half-sisters," Lucille explained. "Same rakish father."

"Oh, I see."

Gina wasn't sure but she thought the lady's nose did tip a little toward the ceiling. "I don't want a full skirt in the front, " she said as kindly, yet as off-putting as she could manage without laughing.

The sales lady simulated her delight. "I appreciate defining information. We won't waste time showing you any bouffant skirts."

The next dress was strapless.

"Sleeves," Lucille directed.

"Thank you," Gina agreed. "I've seen too many brides tugging at bodices."

"I liked the beadwork," Dolly offered.

"And a draped back for a lacy train," Gina hoped she was being helpful.

The resulting satin creation combined a cascade of embroidery: appliquéd roses with pearl centers entwined among ribbon leaves onto lacy long sleeves. The slim skirt gathered efficiently at the waistline in the back to produce a two-foot train with a hem of climbing roses to match the bodice. The bridal cap repeated the rose and pearl design as did the flowing lace of the long veil.

When Gina sheepishly raised her eyes to the surrounding mirrors, she beheld a beauty. The clean smell of the new materials won the battle with her lilac perfume. As her chin lifted with pride, she felt a slight pressure on her cheek. Her mother's kiss of approval.

Lucille and Dolly laughed and wept half-way back to Geneva.

"Mother's friends are going to drop dead with envy," Dolly pronounced.

"My mother's might just shout." Gina laughed.

* * *

Sunday, December 8th

Reverend Lorna Hale agreed to prenuptial counseling for Tom and Gina after St. Andrew's mass. Her office was small, crammed with filing cabinets with barely enough room for two chairs to fit between her desk and the door. Tom moved the back of his chair next to Gina's, spreading his long legs into the space thus provided. Gina put her hand on his massive shoulder. Proud she was of her happy, smiling giant.

Lorna's crown of tight dark curls sparkled from the stained-glass window's rainbow of colors. "I've borrowed my method of agreeing to marry people from Father Joe Fix, a Roman Catholic priest who is familiar with the Twelve Step Program."

"I didn't know Gina had told you I am a recovering alcoholic," Tom said.

Lorna smiled at Gina's denial. "Tom, Gina has not broken your anonymity. You just did. I was explaining my wedding selection method of which asking about substance abuses is number four."

"I'm glad you understand this added complication." Tom said. "I was planning to mention AA."

"Trust issues have come up before," Gina said, reaching for Tom's hand.

Lorna nodded. "Well let's get started. Who hustled who?"

Gina sucked in a breath. "I guess I'm the culprit. I've known Tom and his brother since high school. But the bank robbery--."

Lorna laughed. "I was joking, Gina. I did read you two were tied together as hostages."

Tom said, "I initially thought we were holding on to each other because of my loss, then Gina's mother died."

Lorna said, "You must both have been terrified during your kidnapping, Gina."

Tom looked at her. "Did you feel any fear at all?"

"The gun was frightening; but once my hands were on the wheel, I prayed the Lord would see me through." She touched her upper lip.

Tom shook his head. "I can hardly tell where the scar is."

Lorna said, "I have eight questions to ask? Gina, what do you like about Tom?"

Gina laughed. "Besides his size? He seems to know who I am. I don't want to live alone and I want to know more about him, his future – with me."

"She's so beautiful. My brother's widow adores her. Gina needs me, as I do her. Most of all, I know she loves me, even when we have a misunderstanding…and there have been a few."

"Okay, number two," Lorna said. "What do you do on your dates?"

Gina laughed with Tom. "We only really had one restaurant date, and I paid the tab."

"We've been going to funerals, family holiday dinners, and jury selections. We both love to walk around Johnson's Mound. I do *not* like riding with Gina when she's racing, breaking speed limits."

Gina lowered eyes, but added with a hint of pride, "You were never in any danger."

"Most of your racing friends are dead!"

"Something to work together on there," Lorna said. "Number three: what do you like to do alone?"

Gina laughed. "I don't like it, but I attend Alanon meetings when Tom's at his AA meeting."

"She likes her driver's education job." Tom reached up to touch her hair. "And my job is challenging."

"I was going to ask," Lorna said. "It's number six on the list."

"I'm a parole officer with a therapist degree."

"Isn't that great," Gina said. "We all work with people instead of widgets."

"Any jealousy or possessiveness between you two so far?"

Gina had no problem telling all. "I was an idiot. Tom was rooming at my mother's house and the day he moved out, I saw him open the door for a beauty ten years my junior."

"My new landlady's granddaughter was showing me where the place was. But during the trial, I really hatred Sergeant Muller."

"Because he's involved with your sister-in-law?" Gina asked.

"No. It was you. Muller questioned you first. You're both the same height. I wanted all your attention. My emotions were all over the place, hating Danny for killing my brother. I know, I know, his uncle was the murderer. And when you were helping Danny, my grieving process didn't allow control of my emotional state."

"How are you now?" Lorna asked. "Is this wedding too soon? What does your sponsor say?"

"Danny will be my best man. I love you, Gina." Tom put his arm around her shoulder. "I want to begin our life together as soon as possible. I'm not sure why I still feel real animosity for Muller. Stan will probably make me do a fourth step about it."

Gina did understand. "Muller's replacing your brother, but Dolly has a right to be happy, too."

"Okay." Lorna said, "Be honest. Tell me the things you don't like about each other. And remember no one will change after the wedding."

"Driving too fast," Tom said. "—and always being right."

"I don't know. He cooks, he's gentle and beautiful. I wish he wasn't an alcoholic. I know he doesn't graduate from recovery. Is it genetic? Will our children have a pre-disposed nature?"

Lorna nodded. "No one really knows, but your children will be thankful for their father's program, as well as your own in Alanon."

"I hope we have a big family." Tom turned back to Lorna. "You visited Marie in her house, there are enough bedrooms."

"Children was number seven," Lorna said. "Remember there is only one voice for discipline, one that both of you must agree on. Number five deals with your families. Are there any issues you haven't worked out?"

"We're both orphans," Gina said. "But we both had loving parents."

Lorna opened her appointment book. "December 15th is available. Your spiritual progress in the recovery programs will help with most of your future decisions. Remember one in two marriages result in divorce, one in fifty for couples who worship together and one in five-hundred for couples who pray together."

Gina kissed Tom's hand. "We're going to start our mornings with an abundance journal."

"She's so controlling." Tom laughed.

"And music," Lorna asked. "for the ceremony?"

"Only Amazing Grace," Gina said.

"Over and over," Tom agreed.

* * *

Saturday, December 15th

Menasha Worthington drew Gina to his side at the back of St. Andrew's in Geneva. "Your mother loved yellow roses."

Gina raised the rounded bouquet to enjoy their fragrance. "I know she's here."

Dolly's ice blue gown matched her blue tipped white rose nosegay. "We're off," she whispered when the wedding march began.

Jeffrey and Timothy squared their small shoulders and marched down the aisle as the white, silk-suited pair of ring bearers.

St. Andrew's had been transformed with white satin ribbons and yellow roses. Garlands decorated each pew facing the runway. Sashes of white wound around each of the 24 pillars along with yellow rose garlands.

The splendor of the nave couldn't compete with the altar's grandeur where tall banks of white and yellow roses provided a backdrop for the groom and his teenage best man almost silhouettes in their black tuxedoes.

Gina kept her concentration on Tom to help her down the aisle of the filled church. But she caught Danny's winked. His white hair accentuated the color of his wedding suit.

Tom's eyes welcomed Gina into his heart, into his life.

* * *

If men got weak in the knees, Tom would have allowed himself to acknowledge the power of seeing Gina dressed as a goddess. Instead he let the sweat drip down his spine as he strove to keep his body from reacting to the vision coming towards him. The soft blue of her eyes outshone her finery as far as he was concerned, but he had to admit all the white perfectness intimidated him. How could she decide he was the man to share her life, to be the focus of her love?

All the doubts he had entertained about her not putting his feelings above her own were swept away with the realization of the gift she was offering as his life mate.

* * *

The photography session and the reception at the Baker Hotel were a blur of faces behind the one happy countenance within Tom's focused view. "Gina." He placed his hands on her delicate cheeks. "Time to head for the airport."

Gina wrapped her arms around his neck, standing on tiptoes to meet his kiss. Her lips quivered with excitement and her warmth promised more. She pulled herself away, tossing her bouquet into the dancing crowd. Then they ran for the stretch-limo Menasha had arranged to take them to Geneva.

In the back seat Tom drew his perfumed wife to his side. "All that white is as unapproachable as the wings of an angel."

Gina's hand caressed his knee. "We only have time to change." Her eyes reflected his goals.

"A bed and you," he whispered as he helped her detach her lacy skirts from the limo.

"Dolly's waiting to help me out of this mountain of clothing." Gina ran for the house with her skirts held high.

Tom caught the driver enjoying the show of long white nyloned legs. "The luggage is in the hall," he told the chagrined driver. "I'll give you a hand after I change."

* * *

Riding to the airport with my husband. Gina repeated the mantra. Tom's left arm was around her waist with his right arm lying across her lap. She traced the bulging veins on his huge hand.

Dolly promised to take care of her discarded wedding dress. "You two deserve to be happy," Dolly said through good-bye tears. "Don't hang on too tight to each other."

That's all Gina wanted to do. Climb up in Tom's lap and hold on for dear life. "I can't relax," she whispered in his ear.

His boutonnière smelled as sweet as her bouquet had.

Tom rubbed her knees. "Maybe you can sleep on the plane."

Gina couldn't imagine sleeping, not with this exciting man caressing her. "My husband," she said.

"And don't you forget it." He laughed.

Gina tried to see into the future. Their home in Geneva would swarm with children, theirs and neighborhood kids. Lonely would be an unused word in her world. She wanted more than one child. She didn't want any of her children to feel as alone as she had. Friends were fine, but where were friends on the holidays, or when bad things happened?

Family really showed up when life got too real. Then she thought of her mother's friends and their constant loyalty. Not that she would think of discounting their deeds, but her children would have each other. Maybe, ten brothers and sisters would be enough.

* * *

After Tom gave their luggage to curbside check-in, he accompanied Gina to the first class waiting room. He couldn't fill his mind with enough awareness of her. This poised beautiful, gutsy woman was his wife. The wind had disarranged the careful curls peeking out from under the cap of pearls and satin flowers that her veil had cascaded from. Her blue eyes matched the silk sleeveless jacket she wore. Her white wool slacks accented her flat stomach and slim hips. She wore the blue boots she had on the first day they'd met. The memory of the robbery and murder needed a deep pocket for today; this was their day of celebration.

"Did you race cars on Maui?" Tom asked to disengage his negative thought pattern.

"No, but the roads would be ideal." Gina pulled on her bangs, as if aware he had stared at her hair. "The brochure says bicycles are the best way to travel up to the crater."

"Are you blushing?"

"I think I am." She laughed. "I was just wondering about not being able to bicycle in bed."

"There's my angel." Tom pulled her to him for another kiss. "We can't stay in bed for seven days."

Other passengers in the lounge were smiling at them. Tom nodded at their approval before telling Gina, "Danny said he was too shy to tell you, but he hopes you'll be a happy wife."

"He looked stupendous."

"Very handsome for a young man," Tom admitted.

"He was getting a lot of attention from the girls at the reception."

"They were lining up to dance with him. I cautioned him to wait until his degree is accomplished to pursue a particular woman."

"Good advice." Gina giggled. "Do you think he'll wait?"

"No," Tom laughed, "but it was good advice."

On the plane Tom settled into his seat as if he were becoming comfortable with his happy future. "No guarantees," he said out loud without realizing it.

"Sure there are," Gina answered his doubt.

"Life holds a lot of curve balls." He was thinking about his twin, about Gina's mother, about the miracle of this woman loving him. Tom squeezed her hand.

"There is integrity." Gina met his gaze.

"Yes," he agreed. "And love."

"Is it possible love is all there is of God?"

"I don't know anything." Tom struggled with all the verbiage in his head about gods and his personal Higher Power. "A willingness to reach for our highest aspirations, to follow God's will, seems the only fit thing to do."

"Is doing as important as being?" Gina sipped at the coffee the flight attendant had provided.

"I think the word love is a verb." He said, watching her throat as she swallowed. "I want to spend my life doing for you." Tom's mouth watered as he thought of kissing her neck.

"When you're not serving as a probation officer?" Gina elbowed him gently.

"Even when you're pregnant with twins," Tom laughed.

Gina held her arms out in front of her to simulate a large pregnancy. "Oh, twins is it?"

Twins, he thought. Tom was sure his state job as a probation officer would have good medical benefits, but college for twins. He glanced at the side of Gina's still smiling face. She'd want more than two. The rooms in the Geneva house appeared before him, bedrooms and bedrooms to fill with their babies, not counting that mammoth attic bedroom, which they would keep for themselves.

Put a computer up there. Maybe a cash register? Money, he was starting to worry about the money already. *God's will be done,* he prayed as willingly as he could. Well he could go back to school while Gina was pregnant. A law degree and his court connections might promise a higher paying job. Nothing to think about now. Now all he had to do was enjoy his new bride.

* * *

Hawaii, December 15th

The landing on the Big Island and transfer to the shuttle plane proved uneventful. The small islands bravely danced in an unending blue ocean.

"Where to?" Tom asked as he headed their rental car out of the Kapalua airport on Maui.

"Our hotel in Kahalui is to the left," Gina adjusted her sunglasses. "Let's go around the island once." Her insides were shuddering.

"Putting off the inevitable?" Tom kidded.

Gina smirked. "I thought at least we could say we saw the entire island."

"Good idea," he said consulting the map. "We can lunch halfway to the hotel, at Hana."

"The guide book says Hana has a beautiful view of Hawaii." She watched his soothing profile as he centered his attention on the ocean, as if trying to permanently imprint the sight.

"Next stop, Lahaina." Tom said, then added, "When I'm facing the concrete blocks in my office in Geneva, I wonder if I'll remember any of this."

Gina touched his thigh. "I promise you'll remember some of it."

"Maybe you should drive." He grabbed her knee.

"You keep both hands on the wheel." Gina slapped his hand away and consulted her guide book. "When this road becomes Office Road, there's a little turnout with a view."

"We'll never get to Hana in time for lunch if we keep stopping at every few feet."

"Here, here," Gina coaxed him to turn into a small parking lot.

The wind whipped at their clothes as they walked toward the shoreline. A slight drizzle accompanied the wind blowing up from the ocean. "These are called Dragon's Teeth," she said.

"The salt spray must bleach the lava here." Then Tom pointed to the west. "Look how calm the bay is."

Gina continued to read the guide with her back to the wind. "This lawn holds the remains of nearly 900 Hawaiians. More!"

Tom looked at the unmarked lawn. "How do they know?"

"A Hilton Hotel tried to dig them up to build here, but the natives fought the excavation of the graves."

"Sacred ground," Tom said as they quietly resumed their drive.

The church interior of St. Patrick's came to mind. Gina counted the hours involved in writing thank you notes to everyone for their gifts. Personal comments would have to accompany most of them. Menasha's gifts were the flowers for the wedding and reception, and the stretch limo. She'd have to specifically give him effusive credit for the Baker Hotel dance hall. The roses draping the balcony which encircled the room reminded her of his weaving yellow roses around her mother's morphine drip stand the last time they had had a dinner party.

"Mother kissed my cheek at the wedding," Gina remembered.

Tom didn't reply immediately. "Belief in ghosts is beyond my ability to suspend disbelief."

Gina raised her blue eyes from the book to shine them on Tom's resolve. "We have to stop at Black Rock. That's where the souls 'uhane' leave the earth."

"Souls I can handle," Tom said, "but ghosts. . .."

"I didn't see Mother," Gina explained. "I just felt the kiss."

They walked over to the volcanic formation. Tom bent down to pick up a black stone from the sand as a keepsake.

"Don't do that," Gina said, knocking the pebble from his hand. "If souls don't have a family to receive them, they wait around here, even attach themselves to some of the rocks."

Tom tried *not* to show his negative appraisal of her statements. "Okay, okay. I don't feel inclined to test your theories."

"They're not mine," Gina tapped the book.

They held hands as they watched the backs of snorkelers move over the coral beneath the surface, before returning to the car.

"Do you swim?" they asked each other in unison. "No," they both answered and laughed.

"We're crazy to choose Maui if neither of us swims," Gina rested her head on his broad chest.

"No, we're not," Tom kissed her before she got in the car. "I love the water: seeing it, walking in it, sitting in it."

"An instructor once told me I can't relax enough to swim." Gina ruffled her curls.

"We probably both drowned in a previous life."

"You believe in reincarnation but not ghosts?"

"I was kidding," Tom rubbed his throat. "but I did nearly drown when I was two,"

Gina reached for his hand, taking it away from his throat. "I was four. When the water touches my neck if I can't plant my feet on something firm, I freeze up."

They turned to each other.

Tom said, "We're a pair."

"You could be the other half of my soul."

Gina chewed on the idea of a soul-mate on the drive to Lahaina: past the never-ending beach, past the steep cliffs protecting the interior of the island. Being half of another's soul was way too much responsibility for her. Mother said she needed to keep her hands off Tom's motivations to over-indulge; but the subject was hard to avoid within a marriage. "How are you different from other people who drink?"

Tom glanced her way, before maneuvering the car around a slow truck on the busy highway. "Other people can stop. I can't. Have you ever had a mixed drink?"

"Sure, I drink."

"Why do you waste the time with a mix? Alcoholics take it straight, all the way to drunk."

"You get drunk every time you have a drink?"

"No, sometimes I have a glass of wine and stop; then I have two glasses of wine a week, then three, then I decide to see how many it takes to get me drunk. Fewer all the time after I'm sober, more if I'm not for a very long time. I drink to get drunk, not to be sociable."

"Why?"

Tom knew the answers but not the core issues. "Actually I leave a lot of the answering to my Higher Power."

"Should I keep going to the Alanon Meetings?"

"You might want to, but that's not my business."

Gina touched his knee again, and he flinched. "Sorry. Bad subject. Mother told me to shut up about it."

"At the wedding?" Tom asked.

"No silly, after you went out with Menasha."

Tom nodded his head. "Bad time. The fumes of the alcohol seduced me."

"Wow," Gina said, determining never to bring up the subject again.

* * *

In Lahaina they only had time to marvel at the roots of the Banyan Tree and stand on the second floor porch of the old Plantation Hotel. Sky-surfers with colorful parachutes tied to speed boats swept by. A Navy submarine could be seen letting sailors disembark onto rubber rafts for shore leave. A group of women stood on the long pier, waiting or waving.

"I'm getting hungry," Gina complained.

Tom checked his watch. "Eleven. Do you still want to have lunch in Hana?"

"I do," she said.

"I've heard that before." Tom embraced her. "You were dressed all in white, like an angel. He kissed her to make sure the reality was Gina. "Recovery is a blessed thing."

"I'm thankful for it too," she said returning his kiss and affection.

In Hana they stopped for tentative wading in the Blue Pool. Tom didn't know which way to turn after he'd rolled up his pant legs and tucked his socks into his tennis shoes. He placed them as close as possible to Gina's blue sandals. The waterfall was behind them and the ocean in front, but the view of Gina bending over to wash her hands and wet her fly-away curls was far and away the best of either scene.

"I wish I had a postcard of you," he said, grabbing her by the waist and hauling her to shore. "Aren't you hungry yet? My stomach feels like someone cut off my head."

Gina kissed him, longer than his body could stand in polite company. "Nothing wrong with your head." she laughed.

The Hana Ranch Restaurant was listed as the worst place to eat in Hana, according to the guide book, so they opted for Tutu's Snack Shop's hot dogs and fries. "That wasn't very satisfying," Gina said. "I guess we're supposed to feast on the view."

"Can't beat this," Tom stretched his arm out to the expanse of sea and sky. The view of the big island gave texture to the perspective of endless ocean.

"I hope I can satisfy you sexually," Gina kept her chin down, paging through the endless guide book pictures.

Tom lifted her face to his, kissing her slightly greasy mouth. "Our love guarantees sexual gratification. Now you will know how it feels to be replenished." Tom kissed her, not hurrying even though the waiter came to take their plates away.

Gina said. "I like honeymoons."

"One," Tom laughed. "Maybe when were in our seventies, we'll have another."

* * *

Gina stepped away from the table on the deck surrounding the restaurant to hunt for the restroom. She had to walk to a nearby hotel and returned to the table to tell Tom she'd be gone for a minute. When she didn't find him at the table, she trudged off to the hotel, thinking he would be on his way too, but she never saw him on the path.

As it turned out the Snack Shop was only open for lunch. The chairs were stacked on the tables by the time she had returned. No Tom. She banged on the restaurant's door, but no one answered. She waited at the car for half an hour. When he didn't return, she increased her worry by walking up and down the beach with the car in view, waiting.

When she decided to find a police station, Tom turned the corner of the restaurant.

When he spied her, he took off running toward her, stopping an inch from her feet. "Where have you been!" he yelled at her.

Gina burst out crying from relief. She pushed him away angry that he would raise his voice.

Tom dropped to his knees, encircling her waist with his arms, holding on as Gina wept. Finally she started to stroke his hair. "I thought I'd lost you," she said.

"Where were you?"

"I used the restroom at the hotel and then I waited by the car." She sniffed. "Where were you?"

"I didn't ask the waiter where you'd gone, but I visited the gas station down the road, thinking that's where you'd be."

"Where were you for the last half-hour?"

"In front of the restaurant, waiting for you." Tom got up and brushed the sand off his knees.

"Next time, we'll wait in the car, okay?"

"Good idea." Tom hugged her to him. "My mind went blank when I tried to remember what you were wearing." He checked out her blue sleeveless blouse and white slacks. "I could have told them you were wearing blue shoes."

"I love you, you nut." Gina said.

They continued their trip to the Kalahui hotel in silence. Each was sobered by the recent stress and their reunion.

"If God is love," Gina finally spoke, thinking of the unhelpful waiter, "why does he love all of us?"

"I think he was alone and created us to fill the void." Tom re-focused on the ocean. "Alone isn't bad, but it's hard if there is no one to share beauty and joy with."

Gina knew her love would outlast both of them.

* * *

Tom could feel the tension falling from his shoulders when he walked up to the Maui Beach Hotel. The grounds were impeccable. No trash or dead flowers were in evidence. The hotel designers, management and staff did everything right. The lobby and rooms were immaculate. Gina picked up a half-inch rubber duck sitting on a stack of wash cloths. "Tom, they've thought of everything."

Room service knocked and asked if they needed anything. Tom asked for more packets of coffee and was handed them while the door was still open. A list of free services included daily aerobics, yoga classes, a business center with free internet use, scuba lessons, and free cabana chairs. "Menasha said your mother picked this place out for us," Tom sat on the king size bed.

"She was set on my marrying you."

"Smart dame, your mother."

"Well, you have to give me credit." Gina plopped on top of him. "I agreed with her."

"Smart lady," he said, unbuttoning her blouse.

CHAPTER SEVENTEEN

Saturday, December 22nd

At O'Hare airport Dolly Woods moved her van for the fourth time as she waited for the newly married couple to arrive from Maui. Horns continued to blare as impatient drivers jockeyed for temporary spaces. Dolly strained to catch a glimpse of Gina or Tom. The windshield wipers couldn't keep up with the downpour. The defroster wasn't much help clearing the inside of the windows either.

Jeffrey and Timothy had agreed an afternoon spent with their grandfather's horses would be more fun than meeting their uncle and new aunt, Gina Woods, in the rain.

Dolly marveled her half-sister and she would finally share the same last name, temporarily. Because, Sergeant Steve Muller insisted on Valentine's Day Dolly's name would change to his.

She wasn't ready to embark on a new life of marriage. Steve was a fine, gentle man but marriage with the boys' father hadn't enamored her of the marital state. Besides her boys needed time to adjust. Her brother-in-law deserved to enjoy his new wife, before Dolly could summon the necessary courage to approach him with the news. Dolly had agreed to marry Steve. Was she being fair to him if she wasn't sure she loved him?

Dolly tapped the automatic window button and caught a glimpse of a tall man bending to lift shoulder bags from his wife. Her throat clutched as she realized her first reaction was to wonder who her husband was helping. Even in death Jonas's image entrenched itself in her heart, brain and body.

That would be Tom, she reminded herself, beeping her horn before climbing out of the van's door and waving like crazy. "Gina, over here."

Gina stopped in her tracks. Tom had to catch her back. She acted as if she was going to faint as she turned in Dolly's direction. Then she was all smiles.

As they packed the suitcases into the van, Gina explained, "Only my mother ever called me Gina."

"Oh," Dolly dropped a suitcase and hugged her sister. "I'm sorry. Did I upset you?"

"I was just surprised," Gina said.

"She's been thinking of her mother most of the trip." Tom said. "Did you know your half-sister believes in ghosts?"

"Do not."

"Do too."

"Well," Dolly laughed. "I can see married life has matured both of you."

* * *

Gina sat in the back of the van, giving Tom the passenger seat next to Dolly. "You've been up to something while we were gone."

Dolly braked too hard at the toll booth. "Sorry." She turned around to glare at Gina. "What makes you say that?"

"Your voice has gone up an octave," Gina smiled at her and winked, "since I first met you."

The three of them were probably thinking the same thought, Jonas's murder.

Gina wished she'd kept her mouth shut. "Sorry," Gina said. "What are the boys up to today?"

Dolly seemed relieved at the change of subject as they got on 64 for the drive home. "Horses. They're both in love with riding horses right now, when my dad lets them."

"How's the house in Geneva?' Tom asked.

"I'm still living out in Wayne. The newest thing is that Mother hired Florence to help with my boys. She says I need time away from them."

"Do you?" Gina asked.

"Mother says we ought not to live for children. It's better to share a full life with them." Dolly laughed nervously. "Mother's afraid I'll become an old maid."

"You're hardly an old maid." Tom was getting irritable,

Gina could tell by the spacing of his words.

Tom grumbled, "Jonas hasn't been gone for more than a month."

"Five," Gina said, then wished she could bite off her tongue.

"Mother expects you two for supper this evening," Dolly said. "The boys miss you, Tom. Menasha will be there."

"I'm supposed to get them together."

"Who?" Dolly and Tom asked.

"Menasha and Florence. Mother decided before she died that the two of them liked each other and shouldn't be living alone."

"No wonder he's been calling," Dolly laughed. "I thought he was concerned about you two."

Gina didn't tell Tom but she was glad to be home. They had hardly left the motel room for a week. Not that she didn't like making love with her beloved Tom; but enough was enough.

They hadn't seen anymore of Maui, except on the ride back to the airport. After every stint of love-making, Tom would sleep for hours. Gina was happy Dolly had packed Steve's present of "Swerve" and "The Nature of Things" in her suitcase. She skimmed "Swerve" finding the search for classical manuscripts fascinating. In Part III of "the Nature of Things," Gina marveled at how closely the Psalms followed the poet's line of thinking.

> "O Thou who first uplifted in such dark
> So clear a torch aloft, who first shed light
> Upon the profitable ends of man,
> O thee I follow, glory of the Greeks,
> And set my footsteps squarely planted now
> Even in the impress and the marks of thine—
> Less like on eager to dispute the palm,
> More as one craving out of very love
> That I may copy thee!"

Surely, Lucretius was thanking the Lord on high for all the magnificence of nature. She wondered how Muller could read the lines in error. Even the word 'swerve' was used as a synonym for miracles in the universe a world without the Lord to watch and know her seemed unthinkable. at least unlivable to her. Courage was one thing, but acknowledging the aloneness of chance for her existence went beyond her comfortable world.

Gina walked up the steps to her home, bringing her share of the bags. She unlocked the door to find Dolly had been busy. The foyer was lavished with Christmas garlands. When Gina turned on the lights in the living room, a mammoth tree in front of the windows burst into a flurry of blinking blue and white lights.

"Oh, Dolly," Gina said. "What a homecoming!"

"Monday night, we'll open presents in Wayne," Dolly said. "You have to be there. The boys wanted Tom and you to be ready for Christmas."

"They did a bang-up job," Tom said.

"Should I wait for you to freshen up to drive you out to Wayne?" Dolly asked.

Tom nearly pushed her out the door. "What time is dinner?"

"Seven."

"We'll be there in less than an hour, right, Gina?"

"Sure, sure." Gina kissed Dolly good-bye but wanted to put off going anywhere for maybe another week.

"I love this house," Tom said. "Can I make you a cup of coffee while you change?"

"Husband," Gina said. "You are exactly what I need in this old house."

"Get ready. I'd better stay down here or we won't be making our commitment to Lucille.

In their attic bedroom, Gina appreciated the familiar scent of cedar. She refused to unpack. Instead she slipped into her mother's old bedroom and ransacked her closet for something decent to wear to dinner. She found a black satin sleeveless dress with a scoop neck which fit like a glove. "Thanks, Mom," she said as she surveyed the result.

* * *

Tom turned to find Gina dressed for dinner in a revealing cocktail dress. "Wife," he said nonplused. "You're beautiful. Let me run up and put on a clean shirt and tie."

When they were well on their way and Tom's hands were glued to the steering wheel, he ventured, "Every time I think I have an image of you nailed to my heart, you slip into a different persona."

"Mother called me a changeling." Gina played with the hair on the back of his neck.

He shivered. "I have to drive."

"Right," she said, pulling a bit of satin and lace over her knees.

Tom had noticed and his body reacted without his leave to do so. "Maybe we could make it a short evening."

Gina shook her head. "Your nephews will have my hide if I drag you away from them."

He smiled at her. His life was getting fairly perfect.

* * *

Gina thought it odd that Lucille and Henry Stone had invited the Sergeant Muller, until she noticed Muller's attention to Dolly. Dolly's face was flushed. Gina shrugged her shoulders as if to ask what the problem was. Dolly nodded in Tom's direction. He was busy with Jeffrey and Timothy's differing renditions of riding with their grandfather.

"The horses know when you should duck for the tree limbs," Jeffrey stated.

"They don't either," Timothy argued. "They just don't want to hit their own heads."

"Horses are pretty smart." Tom made both boys feel he had agreed with them.

Menasha, her mother's old beau, sat next to Florence whose face was as red as Dolly's. When Menasha turned toward Gina, he placed Florence's hand in his lap. "Your mother told me Florence was a great girl."

Gina smiled as hard as she could at Florence, willing her to know everything was fine. "I'm sure she told Florence you were the best man she had ever known."

Florence's eyes widened. "I thought you would disapprove."

"Nonsense," Gina said. "I'm happy for you both."

* * *

Monday, Christmas Eve

Tom asked Mr. Stone, Henry, to speak with him in the den. The crowd in the living room had finished opening all the presents and were getting way too noisy to speak in confidence.

"What's the problem, son?"

Tom wanted to beat around the bush, but he couldn't think of a way not to come right out and say what was eating at him. "Do you approve of Dolly's interest in the policeman?"

Henry laughed, then he realized Tom's loyalty for his deceased brother was the problem.

"Jonas would not have wanted Dolly to live alone."

"She hasn't been a widow for three months."

"Nearly six, Tom. I thought we cleared this up when I asked you to become my trustee for the boys."

"I didn't know her marriage was in the offing."

"Not until Valentine's Day."

Tom sat down hard. "That soon."

"Pull yourself together and go out there and congratulate them. I will not have my only daughter made unhappy by the brother-in-law she loves as much as any member of her family. I will call your sponsor, if you are not on your feet in two seconds."

"Call my sponsor. Henry, I'm not a child."

"Then stop acting like one. Jonas would be rolling in his grave!"

Tom got to his feet. "Have you heard about this book he's been talking about that proves there is no God?"

"Nonsense. Dolly's business is not yours."

"He's making it my business. Gina's already read the book and thinks the author just misunderstood what he found."

Henry put his hand on Tom's shoulder. "Books with the exception of the Bible are not coming between any member of my family. Do you understand?"

Denial, Tom thought, but smiled and headed back to the scramble of people filling Lucille's living room.

Dolly sidled up to Tom. Henry gave him a final thump on the back. "I want you to love Steve as much as I do," Dolly whispered.

Tom smiled. There it was, a quandary. He didn't like the smaller man. Not only because he was taking Jonas's place with Dolly and the boys. He hadn't liked him the first time he heard Gina laughing with him. Maybe he better call his sponsor. Tom recognized his thinking was all wrong. The Lord certainly never excused hating anyone. "We certainly need to be friends in this small of a family."

Dolly smiled at Steve, who seemed to think the coast was clear.

He came right over to Tom and brought up the terrible book. "Have you read it yet?"

"Not yet, Steve." Tom smiled at him the way he thought his Savoir might want him to, "but I intend to."

"Been kind of busy on your honeymoon," Steve said.

Tom doubled up his fist, but he kept it behind his back. *Please, Lord,* he prayed, *don't let me forget myself and You.* "I understand congratulations are in order. Valentine's Day is the big day?"

Steve wove his arm around Dolly's waist. "I was hoping you would be my best man."

"He'd be glad to," Gina said, joining them.

Tom smiled down at her. "I love weddings."

* * *

Saturday, December 29th

After only half a week back on the job as a probation officer, Tom found himself in the basement of his new home in Geneva. He'd already started a pork roast for dinner. His hands itched for a piece of wood. Sawdust would wash off the seamy side of his job. He didn't want to think of the raped eleven-year-olds, or the unloved youngsters who now populated his world as grownup felons. Without love they had developed as rank weeds outside the fence of affection which should be the divine right of every child born to earth's greatness.

For an hour he listened to the table saw's whine as he cut a large plank of oak, left over from the shelf he made for Gina's mother. He planned a wall of bookshelves for their bedroom.

His wife's voice sounded as sweet as summer rain. "Coffee?" she asked, handing him a steaming cup.

"My life would be perfect," he said dusting off his hands and sipping the brew. "If there was no evil in the world."

"Hard day?"

"Not as hard as it is for some of my charges." He slipped his arm around her waist and kissed her willing mouth. "And you? How did those rambunctious teenagers take to your driving directions?"

"They're all angels." She rolled her eyes. "I'm having a ball. They think I'm quite the hot rod and listen to every word out of my mouth."

He loved to hear her laugh, washing every resentment out of his soul. "All this equipment." Tom swept his arms around the room. "I was wondering if the kids would find it as ameliorating as I do."

"Sawdust does have a clean fresh smell."

"I thought we might invite Danny to take a stab at building something?"

"He'd love it," Gina purred. "You are the best man I have ever met."

"That's good," Tom laughed. He could see the workshop filled with men and women, young and old, carefully building simple pieces of furniture. They might develop a pride in their accomplishments under his careful instruction. "We could keep quite a few cons busy here."

"Finally," Gina dusted the wood shavings from his hair. "A place to care for those who haven't shared the love we've been blessed with. Now hurry and wash up. Dolly and Steve will be here in an hour."

"Why are they coming over?"

"When you said you were making a roast, I thought there would be enough for four. What's the problem?"

Tom laughed. "He's too short."

Gina tipped her head, "Not as tall as Jonas?"

Tom whacked her bottom, then pulled her close. "Looks like I'll need to stay later tomorrow night, writing out a Fourth Step for Muller."

"Remember, Rev. Hale said couples who pray together have a one in five-hundred chance of divorce? When should we pray? We're too rushed in the morning."

Tom followed Gina up the basement steps, wishing they could be alone for the night. "We could pray before meals, except when we have Muller over. I can just see his face when I ask God to forgive my hatred for him."

"You don't hate him, do you?"

"Naw, he's too short to waste my emotions on." But Tom asked himself why he so disliked the poor guy.

CHAPTER EIGHTEEN

Maybe Muller would choke on the pork roast. Tom could only hope. *Showing your resentment a bit aren't you?* he asked himself. Tom smiled at Gina sitting on his right, then towards Dolly, who didn't notice his attempt at civility because she was fixated on Muller.

Tom's sponsor, Stan, would point out which of his many character faults was currently taking hold of his good sense. Tom tapped the table next to Dolly's plate to capture her attention. "Tell us a story about the boys."

Gina passed Muller more roasted vegetables to accompany his third helping of pork. "Steve, how do you get along with Timothy and Jeffery?" Gina asked him.

"Jeffery is such a serious little man," Muller said shaking his head. "I do wonder at times what he's thinking."

Probably about his dad, you short idiot! Tom thought, but could not say.

"Jonas always tickled Jeffery, telling him the *'judge'* needed to leave town." Dolly turned to Tom with a genuine smile. "You are such a great cook, Tom. Gina's so lucky."

"The peach chutney helps," he answered humbly. "But I think I must have salted the pork twice." At least he could report to Stan how he hadn't acted on his hostility toward Muller.

"Pork never gets salted properly," Muller said in nearly a teenager's twang. "I loved it."

But somehow Gina must have picked up a clue of Tom's growing rancor. "Tom, are you catching a cold?" she cautioned. "Your voice has dropped two octaves"

Tom reached for her smooth arm to calm himself. "Don't think so."

Gina cleared away their dishes and brought in a pot of coffee and a strawberry cream cake. "The Blue Goose bakery has the best cakes."

Dolly watched Tom too closely as he cut pieces for his guests. "Timothy says Steve spends more time with them than he does with me."

"They are great kids, Dolly." Tom hoped the air was cleared. His soul still raged against the substitution Dolly had so easily made for his brother. Sure, maybe Jonas wasn't the most empathetic person, but he was a hard worker, mainly because he never accumulated enough money to spend at the rate he wanted.

When they left, Tom thought he was safe enough to sigh as he loaded the dishwasher.

"What is it? Are you not feeling well?"

"Just insane." Tom dried his hands before bringing her sweet smelling body closer to his. He placed one hand behind her head and one under her chin. "You married a crazy person."

Gina's warm kiss proved she wasn't deterred. "Muller isn't Jonas."

"Not by half-a-foot!" Tom laughed and Gina joined in.

"But, you know, Tom, he loves Dolly. We couldn't ask for a more honest or devoted husband for her."

Tom put on his jacket at the back door to haul out the smelly garbage and move the plastic bins to the road.

Lord, he prayed. *Help clear my soul of these useless hatreds.*

* * *

Dolly had warned Steve Muller about the possibility of Tom's jealousy. He'd shrugged the information off, as if the emotional mine field he was about to enter was beneath his notice. "Don't tell him about taking the boys to Disney World when we get back from our honeymoon."

"Do you think his feelings are hurt because I asked Jerry Hoffman to be my best man?"

Dolly couldn't share the relief his choice had brought. "Maybe." Why she wasn't completely honest with the man she was going to marry in less than two months? "I know he thinks his nephews are the only family he has left."

"What's Gina, chopped liver?"

Of course, he made her laugh. Life was going to be sweet with laughter ringing through the new house they were building in Walden Hills just west of Randall Road. The boys would have separate rooms with their own full baths. Their new set of grandparents couldn't be any warmer to the boys. If only Tom could get his act together and not worry them about their only uncle.

Gina met them at the door. "Ah here they are, my favorite couple."

"Blue becomes you," Steve said, helping Dolly off with her coat.

"And, Dolly," Gina said, "Red makes you look like Marilyn Monroe."

"Oh, I hope not." Dolly could feel a blush rise to the roots of her blonde hair.

Tom turned his frown into something resembling a welcome. "Hope you're both hungry."

Gina had taken the evergreen garlands down from the stairwell, but the Christmas tree was still cheerfully winking at them. Dolly had trouble letting go of Gina's embrace. They had both suffered major losses. "The Lord's been good to us, Gina. Tom's right, I like the smell cedar in your clothing, too."

"We've both been given someone to love," Gina said.

Dolly wished she had told Tom at some point how unhappy Jonas had made her at times. Of course she loved Jonas; but all the money-grubbing thirst of his quite dampened her initial attraction to his height and youthful beauty. He never listened to her hints about wanting him more than any amount of money. Jonas never believed she loved him for himself. And now his pig-headed brother would just as soon she stayed a withered up old maid than be happy with the gentle lover she'd been lucky enough to find. Of course it was soon after Jonas's death, but somehow she thought even Jonas would understand. Why not Tom?

When he asked her to tell him about the boys, she winked at Steve to clue him into Tom's favorite subject. Gina's question about how well Steve got along with the boys should have alerted him further. After Steve mentioned how serious Jeffery's personality was, she thought Tom was going to jump off his chair.

He did calm down somewhat when she complimented his cooking skills. Then Steve followed her lead and mentioned how much he enjoyed dinner, but Tom, of course, took umbrage.

Her dear sister, Gina noticed and called Tom to task for his rudeness. And Tom did apologize when he was cutting the cake by saying Jeffery and Timothy were great kids. Nevertheless, Dolly asked the Lord to intercede, *Lord, my boys need the men in the family to get along.*

Before they left Dolly invited Gina and Tom to join them for New Year's Eve. "We're all dressing to the nines."

"I haven't returned my wedding tuxedo," Tom said. "Will that do?"

Dolly and Steve laughed together. "Wonderful," they said in unison.

Steve didn't start the car right away. "Give me a hug, Dolly. You were right Tom's still grieving for his brother and our marriage is a problem for him. He sent me the evil eye more than once."

"You don't believe superstitious rot, do you?"

"Not yet." Steve patted the dashboard of his Honda as if he were encouraging a faithful steed.

* * *

Gina shut the lights out in the kitchen, before Tom returned. She didn't want him to see how angry she was. After Tom stumbled in and hung up his coat in the dark, she startled him. "Dolly is my only family, besides you."

Tom reached for her but she stepped away. "I thought I acted all right."

"No. You didn't."

He sighed and walked past her into the living room, where the Christmas tree still held its twinkling promise of eternal love. "I'm sorry. You know I can't stand the little creep."

"You don't sound like you're in recovery."

"And you don't sound like you've even heard of Alanon. Come and sit down," his low voice lulled her into his ken.

"We're a mess and we haven't been married a month."

"Let's kneel down and ask the Lord for help." Tom knelt down first.

They knelt with their backs to the tree, their folded hands on the cushions of the couch. Each waited for the other to start.

"Lord," Gina began reaching for Tom's hand. "We're lost and don't even know how to voice our prayer, but our hearts are not at peace."

"Make me a channel of your peace," Tom began. "Where there is self-hatred, let me sow seeds of love. Where there is wrong, let me extend the spirit of forgiveness. Where there is sadness and fear let me bring joy and trust. Where there is darkness let me bring light. Where there is conflict let me bring harmony. Where there is despair let me bring hope. Where there is doubt let me bring faith. Where there is error let me bring truth. Lord, grant that I may seek to comfort rather than to be comforted, to understand rather than be understood, to love rather than to be loved, for it is by giving that we receive, by forgiving that we are forgiven, and that by self-forgetting that we find, and by dying we awaken to eternal life."

Gina moved to sit on the couch. "What were we arguing about?"

"I acted like a fool the night our first guests arrived for dinner."

"And I don't understand why?"

Tom laughed. "I think it could be Muller is too short for me. I want Dolly to marry a man as tall as Jonas."

"Well that's ridiculous."

"I know. Isn't that great?"

* * *

Sunday, December 30th

In a St. Patrick's pew, Tom bowed his head when the eight o'clock bells began to ring. "Please, Lord, keep me near your heart. Forgive my hatefulness and restore my soul to sanity."

Gina's head was bowed too. What she was praying for? Stan would have said it was none of his business. She was beautiful in a blue long coat and a rimmed felt hat that matched the collar of the coat and her gloves. He thanked the Lord for his good fortune, even for Danny's foresight in first tying them together.

Gina brought her own prayer book from home. Post-it flags stuck out of the top and sides of the book and she easily turned to relevant pages to follow the service.

Tom tried to listen to the Collect of the Day, but he missed several words. When the page number for the Psalms was announced, he read aloud with the rest of the handful of parishioners. The ten o'clock service with songs and organ music was too late for Gina's noon Alanon meeting. They listened to the readings from the Bible and stood facing the black, female priest as she read from the Gospels. Tom tried to listen to the sermon but his mind was whirling with unresolved issues: Muller's marriage to Dolly, how Timothy and Jeffery might fare under a *new* father, when he should start his own family, should he ask Gina about Danny's future. His mind went around and around as if he were dreaming a familiar lost scenario, where the roads had no names and ice threatened every bridge.

Gina nudged him. The sermon was over and they read the Nicene Creed together. The Prayers of the People seemed never ending, but Tom threw in a request for his nephews and his marriage…and prayed for Jonas to find the light of eternal salvation in the great beyond.

During the Peace ritual, Tom hugged Gina, who pushed him gently away to greet the other churchgoers.

Communion always touched Tom. All over the world, people were remembering the Lord and celebrating his great sacrifice for the redemption of people on earth. Surely, the Lord heard their thanksgiving praise. The Lord's Prayer reminded Tom he would need to ask Stan for extra time in the evening to help him come to terms with his Fourth Step for Steve Muller. And he needed to forgive Dolly for even liking the man.

* * *

Dolly greeted Gina as she arrived in the basement of the Methodist Church. "Over here. We're already started."

"We went to mass," Gina whispered. "Tom is sorry he acted so badly."

Dolly only nodded, because David was reading a lesson from <u>Hope for Today</u>: "I like how Step Three begins. It states, 'Made a decision…,' This means I have an active choice to turn my will and my life over to a Higher Power. No one is going to force me. No one is going to make me do anything. My recovery is my choice. What I choose to do with my will and my life is my decision, and today I choose to turn it over to the God of my understanding."

"What a relief it is to finally make that decision and to realize that I don't have to do or fix everything. I have begun to learn what is and isn't my responsibility. I feel lighter knowing that my Higher Power is with me twenty-four hours a day to help me with my life and its challenges. From the smallest decision to the largest, I pray, 'God, what would you have me say and do today?'"

"This process of turning my will and life over to God sounds so simple, yet it certainly didn't happen at my first meeting! Actually, it didn't happen for a long time. I had to build a foundation for my Step Three decision, first by diligently working Steps One and Two. Taking Step Three was a natural outgrowth of that groundwork."

"Along the lines of 'Progress Not Perfection,' my relationship with my Higher Power evolves day-to-day, one day at a time. What a gift I have been given! Turning my will and my life over to a Power greater than myself provides me with a bottomless well of love, peace and serenity, if I choose to drink from it."

Gina could feel herself blushing. When she first awoke a rebellious thought presented itself, 'Why can't I have it my way?' She couldn't even get through the first month of marriage without fighting with her husband.

David looked her way. "Did you want to share?"

"Not yet," she managed, hastily wiping away a tear. "Marriage is not a perfect state of being."

The other women laughed with her.

Dolly said, "Don't tell me that. You know my marriage is coming up in two weeks."

Helen looked from Dolly to Gina. "Why didn't you have a double ring ceremony? Sisters often do."

"Our husbands," Gina and Dolly said together and then laughed as if the fact was not a painful one.

* * *

Tom drove out to Wayne to pick up Timothy and Jeffery. They were waiting at the front door with their coats on. Tom asked Lucille, "Am I that late?"

She patted his back. "They really like spending time with you, Tom."

On the way back to Gina's house, his home, Tom didn't really listen to the boys' chatter. He was rehearsing how he might bring up Muller without specifically asking how they felt about their mother's new husband to be.

Timothy talked more than Jeffery. "Boy, we're going to be ring-bearers again. We'll wear those white suits we wore at your wedding."

"Do you see your best man very often?" Jeffery asked.

"Danny's lives in a home in Elmhurst for young men on parole," Tom explained.

"What's parole?" Timothy asked.

"He was involved in the bank robbery."

Both boys quieted down with the memory of their father dying in the bank robbery.

"He didn't have the gun," Tom explained to himself why he'd allowed the felon to be the male witness for his marriage.

"Couldn't Steve have been your best man?" Jeffery asked.

"I don't know Muller very well."

"Who is Muller?" Timothy asked.

"When Mom marries Steve she'll be Mrs. Steve Muller."

"Not our mother?" Timothy voice sounded shrill.

"Of course, Dolly will always be your mother, Timothy. Just like I'll always be your favorite uncle."

"We only have one uncle," Timothy said from the backseat. "And you don't want us to call you Uncle Tom. Can we still call Mom, Mom?"

In the rear view mirror, Tom watched Jeffery slug Timothy's arm. "Don't be a baby. We only have one Mom."

After a decent interval, Timothy said, "I like Steve."

"You like everybody," Jeffery patted the shoulder he had struck.

"And you?" Tom said, not being able to say Muller's name again.

"He's so short," Jeffery said. "Will he grow soon?"

Tom laughed. "No. That's it. Your father and I are taller than some men. You'll stop growing when you're about twenty-one." Tom wondered if the boys would notice he'd mentioned Jonas as if he were still alive.

"Steve likes to throw footballs even in the snow." Timothy said as his evaluation of the man's worth.

"Mom smiles more when Steve's around," Jeffery said. "I like to see her happy."

"Me, too." Tom added just in case his interrogation had shown resentment of the man to marry his brother's widow. "Would you like to see my basement workshop?"

Before Tom persuaded the boys to go downstairs, they spent a considerable amount of time with Sweets, who hadn't yet been fed. Tom finally picked up the kitten and the boys followed them down into wood-working shop.

"Wow," Jeffery said. "This is grand."

Timothy remained half-way down the steps. "Grandpa says he married Grandma because she was rich. Is this why you married Mom's sister?"

Tom barely had time to appreciate the smell of clean lumber before going over to the six-year-old boy and lifting him to the floor. "Your grandpa doesn't like to talk much about your grandma, but I know his heart skips every time he sees her walk into a room."

"Love does that," Jeffery explained to his younger brother. "Remember. Steve said his heart goes all a flutter when he sees Mom."

They all heard Dolly and Gina open the back door.

"Mom's here!" Timothy ran up the back stairs.

Dolly's woolen scarf was wrapped around one eye, because Timothy's hug hadn't waited for her to finish taking off her coat. "I love you," Timothy said still gripping her shoulders.

"I love you, too, honey."

Timothy finally let go. He turned to his brother. "You're right my heart is beating faster."

Dolly shook her head knowingly at Tom. "Men talk?"

"Sort of," Tom hugged Gina. "How was your meeting?"

"Helen asked Dolly why we, sisters, hadn't had a double-ring ceremony."

Right back to Muller, Tom's insane brain prompted. He took refuge from Gina's probing eyes by hugging Dolly. "The boys like Steve."

"Who wouldn't?" Timothy asked.

* * *

As Tom drove his Escort to the AA meeting at Mrs. Burns' home, he wondered if his natural dislike of Muller could drive him to drink. Stan would help.

Norma was never going to stop talking. Tom concentrated on the purple lace ringing the collar of her sweater, hoping he looked interested. Jan complained she should have attended Alanon in the morning, but was too busy fighting with her hung-over husband.

Connie's face was rigid. "I'm Connie. They are making such a fuss over that singer's suicide and they don't even mention she was a prescription-drug addict."

Jimmy and Todd sat side by side. Jimmy said, "We just want to remember her voice."

Todd said, "Jimmy's right. My name is Todd by the way. I know we're not supposed to cross talk, but I agree with Connie, too. Young people are going to think they need to take drugs to be successful."

Connie shook her head. "My addiction is probably coloring my view of the situation. But the media does seem to glorify drug addiction."

June and Judy seemed to understand Norma had used up a lot of time talking about the loss she felt when her dog died and passed when it was their turn to speak.

Ron said, "My name is Ron. I'm so glad to see you boys return. I prayed for you both. And with that I'll pass."

Tom looked at Stan. "My name is Tom. I'm dealing with a crazy resentment against the man who is marrying my brother's widow. I know it doesn't make any sense. I don't want her to be unhappy for a specific number of days, but I don't want her to forget Jonas either. And the man is shorter than my brother."

Stan laughed and the rest of the group joined him, finally Tom recognized how laughable his thoughts were, got the program and entered into the merriment, much relieved.

CHAPTER NINETEEN

New Year's Eve

"Lord, keep me sane," Tom prayed as he straightened his tuxedo's bow tie. Muller would be at the Stone's party and he wanted to be gracious in front of his nephews…and Gina…and his Lord.

Gina turned her back to him. "Zip please and careful the silk doesn't get caught in the zipper.

Her sleek coppery-red gown clung to her elegant curves. Fastened at the neck, the halter top of the gown left her sleek back bare to the waist.

"Will you be warm enough," he asked, not really willing to share all of her beauty with the crowd at the Stone's. To answer she wrapped a stole the same color of the gown around her shoulders and held out an end for him to touch. He was surprised because its shimmering material was woolen. "You are beautiful."

Gina stood on her tiptoes to kiss him. "We're not really late, but the roads might be icy."

When they arrived at the dinner hour all the lights in the Stone house blazed. Old-fashioned oil beacon lamps swathed in evergreen garlands marked every three feet of the driveway up the long hill to the mansion.

The valets, butler, and servers, male and female, wore festive uniforms of blue and white trimmed with gold.

At least fifteen Christmas trees, each with its own toy theme circled the walls of the brightly lit main hall. Teddy bears, trains, dolls, tops, miniature houses, lighthouses, boats, musical instruments: harps, violins, drums, and horns; sports equipment: baseball, soccer, football, and tennis were dedicated to separate trees.

The staircase posts sparkled with white blinking lights. The fireplaces in the main hall, ball room, side sitting rooms, and the dining room were lit and their mantles trimmed with enough holiday paraphernalia to tempt Santa Clauses from the surrounding five counties to scorch their bottoms.

Tom escorted Mrs. Stone into the sumptuous dining room.

Unopened Christmas boxes were set on each quest's chair. Tom counted eighteen places around the table which was lavishly dressed with spilling cornucopias of fruits and nuts and crystal candelabras complete with all candles flaming.

"We're having an open house for our friends and neighbors tomorrow," Lucille explained. "Henry wanted Steve to be comfortable in our home before their wedding."

"I understand," Tom said. Part of his soul rebelled, but he smiled as sincerely as he could. Lucille's daughter, Dolly, deserved every happiness, which held priority over his own wishes for this one evening.

But Muller attempted to ruin Tom's best intentions. Walking Dolly to her seat on the other side of the table, he called across to Tom, "What did you and Gina think of the book we gave you?"

Gina waved her hand, fingers spread as if to stop the conversation. "I've read it but Tom hasn't had time."

Tom said, "The one on the bathtub? I read 'Swerve' when I couldn't sleep. Intellectually interesting, but the author doesn't reflect my beliefs."

Danny Bianco was seated between Tom and Gina. Across from them Muller and Dolly were separated by Jeffery and Timothy's chairs. Dolly's dress was a lace and blue velvet creation as long as Gina's.

Muller kept bringing up the atheist's subject of his book. "Wasn't the poetry of 'On the Nature of Things' clever?"

Tom agreed. 'He used his genius to slide his belief of an uncaring Creator right into the reader's heart."

Mr. and Mrs. Stone sat at opposite ends of the table with Menasha and Florence at each side of Mrs. Stone. Judge Wilcox and Harvey Slemmons were at Mr. Stone's end. Taking up the spaces between, Tom recognized Dr. Pheiffer, Danny's therapist. Jerry Hoffman sat next to her. The prosecutors, Steffen Novak and Ms. Krisch, were also in attendance on Tom's side of the table.

We could reconvene the trial. Tom's stomach growled, resisting his impulse to vacate the premise.

Mr. Stone raised his hand to contribute to Muller's touchy subject. "Friend of mine said she was reading, I think Bradshaw. Was that it, Mother?"

At the other extremity of the table, Lucille said, "Sorry, dear. I remember the conversation with Lydia, but not the author she referenced."

"All right, well anyway, the idea was the important thing," Henry Stone continued. "Seems this author whoever he or she was proposed between the atoms where we all know a void exists. Right, Jeffery?"

Jeffery nodded seriously. Tom's heart went out to the lad. Jonas would have been so proud of his oldest's handling of his grief.

Timothy interjected, "This is like a tennis match on TV, only with words."

Jeffery elbowed him.

Stone was still speaking, "In this limitless space between any two atoms, there is a consciousness."

"Who cares for each and every one of us," Gina said.

Muller cocked his head as if prepared with a ready dispute from the book on the tip of his tongue.

But Danny jumped the gun. "I'll vote for Him," he said. "How could a Creator not wonder what we're all up to."

Dolly smiled her beautiful smile, close to sister Gina's rendition of happiness. "Faith is always a precious gift, not one won by reason."

Tom relaxed. At least the boys would have a decent upbringing even if their stepdad harbored serious doubts about the Lord. Suddenly, Tom felt pity for his designated enemy. How sad not to experience the Lord's affection. "The poetry was superb, Steve."

Steve looked at Dolly as if to communicate the fact, Tom did not hate him for joining the family.

Thank you, Lord, Tom prayed. *for answering my fears for the boys and Dolly'* He was now content to let God, and let go of his adverse opinions toward another of the Lord's creatures.

Dolly blew him a kiss from across the table.

Next to Tom, Reverend Lorna Hale rose to give the blessing, "Lord, thank you for our friends and neighbors company this festive evening, bless this food in remembrance of our recently lost companions."

* * *

Mr. Stone's voice boomed down the table. "Danny, I understand you would like to work for us?"

Danny's eyes blinked. He relaxed as if ready to nod off as the guests directed their attention in his direction. Under the tablecloth, Gina tapped the boy's knee, before answering for him. "What have you offered Danny in way of salary?"

The guests laughed and Danny regained his composure, smiling in thanks to Gina, before saying, "I'd be willing to work for room and board, Sir."

"Never manage your college expenses with that attitude, son. I think a stable manager could pull down a salary of $35,000 a year."

"Here, here," the crowd applauded.

Tom thumped Danny on the back and grinned at Gina. "We expect a great deal from you."

Danny's voice shook with emotion. "If my mother hadn't taught me as a child that the Lord loved me, I would be convinced by the blessings he's bestowed upon me in the last six months. My future is brighter than Mother ever hoped. Today I can count more friends than I've known all the years of my life."

The resulting silence was broken by Timothy, who threw a cherry tomato across the table at Danny. "Don't forget my horse is Flicka, the white mare."

Steve frowned at the youngster and Gina noted Tom fisted his hand resting on the tablecloth.

Dolly had noticed Tom's frown too. "Timothy, who declared a food fight?"

"Oh, Mom," Timothy smiled up at his mother. "Everybody was so grumpy, I wanted to cheer them up."

"And a good job you did there, son," Mr. Stone said. He motioned to the waiters, "More libation, gentlemen."

One of the servers filled Tom's water glass. Obviously the servants had been warned not to serve alcohol to one of the guests. However, Gina relaxed when she saw Tom had turned his wine glass upside down alerting the crew to his preference.

Across the table, Dolly's nerves seemed to require a constant refill.

* * *

After dinner, Dolly shooed her boys upstairs and hastily tucked them in.

Jeffery held onto her hand. "Mom, what's wrong?"

Ever conscious of her moods, she knew the boy wouldn't rest until she'd answered. She sat down on his bed to think.

Then Timothy sat back up in the twin bed opposite. "You drank eight classes of red wine."

"I did not." Dolly laughed. "Did I really?"

Jeffery nodded. "We counted."

"Well I'll go down and drink some coffee right now. I guess I was nervous because Steve was here."

"Because you love him?" Jeffery asked.

Dolly sat quietly. "No," she said. "I can't explain."

"Yes you can," Timothy demanded. "but you won't."

"I try to be truthful with you and myself," Dolly said. "But sometimes being honest creates conflict that can be avoided by silence."

"I understand," Jeffery said as he burrowed under the covers.

"Not me," Timothy said, still sitting up.

Dolly switched beds. "Well, how would you feel if we pray together about it?"

"I like your prayers," Timothy said. "They make me sleepy."

He laid back down and Dolly recited the 23rd Psalm, "The Lord is my shepherd. I shall not want. He maketh me to lie down in green pastures, He leadeth me beside the still water. He restoreth my soul. He leadeth me in paths of righteousness for His name's sake. Yea, though I walk through the valley of death I shall fear no evil, for Thou art with me. Thy rod and Thy staff they comfort me. Though preparest a table before mine enemies. You anointist my head with oil. My cup runneth over. Surely goodness and mercy will follow me all the days of my life and I will dwell in the house of the Lord for ever and ever."

Timothy was right. He was fast asleep. Dolly stood up too quickly and realized the boys were correct, too. She'd had much too much alcohol to drink. *Coffee*, she counseled herself. *Find a cup of coffee, if not a pot.*

Dolly held onto the familiar stair railing in her mother's house. How soon would it be before Steve's new home, her new home would be finished? As she reached the bottom step, she fairly stumbled off the last step, grabbing at a familiar shoulder.

"Jonas," she said, before realizing Tom's shoulder had steadied her.

* * *

Gina helped Dolly into the kitchen. "I think coffee is a great idea."

Dolly's face was red with embarrassment. "Did Steve hear me?"

"Just Tom," Gina said.

Waiters and servers were pushing around them, carrying trays of dessert and after-dinner drinks.

The Stone's cook, Mrs. Mac, brought over a mug of coffee. "Come sit in my room," she said. "We're in the way here."

Gina followed Dolly into a small bedroom off the main kitchen. Mrs. Mac excused herself and retired to a small attached bathroom. When she came out, she pressed a warm cloth to Dolly's forehead and wrists. "You never eat when the house is full of people. Did you drink too much?"

"Jeffery and Timothy said I drank eight glasses of wine." Dolly sipped at her coffee, patting Mrs. Mac's hand. "I'll be all right. What time is it?"

"All most midnight," Gina said. "Tom and I were looking for you. Steve wanted to know where you had vanished."

"Vanished," Dolly frowned. "I was putting the boys to bed. What does he expect a mother to be doing at this time of night?"

Mrs. Mac shook her head and left, shutting the door behind her.

"Never mind," Gina said. "Everything is all right."

"No it isn't," Dolly said. "My head is swimming, the boys think I drink too much, and Tom thinks I'm an idiot. He's right Steve is too short. I probably would have fallen on my nose if Tom hadn't been there."

Gina tried to figure out how everything had gone so wrong in such a short period of time. She tried to remember her Alanon training of not trying to be in control of everyone's life. *Dear Lord,* she prayed. *Help.*

Dolly finished the last of the coffee. "Will you pray a minute with me?"

"Of course," Gina said. She took Dolly's hand and bowed her head. "Lord, grant me the serenity to accept the things I cannot change, the courage to change the things I can and the wisdom to know the difference."

"There's the rub," Dolly said. "How do you know when to fold your cards and let the Lord handle everything?"

"Anytime is a good time to turn your life and your will over to the care of God, as you understand Him."

Tom opened the cook's bedroom door. "Everything all right in here?"

"Of course," Gina and Dolly said together.

Tom joined in their laughter. "You two better get out here. Steve's threatening to call the cops if he can't kiss his wife-to-be when the clock strikes midnight."

"He is a cop," Dolly said.

"Guess who else had too much to drink on New Year's Eve?" Tom put his arms around both their waists to escort them back through the crowded kitchen to the party gaining momentum in the great hall of the Stone mansion.

Dolly stopped them just outside the heated kitchen. "Tom, please forgive me."

He put both his hands on Dolly's face. "No one faults you for allowing your dead husband's twin to lurk around."

"Still..?" Dolly hung her head.

Tom tipped her head up, placing one hand under Gina's face, too. "Now I have twin sisters to love."

Gina and Dolly traded smiles. Then Gina held Tom and Dolly's hands as she made her way through the crowd to Lucille. Mrs. Stone was regal in a black velvet gown trimmed with miniscule white satin roses around her throat, wrists and hem. "I want to thank you for a lovely evening," Gina said.

"Now, Gina," Lucille said. "You know you and Tom are family. You need to come by to check on your young charge, too." She reached behind her where Danny had been eavesdropping, bringing him forward. "You want these two to join us for Sunday dinners, don't you?"

"Of course," he said. "That's very gracious of you."

Gina thanked the Lord for guiding her in the quest to vindicate the innocent boy. Danny had a home now, a future with manhood only a step away.

Dolly swept next to Gina as the clock started chiming. "I wanted to be near my sister to see the New Year in."

They hugged each other but were instantly pulled in opposite directions by Tom and Steve.

Gina could hear Danny and Lucille's laughter as Tom picked her up and whirled her around in his strong arms.

He sat her down as the clock struck again and the crowd began to chant backwards, "Eight, seven, six, five, four, three, two, one!"

Gina stretched up on her tiptoes and kissed her dear husband to begin their life together in the New Year!

Printed in the United States
By Bookmasters